The Christmas Women

Elyse Douglas

COPYRIGHT

So long as the memory of certain beloved friends
lives in my heart, I shall say that life is good.

—*Helen Keller*

For Mrs. Buchy, a passionate teacher.

The Christmas Women

ONE

At 6:26 in the morning, Trudie Parks received a phone call from Ray Howard—a call that would change her life forever.

"Sorry to call so early, Trudie, but I just had to tell you."

Trudie stretched and yawned. "I was up anyway, Ray. What's up?"

Trudie sat on the cushioned kitchen window seat, staring out the bay window at the blurring world of falling snow. Dressed in blue flannel pajamas, heavy pink housecoat, and fuzzy white slippers, she watched a frigid north wind blow a chaos of snow, piling it in drifts against trees and houses, smothering parked cars.

"I went to see Mrs. Childs last night. Bad news. She has breast cancer."

Trudie shook awake. "Oh, no. Is she okay?"

"I guess so, but she didn't look like herself. She's still recovering from surgery and looked so old and frail. It really broke my heart to see her that way. She was always so strong and energetic."

Ray was an English teacher at Deer Lake High School, where he and Trudie had graduated 20 years before.

They'd remained friends, meeting occasionally for dinner at Rusty's, the local hangout. Ray was gay, something he'd confided in Trudie during their junior year, even before he came out to his family and other friends. Mrs. Childs had been their drama teacher. Though she'd retired 10 years ago, Ray still kept in touch with her.

"How old is Mrs. Childs now, Ray?"

"Seventy-six. I was reading about breast cancer on the internet. It's harder for older women to battle it."

"Did she have a mastectomy?"

"No, a lumpectomy, but she had chemo for a while before the operation, so she lost some hair." Trudie sat gazing out at the white face of the morning, suddenly lost in thought, remembering her former teacher's dramatic facial expressions and raised fist whenever she was emphasizing a point. Mrs. Childs was rough on the surface, but motherly and kind underneath, with an expansive heart which she offered to any student who showed an interest in learning.

"Are you there, Trudie?"

"Yes... Yes, Ray, I'm here. It just makes me sad. She was my favorite teacher. I learned so much in her class. I loved the shows we did, especially the Christmas shows our junior and senior years."

"Yeah, those Christmas shows were amazing," Ray said. "The entire county used to come out for them. Remember?"

Trudie smiled at the memory. "Oh, yes, of course I remember."

"And you and Kristen and Mary Ann were always Mrs. Childs' favorites. She got you all together during your junior year, didn't she?"

"Yes, when she took the shows over from Mr. Keane."

Ray laughed. "Yes... Mr. Ka, Ka Keane! The superhero music teacher. White teeth, white sweaters, white shirts. He didn't want any part of those Christmas shows, so he turned the whole thing over to Mrs. Childs. And then she informed me that I'd be in charge of the musicians. She didn't ask me. She *told* me."

"Mr. Keane just couldn't put in the extra hours," Trudie said. "He had four kids and he lived way out in the boondocks somewhere."

They sat for a time without talking, lost in good memories.

"Mrs. Childs knew what she was doing, though, especially when she put the three of you in charge," Ray said. "It made her job a whole lot easier. She'd just sit back and watch the three of you go."

"She convinced us it would be fun and something to put on our college applications. So Kristen and Mary Ann and I made lists and called students and fought over music, boyfriends, food and clothes, and we loved every minute of it."

"She called you the 'Christmas Girls,' didn't she?" Ray asked.

Trudie smiled at the thought, suddenly missing Kristen and Mary Ann. "Yes, we were known as The Christmas Girls."

Trudie glanced over at the digital clock. The red numbers glowed 6:45. She would have to be at the dental office before 9 o'clock, and not a minute later, because Mr. Posier was scheduled for a cleaning. Snowstorm or no snowstorm, Mr. Posier would be sitting in reception bolt upright, like a general waiting for action, his impatient gray eyes narrowing on his watch, just daring her to be late. She could clearly see his white starched face and fixed chin. He was a cranky engine, whose complaining and opinions rattled on unabated until she got the suction tube in his mouth.

"I've got to go, Ray. Thanks for letting me know. I'll try to go see her tonight after work. What's her daughter's number?"

Ray gave her the phone number and address. "I pity you having to go out in this," he said. "They closed school today. Our first snow day and it's only November 18th."

"Lucky you. Got to go."

After she hung up, Trudie remained sitting, watching the wind stir the trees and create little cyclones that went spiraling off down the street. She placed her chin in her hand, as a vast distance filled her eyes. She wanted to be in that cyclone, being blown off to somewhere—anywhere but Deer Lake, Ohio. Not that there was anything wrong with Deer Lake, except that her life here had not gone the way she'd thought it would. Maybe it would be nice to be blown off somewhere else, over a rainbow or beyond a snowstorm.

But in truth, did anybody's life go the way they'd hoped or dreamed or planned? What about her best friends in high school? Mary Ann had married an airline pilot and moved to Denver. Last she'd heard, she was divorced with two teenage daughters.

Kristen had moved to New York, studied for a law degree and married some rich investment banker. Trudie remembered their address, having been very impressed and a little jealous that it was on West 79th Street, in New York, NY. They'd gutted and remodeled a 3-story brownstone and Kristen had posted photos on *Facebook*. It looked fabulous. But the last time Trudie had heard from Kristen, she said her marriage was not going well and their only son was attending a private school in Massachusetts. She worked fourteen hours a day and most weekends. What kind of life was that?

They spoke on the phone to each other maybe once a year. Then there were the obligatory Christmas cards, with no personal news. Kristen always sent a Christmas card with a photo of her now 13-year-old son, Alexander, who was rarely smiling. *From Our Family to Yours* was printed across it, something Trudie struggled not to bristle at. It wasn't Kristen's fault that Trudie had no family, but why couldn't she be a bit more sensitive? And why couldn't she ever include a photo of her and her husband? It was always just the cute blond-headed boy she'd never met, standing alone next to a spreading oak tree with blazing autumn colors. How WASP.

And then there was Mary Ann's version of the Christmas card. Although she didn't like social media, she now sent an electronic Christmas card with the usual blah, blah, Merry Christmas and Peace on Earth and little birds flying around. Not that there was anything wrong with little birds or wanting peace on Earth, but there was no personal news. No information about what was really going on in her life.

They'd been like sisters in high school —maybe even closer than sisters, at least for a time. They'd shared everything, from family secrets, to backseat adventures with boys, to hopes for the future. They had truly loved each other.

Trudie heaved out an audible sigh, missing them and their friendships. The 20th high school reunion that could have brought them back together was cancelled last May after a tornado ravaged the town. Part of the courthouse square, dozens of homes and most the junior high school had been demolished.

Trudie padded off to the kitchen and put on the red

kettle to heat water for coffee. While the water hissed and steamed, she folded her arms and leaned back against the kitchen counter, blinking around at the spotlessly clean kitchen. She scooped a spoonful of instant coffee and dropped it into the cup, pausing before she poured the water. What had that young teenage girl said to her yesterday as she was cleaning her teeth? They had been discussing some middle-aged movie star who had never married.

"Have you ever been married?" the young girl asked.

Trudie gave her the stock answer. "No... never found a man I wanted to live with. They're all so messy, you know."

But that wasn't the truth. Trudie poured the steaming water, filled her cup and stirred. She tipped in some milk and added a spoonful of sugar, then as she poured boiling water into her instant oatmeal, her thoughts returned to Mary Ann and Kristen and their high school days. She'd never forgotten one particular conversation during their senior year. "You'll be the first to marry, Trudie," Kristen had proclaimed. "You and Cole will be married right after high school, have three kids and live happily ever after." Mary Ann had concurred. "Yeah, you're the type. You'll settle down and get married right away."

Trudie sat down at the kitchen table with a heavy sigh. Well, anyway, she *had* settled down, but she'd settled alone. She sipped her coffee, staring blankly into her oatmeal, suddenly uncomfortable with the full array of memories Ray's phone call had brought back. There were happy memories, for sure, but there were also the suppressed unhappy ones, plus her own persistent sense of failure.

Mrs. Childs had cancer; stubborn and sturdy and wonderful Mrs. Childs, whose drama class was as difficult as social studies or math. She made her students memorize Shakespeare monologues and write reviews of movies and TV shows. They had to work in groups to write and then perform one-act plays, as well as audition for both the senior class play in the fall, and the musical in the spring. No, Mrs. Childs' class was not a breeze to pass.

Suddenly seized by a thought, Trudie got up and strode across the polished hardwood floors into the spacious, wood-paneled den that had once been her father's office. She searched the floor-to-ceiling bookshelves, realizing, with a frown and a sweep of her index finger, that she hadn't dusted the shelves in almost two weeks. Her eyes wandered until she saw it: her senior class yearbook. She used the two-step wooden ladder to reach up and pull it down.

Back in the kitchen, she laid the yearbook down before her. She spooned her oatmeal and stared at the yearbook. She sipped coffee, staring at it. She made a steeple of her hands, staring at it. She hadn't looked through it in years. The group photos and senior portraits always provoked both fondness and an aching regret. Some of her classmates had already died. Some had seemed to vanish. Most had moved away after college. Like a lot of Midwestern towns, Deer Lake had suffered manufacturing losses and most of the young people had fled to the cities for better opportunities. It was only in the last three years that the town had managed a sort of renaissance, mainly because a company called *CodeMobile* had moved into an old, abandoned factory on the edge of town and, miraculously, it had flourished, hiring programmers and IT professionals from all over the country. The company had become a leader in mobile IT services and internet security. As a result, Deer Lake was flourishing again.

Trudie had never considered moving away, even during the town's lean years. Right after she graduated from college with a degree in dental hygiene, she landed a job with their family dentist. She had hoped to live with her parents only until she could afford her own apartment, but tragedy struck: her mother died suddenly of a ruptured brain aneurysm. Since her older brother, Tommy, had attended college in Maine and fallen in love with a local girl, he'd decided to stay in Portland. Trudie did not have the heart to leave her father alone, especially when he asked her, in his quiet, unassuming way, to stay and keep house for him for just a little while, until he got adjusted to living alone.

Her father, Thomas Parks, was not a social man, and they both knew he would never remarry. He worked as an accountant for a supermarket chain. A shy, bookish man, he retreated even further after his wife died. Trudie lived with him all through her twenties, always dreaming about striking out on her own, but never meeting a man who would give her an excuse, and never thinking it was worth the expense to pay for a small apartment when she had almost an entire house rent-free. She and her father ate dinner together most nights, and then he went into his study and she went upstairs to watch TV or read, except for the nights she tutored local high school students or went out to dinner with co-workers. Sometimes on week-ends, she and Ray went to plays or concerts in Cincinnati.

Shortly after her thirtieth birthday, her father developed a rare form of bone cancer, and Trudie cared for him during his long, unsuccessful battle with it. She celebrated her thirty-second birthday a few days before he died.

And so here she still lived, in the grand Victorian

house on Oak Street, with its gables and turrets and wide, wrap-around porch and formidable wrought iron fence and gate. The house had been in her father's family since 1900 and Trudie loved it. When her father died, she bought her brother's half of the house and became the sole owner. She'd surely live in the old house for the rest of her life.

Trudie pushed the bowl of oatmeal aside, turning reflective. She was 38 years old, galloping toward 40. Lately, as she rambled through the three-bedroom house, it seemed larger and quieter, absent of any real life, as if its glory days were far behind it and an uncertain future promised much of the same old, same old. How lonely the house had become. How fast the years had flown.

Trudie ran the flat of her hand across the surface of the royal blue yearbook with the raised embossed letters, *Deer Lake High School.* She was reluctant to open it, as if it were some Pandora's Box that would release unwanted dark spirits from its dusty old glossy pages. The yearbook documented an important phase of her life—a crowded and restless senior year. The static images catalogued frenetic activity, sexual awakenings and secrets she'd never shared with anyone. There was that cool autumn night with Jon Ketch at the "haunted house" in the ghost town ten miles away. There was Cole Blackwell, the 6-foot 6-inch star basketball player she'd fallen for. He'd made the vow that he would always love her, so why shouldn't she sleep with him? He loved her. They'd get married right after high school. But that was in early November of their senior year. By late April, it was all over. Cole had moved on.

And then in early May, Mary Ann had let it slip that Cole and Kristen had been dating for weeks behind Trudie's back. Trudie went ballistic, refusing to speak to

Kristen for a month. In fact, the memory of that betrayal still nearly nauseated her. But with Mary Ann's pleading that The Christmas Girls were meant to be life-long friends, Trudie reluctantly reconciled with Kristen right before graduation. It had helped that Kristen and Cole had not flaunted their relationship by going to the prom together. Trudie, too, had stayed away, unable to bear the indignity of not having a date, after the entire class had assumed that she and Cole would be together forever.

But all that had happened a long time ago, Trudie thought. She and Kristen had talked it all out a few years later, and when they met for their ten-year high school reunion, Kristen had again apologized repeatedly, and they had finally decided to lay it to rest. It had happened in high school, after all. Like most things that happened during their teenage years, it was an old, moldy memory. Over time, old relationships and old hurts become blurry, confused and mostly forgotten. You learn to forgive and forget and, hopefully, you grow up.

But there it was—the yearbook—staring back at her—beckoning her to open the cover and dive back into the past. It seemed to steal all other thoughts from her brain, demanding her entire interest. With an unsteady hand, Trudie slowly opened the yearbook's cover, unaware that she was holding her breath.

TWO

Trudie stared at the pages, absorbed in the images and titles. She carefully read her classmates' inscriptions, written right after graduation, before they embarked on their shiny, new, promising lives.

To a really smart and sweet girl. Keep your warm, sincere smile, Trudie, and you'll never have trouble finding friends, or keeping them. — Lots of love, Connie Baker

To a great girl, with star quality. What is it about your great smile and deep blue, penetrating eyes? Always thought you could see right through me. —Best of luck in all you do. — Molly Cahill

Hey Girl: Loved those Christmas shows! Maybe I'll major in stage managing. You Christmas Girls were the best. The year just raced by like a dream. A wonderful, crazy dream —good luck! Liz Tyree

Trudie Love: I have been in love with you since we were in the 7th Grade. Hey, I can say that, now that we're graduating and I'm going off to college. Remember me sometimes when I'm famous. And yes, I was always jealous of Cole! Why the hell didn't you love me!? — I was always in love with you! Kiss me, sweetheart! — Jon Ketch

Trudie sat back in the kitchen chair and closed her eyes. Jon Ketch. She could see him clearly, as if he were standing in front of her. He was five-feet seven inches tall, with a mop of long black hair, a clean masculine face and broad shoulders. His neon blue eyes captured and held you with a magnetic, calm intensity. He was volatile, clever and unpredictable. He had become the movie star he'd always dreamed about—the most famous graduate in the class.

In Hollywood he was known as a sarcastic and charismatic guy, who took on edgy, sometimes violent roles. In New York, on and off-Broadway, he started out performing Shakespeare and other serious drama, and then he surprised everyone by doing a comedy, for which he received rave reviews.

His father, a wealthy banker, had sent him off to a private high school in Chicago. But when he learned Jon was skipping most of his classes to hang out with actors and go to the theatre, his father yanked him back to Deer Lake High School. Jon loved to imitate his father, his eyes bulging, fists clenched, eyebrows arched, in outrage. "I'm not going to waste my money so you can become another unemployed actor!"

So Jon auditioned for the school plays and was, by far, the best actor the school had ever seen—or probably would ever see. Jon and Mrs. Childs formed a special bond during his senior year. She believed in his talent, and she was the only person Jon ever listened to about anything.

Trudie had looked him up on the internet just a few months ago. He'd been in 15 films, and was married and divorced twice. He had three kids, all daughters, and he lived just outside L.A. He was notorious for getting into fights with "insulting" strangers and the Paparazzi, as well as with other cast members, when he felt they were lazy, or content to live off their celebrity.

Some directors refused to work with him. Others adored him and considered him one of the great up-and-coming American actors. That's the way it was with Jon. You either liked him or you hated him. Trudie had always liked him. Maybe she'd secretly loved him, too. Maybe she loved him because he was her opposite. He was a rebel, a thrill ride and a time bomb always about to go off. He scared her and he attracted her.

A few years back, Kristen had seen him in a production of *King Lear* in New York. He'd played the Fool brilliantly, according to Kristen, who had gone back stage to see him. "Jon was as wild as ever," she'd reported on the phone. "He gave me a big wet kiss and said, 'Look at you all dolled up and ready for love.'"

About two years ago, Trudie had driven to Columbus, Ohio to see Jon in an independent film entitled *Two for My Baby*. He played the father of a troubled teenager and, on the screen, he was explosive, daring and riveting. He'd been praised by the critics. Trudie had clipped the review from the newspaper.

"Jon Ketch comes crashing onto the screen with noise and color. He plays a sober, hard-working, volatile, faithful husband, who tries to keep his drug-addicted teen daughter from spiraling out of control. Mr. Ketch seethes, barks and burns with outrage, aches with compassion and, finally, he breaks your heart. It is a virtuosic performance that is both disturbing and hypnotically alluring."

Jon had been nominated for both a Golden Globe Award and an Academy Award for his role in *Two for My Baby*. He didn't win either. Maybe it was because he'd made enemies. Maybe he was just too outspoken.

According to his recent photo on the internet, he was still thin and in good shape, but graying and thinning on top. He still had that special something—that magnetic something certain people have: an irresistible rakish charm and sexy appeal. Trudie had thought of emailing him after she saw the movie, but she didn't. What would she say? Remember me? He'd probably never respond.

They hadn't seen each other in 15 years. The last time was before he was a star, when he'd come to visit his parents. But they had long since moved to Florida and he'd never returned to Deer Lake. Why should he?

Trudie pushed aside her half-eaten oatmeal, peeled a banana and found Kristen's and Mary Ann's yearbook entries.

Sister Trudie: God, what a year! Boyfriends, football games, the Christmas show with the Christmas tree catching on fire, (Jon Ketch!) Mary Ann spraining her ankle during our Rockettes' rehearsal and the senior class play and... Oh, God, all the fights and hugs. We'll always be friends, Trudie dear... We're sisters, you know. The best of sisters. Closer than sisters. Love ya, Kristen

Trudie fell into timelessness, not noticing it was 7:30. She heard the furnace kick on and felt the slow rising heat, but she was lost in thought. She read Kristen's entry again, a faint smile forming. *"The best of sisters."* Trudie frowned. Even though Kristen had betrayed her like that in high school? Had Trudie really forgiven Kristen for that?

They hadn't seen each other in ten years.

Trudie read Mary Ann's entry.

Dear Trudie: High School is over but we will never be apart. Don't forget how much we've been through together and how much we love each other. After all, we are The Christmas Girls, always merry and filled with peace and love. God bless you, sister dear.

We will always be close, because we are truly sisters.

There were more entries, but Trudie skimmed over them. Finally, she turned the pages, lingering on some and flipping through others, as she took in the smiles and poses—images that brought a startling palette of emotions. The minutes expanded in the silence as she studied the faces, all looking so young, so hopeful and so confident.

She felt like she was on a train—thundering down the tracks, smoke billowing, whistle blowing, racing past familiar towns, winding roads and waving people—forced to recall old conversations, old loves and old regrets.

Trudie turned a page and paused, captivated by a photo. There they were, the three of them, Kristen, Mary Ann and herself on stage performing a Rockettes' style kicking chorus to *Jingle Bells.* They were wearing Santa hats, little red skirts, heels and white blouses with padded shoulders. In another photo, they were giggling and posing next to a tall Christmas tree. Jon Ketch was crouched beside them, making a silly face, dressed as an elf in tights and green pointed ears.

Trudie laughed out loud. They'd had so much fun. She missed those days. Feeling light and warmed by the memories, she wanted the moment to expand. She didn't want to go to work. But she sighed and reluctantly closed the yearbook. After finishing her banana, she stared for a time into the middle distance seeing nothing, hearing the kitchen wall clock tick away time. If she didn't get up and shower, she'd be late for her cleaning with the grumpy Mr. Posier.

In the hallway at the stairs, Trudie paused to stare at herself in the full-length mirror. She was a tall, willowy blonde who could still pass for 32-ish. She straightened her shoulders more, then immediately tried relaxing them, wondering if her posture might be a bit stiff and even a little defensive. She turned sideways and tightened the belt on the silly, frayed housecoat she refused to throw away because it was so soft and warm. She'd lost weight and her tummy was nice and flat. Then she faced the mirror again, up close. There weren't too many lines around her cool blue eyes. She still had a pretty, diamond-shaped face.

An objective observer might say that her expression was aloof and distant, as if she had no idea what was inside her or what made her tick. But Trudie didn't know this. She only knew that when she tilted her head, staring, she heard a lonely, pulsing silence.

By the time she left the house for the garage, David, the high school junior she hired to shovel her walk and driveway, was hard at work, scraping a path up the front walk to her entrance. She gave him a wave of her hand.

Although the wind was sharp, the snow had turned to flurries. She climbed behind the wheel of her Audi and cranked the engine. She'd already decided that on her lunch break she'd call Mrs. Childs' daughter and ask if she could visit her mother, who was staying with her. If she agreed, Trudie would drive north to Columbus right after work.

As Trudie switched on her wipers and crept out of the driveway, she also decided she'd call Kristen and Mary Ann that night. They'd want to know about Mrs. Childs. They loved her as much as Trudie did. Would they come for a visit? Who else should she call? Jon? That was an exciting thought. Ray surely had his number. And there were so many others she should call. They'd all want to know. Of course they would.

16

THREE

As darkness fell, Trudie turned onto a quiet, tree-lined road, craning her neck, searching for the right address. Since the roads had been plowed and salted, it had taken her only about 20 minutes to drive from Deer Lake. The storm had dumped 8 inches of snow then moved swiftly east, leaving behind frigid temperatures.

Trudie drove past two-story homes with shoveled walks and driveways, finally finding Mrs. Childs' daughter's light grey house at the end of the block. It was a modest home with a two-car garage, shrubs heavy with snow, and blue shutters on the windows.

Trudie managed to park at the curb. Placing a careful foot out on the street, she got out, chucked the door shut and gingerly made her way to the sidewalk, crunching through fresh snow. She strolled up the front walk and took the stairs to the porch, careful not to crush the paper-wrapped yellow roses she'd purchased for Mrs. Childs. Trudie stamped the snow off her boots and rang the bell.

She was greeted by a stout woman in her 50s, with a friendly face, steady dark eyes and medium brown hair.

"I'm Julie," she said, stepping aside to let Trudie in,

closing the door behind her. Trudie wiped her feet on the brown foot rug and glanced about.

"It's so nice of you to come," Julie said, and Trudie saw that she was sincere.

"Your mother meant a lot to us," Trudie said. "She was my favorite teacher."

"Well, she was a little scary to my brother and me. She could be so stern and dramatic. But we always knew she loved us, and she was very devoted to Dad."

Trudie pulled off her woolen cap and presented Julie the flowers. "I brought these for her. She always had fresh flowers on her desk at school."

Julie took them. "She'll love them."

Julie hung Trudie's coat in the closet, while Trudie smoothed out her white turtleneck and finger-placed her hair, which had flattened under her hat.

"Would you like something hot to drink?" Julie asked.

"Tea would be nice, if it's not too much trouble. How is she?" Trudie asked.

Julie smiled, thinly. "She's resting. She was so excited you called. She kept saying how much she loved you and your friends. I believe she called you The Christmas Girls."

Trudie nodded, with a smile. "Yes. There were three of us. Your mother put us together in our junior year to organize the Christmas shows. We begged the school board for money; pestered the football players to sing and dance; pulled in freshmen and sophomores to help build and paint the sets; and bullied the band teacher and the band to stay late every night for weeks, while we re-hearsed. It was a lot of fun, and it was the highlight of the year for a lot of people."

Julie smiled. "Oh, I remember. I was there. The per-formances were wonderful. But Dad said Mom was a nightmare to live with during those last weeks in December, when rehearsals were going on. My brother and I made sure to stay out of her way, and we were in our 30s by then."

Trudie lowered her voice. "So, how is she?"

Julie lowered her gaze. "She's weak. The surgery was harder on her than we all anticipated, and now she's getting internal radiation therapy. They say it's better than traditional radiation, but it's still powerful."

Trudie nodded and glanced toward the gleaming fire, feeling the warmth of the room.

They were both lost for words, so Julie led Trudie to a back bedroom and gently opened the door to a small, square room with a deep, royal blue carpet. A vase of daisies sat on the night table next to the bed. The cream-colored walls held spring landscapes in gilded frames, and a chest of drawers displayed framed family photos and a 22-inch TV, with some DVDs scattered about it. It was a quiet, private room. A comfortable room, with a recliner in the corner facing the bed and a ladder-back chair beside the bed. Trudie glanced at the DVDs. They were old Christmas movies: *The Shop around the Corner* starring Jimmy Stewart, *Holiday Affair* starring Robert Mitchum, and *You've Got Mail*, starring Tom Hanks and Meg Ryan.

Trudie noticed a framed movie poster hanging on the wall, just above the TV. It was an original poster from *Holiday Affair*. She studied the 16" x 24" midnight blue and black poster of Robert Mitchum and co-star, Janet Leigh. Mitchum was wearing a gray suit and a brownish red tie, spilling from his coat; his hat was pushed roguishly back off his forehead. He's reaching down, seizing Janet Leigh by her arm. She's wearing a red dress with a sexy plunging neckline, her luscious brown hair gleaming. She looks back at him with cool trepidation.

The poster reads:

MITCHUM'S LATEST!
It Happens in December
But
It's Hotter than July!

Trudie smiled.

Julie came over. "Mom bought that for me about ten years ago. We both love Robert Mitchum."

Trudie turned toward the bed. Mrs. Childs was propped up against pillows, her face half turned away from the dim lamp light.

"Mom," Julie whispered. "You have company."

Myrna Childs slowly turned her head toward her daughter's voice. Her eyes fluttered and then squinted as she worked to focus. Her eyes opened on Trudie with a pleasant confusion.

"Hello, Mrs. Childs," Trudie whispered, a bit taken back by her teacher's pale, wrinkled face and soft, watery eyes. She was also much thinner than she'd remembered.

Mrs. Childs exhaled a soft breath of pleasure. "Mrs. Childs? Oh my goodness, that makes me sound like an old, wizened school teacher, doesn't it?"

Her eyes opened more fully. "Is that you, Trudie?" she asked, lifting a thin arm and shaky hand.

Trudie stepped forward and took it. "Yes. I'm here."

A smile formed at the corners of her mouth. "How nice."

"And she brought you flowers, Mom," Julie said holding them up.

Mrs. Childs smiled and her face looked young again. Trudie fought tears. There were so many emotions attached to her old teacher.

"I'll go put the flowers in water," Julie said. She

backed out of the room and Trudie eased down in the chair next to the bed, still holding her teacher's cool, thin hand.

Mrs. Childs' gray hair was combed softly back from her forehead, and in the dim light, Trudie noticed her steely strength was still present in the eyes and firm mouth.

"How do you feel, Mrs. Childs?" Trudie asked.

Myrna retracted her hand with a frown. "For God's sake, Trudie, call me Myrna. I never liked my last name anyway. Makes me sound adolescent or something. Ironic that I used my married name and taught kids. I don't know why I did. Curt, my husband, wouldn't have cared if I'd kept Lewis, my maiden name."

And then there was perplexed reflection. "Curt was a good man, though. A fair man, and I wasn't easy to live with. Oh my, he's been dead more than five years now."

Myrna shrugged and looked resigned. "Well, anyway, right now I feel like the air is running out of the balloon, Trudie. On the other hand, I remember what that comedian Steven Wright once said. He said 'I intend to live forever. So far, so good.' I intend to go on living, Trudie, because I like living. I just need to regain my strength and then I'll fight this thing and get on the other side of it. You watch me."

Trudie thought, *Yes, this is the woman I knew and loved in high school.*

Myrna reached out her hand again and took Trudie's. "I'm so glad you came. I'm glad Ray called you."

She closed her eyes, as if needing to rest. Then she made a little sound without opening her eyes, as some old image flickered across the screen of her mind. "You were my favorite girl," Mrs. Childs said.

Trudie lifted a doubtful eyebrow.

Myrna's eyes opened. "You *were*, you know."

"Oh, I'm sure you say that to all your old students," Trudie said, going for a little joke.

The silence lengthened as Myrna examined Trudie's face. "You're still pretty, Trudie, with your blonde hair and soft blue eyes. Are you eating enough? You look so thin."

"I've been dieting. I lost 15 pounds."

"Put them back on! You're too thin."

"Ever the director," Trudie said, with a smile.

"Well, yes, bossy and overbearing as always. Poor Julie was in therapy for 5 years because of me. My son, Nick, left town to get away from me and he only comes to see me at Christmas. What does that say about me? Never was the model mother."

Myrna squeezed Trudie's hand, and it was surprisingly strong. "But you *were* my favorite, Trudie."

"I doubt it," Trudie said, squeezing her hand.

"You never did believe in yourself, did you? You were always so guarded and secretive. Did you know how pretty you were…and still are?"

Trudie looked down and away. "Well, thank you. But I won't call you Myrna. I'm sorry; my mouth just can't form the word."

"Are you married?" Mrs. Childs asked.

Trudie didn't look at her. "No… I came close a couple of times but… No."

"Well, that doesn't matter," Mrs. Childs said, watching her closely. "You still have it, Trudie. It's still there."

Trudie looked at her, tentative. "And what is that?"

"An elegant reserve, a remoteness that used to drive the boys wild. They never knew who you really were. You were so mysterious and aloof. Men like that, you know."

"Oh, I don't know about that, Mrs. Childs."

"Remember Jon Ketch?"

"Of course. Who could forget Jon?"

"He was wild about you. So were Cole Blackwell and any number of other boys. I think you scared most of them away because they just couldn't figure you out. Actually, truth be told, you were too smart and mature for them."

"Mrs. Childs, this is not the conversation I imagined we'd have."

Julie entered, carrying a silver tray with a teapot, cups, a pitcher of milk and a sugar bowl.

"Is mother badgering you, Trudie?" she asked, as she eased the tray down on a TV tray table.

"We're just getting caught up," Myrna said. "Oh, isn't this nice! Tea. Thank you, Julie. I would love some tea. Earl Grey?"

"Of course, Mother."

"Wonderful."

Julie poured tea and milk for Mrs. Childs and Trudie, and then helped her mother sit up, adjusting the pillows behind her back. She served herself some tea and lingered for a few moments while they all discussed the weather and the up-coming holidays. When the telephone rang, she withdrew to the living room. "I'll be back with the flowers," she said.

Myrna shut her eyes again.

"Are you tired? Should I go, Mrs. Childs?"

Myrna drew a breath and opened her eyes. "No, Trudie. Please stay awhile longer. I just have to take these little interludes now and then." Mrs. Childs adjusted herself and looked pointedly at Trudie, her eyes shining and alert.

"I can see all of their faces, Trudie. Can you believe

that? That's what I've been doing these last few weeks. Closing my eyes and remembering all my students' faces, just as if I were turning the pages of a photo album. I see them so clearly. I remember them. I see them more clearly now with my eyes shut than if I were actually looking at them standing in front of me. I can see them and *feel* them. Isn't that strange? Well, maybe it's all this lousy medication they're injecting me with. But I see those faces and I remember, and it just makes me feel good. It makes me feel better. Most were such good kids. Some were a pain in the neck, you know, but most were good and fun. Can you imagine me getting sentimental? A woman who doesn't have a sentimental bone in her body?"

"I'd say you have one or two sentimental bones," Trudie said.

Myrna made a little dismissive gesture with her hand. "Are you still working as a dental hygienist?"

"Yes."

"And you like it?"

"Yes. It's not for everybody, but I like it."

"And what do you hear from Kristen and Mary Ann?"

"We haven't stayed in touch all that much."

The words hung in the air, waiting.

"Well now, that's a shame," Mrs. Childs said, with some sadness. "You three were so close. That surprises me."

"They moved away, got married and had families. Life happens."

Myrna turned reflective. "Kristen was so driven, so hell-bent on proving herself all the time. She was a terrible actress, but she sure could get things done, even if she did piss people off now and then. I always thought she and I had a lot in common. Maybe that's why we fought so much. And then there was Mary Ann. I thought of her as Merry Ann. M E R R Y Ann. She was always so up, and smiling, dreamy, and creative."

"She was a good actress," Trudie said.

"Only in certain roles. She lacked fire in the dramatic parts. She always had that far-away look in her eyes, like she was looking for Never Never Land. Well, I hope she found it."

"Was I a good actress?" Trudie asked, instantly wishing she hadn't asked.

"In *The Glass Menagerie*, with Jon Ketch, you were quite good. He brought out things inside you I never knew were there. But then Jon was nuts and would try all kinds of things. But you were wonderful as Laura. Yes. I was greatly impressed by your performance, Trudie."

"Jon scared me," Trudie said. "He was always so unpredictable and wonderful at the same time."

Myrna laughed. "I saw him in a movie just the other day, on DVD. I don't remember what the title was. It was one of his first movie roles and he had a small character part. It was a Tom Hanks' movie, I think. Anyway, Jon stole the scene. He makes the craziest choices, kind of like Brando did. You just never knew what he was going to do next."

Trudie drank the last of her tea. "He was fun though. You couldn't help but like him."

Myrna handed Trudie her cup. "But you three girls made a terrific team. You were the organizer, Kristen the thrust and drive, and Mary Ann the imagination. There was no stopping you three. You should have found some successful business and run it together. You would have been hugely successful."

"Have you been back to the high school recently?" Trudie asked.

"No, not in years. They don't even have a drama department or a music department anymore. They don't have the money. It's just a crying shame."

Trudie placed Myrna's cup on the saucer. "We were so lucky to have you as our teacher, Mrs. Childs."

Myrna smiled her gratitude. "Well, thank you for that, but I was the lucky one. I was truly blessed to have had the students I had."

Mrs. Childs suddenly felt groggy, as if she was walking under water. She closed her eyes again.

Trudie stood. "I'm going to leave now and let you rest."

Myrna's eyes fluttered open again and she smiled weakly. "How delightful to see you again, Trudie. So nice. I'm sorry to be so tired. This has been so much fun."

"You sleep, Mrs. Childs. You sleep and get stronger and better."

Myrna nodded. "As Shakespeare said in the *Tempest,* 'We are such stuff as dreams are made on, and our little life is rounded with a sleep.'"

Trudie leaned over and kissed her old teacher on her warm cheek. "I'll see you again, Mrs. Childs."

"Call the other Christmas Girls and tell them I said hello. Will you do that for me?"

"Yes, I will, Mrs. Childs. I will call them."

At the front door, as Julie handed Trudie her coat, neither spoke for a time. While Trudie zipped up, she noticed Julie's sad, worried face.

"Your mother was always a very strong and determined woman, Julie."

Julie didn't meet Trudie's eyes. "I know, and I have to believe she'll survive this. But she's just not herself. Anyway, thanks for coming. You really cheered her up. She's always so much better when she sees her old students."

Trudie drove slowly back to Deer Lake, lost in thought. She switched on the radio to a country music station, and willed herself out of a dark mood. The visit with her former teacher had been enjoyable, but it left her feeling isolated and sad. For long stretches on the highway, Trudie reran old memories and conversations. By the time she reached Deer Lake, she'd decided not to call Kristen and Mary Ann right away. She needed time to think and decompress after her meeting with Mrs. Childs.

Trudie stopped for a hamburger and salad at Rusty's Cafe, hoping that being at the local bar would cheer her up. She entered, waved to some of her dental patients who were sitting in a booth, then chose a red swivel stool at the gray Formica counter. She extracted her tablet and stared into it, distracting herself with emails and world news.

She was only vaguely aware of a man who sat one stool over from her. She heard him order the fried chicken dinner and a beer. When his food arrived, he asked her if she'd pass the ketchup bottle. She did so, getting her first real glimpse of him. He was lean, fit and quite good looking—handsome enough that Trudie felt an unexpected rush of heat in her chest. He was about her age, with black hair, short on the sides, long on the top, combed straight back from his broad forehead. He wore an olive green dress shirt that set off his light, grayish-green eyes. A dark tie hung loosely about his collar. Trudie liked his clean jaw line and open, friendly expression.

He smiled at her as he took the ketchup. "Thank you.

I don't like ketchup on fries, but I love it on chicken."

Trudie nodded, and then watched him shake the bottle and smother the chicken.

"I just got my flu shot. Did you get yours?" he asked.

Trudie was still eyeing the chicken drowning in ketchup, with amazement. "Ah... yes, I did. Back in September."

"I got the nasal spray. I don't like needles."

He cut the chicken with his knife and fork and began to eat. She turned back to her tablet, her index finger surfing the pages.

"Did you work late?" he asked.

Trudie liked his voice. It was rich and deep. She looked up. "No, I was visiting a friend."

She watched him take another bite of chicken, torn between her desire to be alone and her interest in this stranger. After a moment's hesitation, she allowed herself to be engaged. "So, did *you* work late?" she finally asked.

He reached for his glass of beer. "Yes, we're trying to finish a contract and, as usual, we're running behind."

He turned toward her and extended his hand. "By the way, my name is Don Rawlings."

Shyly, Trudie took his broad, strong hand. She was surprised by a ripple of excitement when they shook hands. "I'm Trudie Parks."

"Glad to meet you." Don glanced down at his dinner, so Trudie started to turn away. But only for a moment.

"Do you live in Deer Park, Trudie?"

She faced him again. "Yes. You?"

"I do now. I moved here about a month ago. Haven't seen much of it, so far. I've just been working."

Trudie was about to ask what he did when his cell phone rang. He snatched it up and was soon engrossed in conversation. Trudie waited for a time, then packed up, paid the check and left, without giving him a passing glance. *I could have waited*, she thought. She could have waved goodbye when she left. But she didn't. Is that what Mrs. Childs meant when she said Trudie was guarded and remote?

As Trudie was about to climb into her car, she noticed Don standing at the front window watching her. He was still talking on his phone. He waved to her and smiled, a beautiful smile that warmed her. Surprised, she waved back and, suddenly, she felt intensely alive; she felt attractive and desirable. For a moment, she had the impulse to go back inside. She sat behind the steering wheel conflicted. Finally, she started the engine and drove away.

FOUR

At the El Conquistador Hotel in San Juan, Puerto Rico, all the tennis courts were occupied. It was Saturday morning, and the humid air was alive with the hollow pop of tennis balls, the sweet scent of exotic flowers and the salty smell from the shining sea. Women dressed in white pleated tennis skirts, white sleeveless blouses, and white headbands swatted at tennis balls, grunting out effort. Men raced and darted in their white shorts and polo shirts.

In the immediate court, a tennis battle was going on between Kristen Anderson Lloyd, 38 years old, and 27 year-old Sean Quinn, the resident tennis teacher.

Sean was wiry, loose-limbed and lithe. His long, curly, reddish blond locks were tied by a red bandana. He was dressed in white shorts and a sky blue polo shirt that carried the hotel's insignia.

Kristen was thin, quick and noticeably attractive. Her smooth muscular legs had good spring. She wore a light blue pleated skirt with a matching sleeveless blouse and a white headband to keep her thick, black hair in place.

Sean had a graceful economy of motion. Kristen had good moves and elastic feet that shifted, bounced and danced. After each assured stroke she found her balance, anchoring, swaying, alert, ready for the next shot.

Sean was a scrambler, filling every empty space of the court, smashing the ball back to Kristen with force. She sprang for it, whipped it back to him with a perfect backhand, and it sailed, skimming the top of the net. Then dropped.

Sean charged it, scooping, lobbing it over her head. She whirled, ran, caught it, pivoted and whacked it back to Sean, a line drive shot.

He lunged, crouched and met the ball, heaving out a "Ha!" as he crushed it with a sharp forward shot. Kristen was there to meet it, her eyes hard with determination. With both hands gripping the handle of the racket, she shot it back to Sean. He calculated distance and position.

Kristen broke for the net as he lobed the ball over and behind her. She spun, looked up and, as if possessed, pivoted and raced for it. Just before it bounced twice, she swung the racket in a beautiful arching motion, caught the ball dead center and fired it back to Sean like a bullet.

Then they fell into a cross-court volley, whipping the ball back and forth across the net in a ferocious battle that drew the eyes of captivated onlookers. Sean charged the net. Kristen's eyes narrowed in sudden alarm and calculation. The ball was like a rope coming at her. She swung and hit it, hoping to make a passing shot and send it right, out of Sean's reach. He lurched, stretched and nicked the ball just enough to set it down far to her left. Kristen broke for the ball, left arm extended, reaching in strained effort and desperation. But it was too late. The ball seemed to float away in slow motion. She missed and it bounced, striking the fence.

Kristen arched back, facing the sky in defeated agony. She cursed, and then slapped the top of the net hard with her racket. "Dammit!" she yelled.

Sean straightened, laughing. Then he bent over, grabbing his knees, gasping for breath. "Goodness gracious, Mrs. Lloyd," he said, with an Irish brogue, "You almost took me out that time. You'll be givin' me a heart attack, you will. It's time you found another teacher, my darlin', before you kill me and send me home to Mrs. Quinn in a pine box."

Back in her room, Kristen showered, belted on a robe and stepped out on her balcony that overlooked the sparkling sea. The hot shimmering air and humidity relaxed her. San Juan was all movement and color. Sexy women dazzled in flashy dresses, tight bright pants and sassy hips. The girl-talk was fast and clipped, and their gestures humming-bird-quick. Flowers shimmered with vibrating reds, yellows and endless gradations of white.

Kristen was fascinated by the azure rolling sea, with its glittering silver and flashing gold, stabbing her eyes with startling sunlight. Seagulls wheeled and lazy clouds seemed packed with cotton. She stared in wonder at the creamy line of the surf and the endless miles of wide beach and quiet palms.

Whenever she strolled the beach, the sun was big and hot and seemed to weigh her down with its heavy force. At night the sprinting brassy music seemed restless and wild, the singers' voices high and pinched with racy delight. Kristen loved this town. This was her fourth visit and she loved it more each time.

Unfortunately, she was there to work, to take the deposition of a doctor who was too ill to travel to New York. His testimony would be key to the medical malpractice case she was working on.

But at least it was a chance to get away from Alan, her

husband. They had fallen into their familiar pattern of arguing over the silliest of things. Where to eat dinner. What movie to see. Even what brand of toilet paper to buy. Which friends were in and which were out. Whenever the arguing sent them both into fuming silence, it always helped to put some space between them. If absence didn't always make the heart grow fonder, then it at least helped to cool the agitation of the relationship.

They hadn't always fought and threatened each other with divorce. It began after Kristen's secret affair with a judge, an older man in his early 50's, who'd been known as a ladies' man. Alan hadn't known about the affair, of course, and after a few months, Kristen broke it off because guilt stabbed at her like a knife.

Then she turned into the worst bitch she'd never wanted to be. She felt dirty and low, and she despised herself. She lashed out at Alan for the stupidest things and blamed him for silly things. When he asked her what was wrong, she'd say she wasn't feeling well and go off to bed or retreat into her work.

Did he suspect the affair afterwards? Probably. She felt it, and saw it in his eyes in private moments. A hurt and wounded look, masked by a thin, resigned smile. But he'd never called her on it. That made it even worse. Either he didn't care or he'd forgiven her, and either way, that made it nearly unbearable. She didn't want to be forgiven. It had happened over a year ago, and their relationship had never been the same.

Kristen stared out into the sea, and her eyes filled with tears. They had been so in love in the beginning, and so in love after their son, Alexander, was born.

She recalled their magical honeymoon in St. Eustatius. They hired a private plane and soared over the Caribbean, under creamy clouds, stunned by the lucid mystic watercolors of yellows, blues and green. She looked down to see ribbons of turquoise and lime, sliding into shimmering waves of electric blue. There was a harbor, dotted with yachts and a dock. There were palm trees and people lounging out on the broad white beach, with cottages nearby. Pure joy pumped through her veins as she took Alan's arm and told him how much she loved him. And she did love him. Truth be told, she still loved him.

Their private two bedroom beach house was white, green and blue, with plenty of windows, which gave them magnificent views of sea and sky.

They found The Captain's Beach Bar and climbed the steps to the veranda, her wearing a skimpy white bikini, a long, peach, diaphanous beach gown, and white broad-rimmed hat. She was sexy and he was handsome. Inside it was cool and shaded, and heads turned and watched them drift to the bar. There were comfortable booths against the walls, and ceiling fans revolved lazily. There was a long mahogany bar with high-backed stools and bottles on glass shelves.

The bartender was Olderson Blake, a tall, thin, black man, about 55, with short white hair and a broad friendly face. He said he came from Barbados.

He looked at the newly married couple as they sat down, and then he narrowed his dark eyes on them and said, "You look like happy people. Happy is good. But in dis life, you must like dee good life and you must like dee bad life, because deh are connected. Yes, my friends."

Kristen smiled at the thought. She and Alan had had the good life, and now they were having the bad life, thanks to her. Despite Olderson's philosophy, she didn't like the bad life. How could she mend the guilt and the hurt she felt? Therapy hadn't helped. Booze hadn't helped. Prayer hadn't helped. How could she stop the self-loathing she felt for betraying Alan and their son?

When her cell phone rang, Kristen snatched it up and saw it was Trudie. Kristen was delighted and surprised. They hadn't talked in months.

"Trudie! What a surprise. How are you?"

"Cold, sleepy and wishing I was somewhere warm."

"I'm going to make you jealous. I'm in San Juan and it's 81 degrees."

"No way! Oh, I am jealous!"

"Don't be too jealous. I'm here for a deposition, until Monday afternoon. What's up? It's been so long."

"I'm sitting by the fire, drinking hot chocolate and looking through our high school yearbook."

"Oh God, not that, Trudie," Kristen said, easing down on a chaise lounge chair which commanded a glorious view of the ocean.

"I went to see Mrs. Childs Thursday night. She had a malignant tumor removed from her breast. Surgery went well, but she doesn't look good."

Kristen's shoulders slumped. "Oh no. I'm so sorry. Somehow I thought she'd live forever. She was always so strong and healthy. She never got sick, not even a cold."

"She asked me to call. She said, 'Call the other Christmas Girls and tell them I said hello.'"

Kristen stood and paced the balcony, suddenly lost in the past, overwhelmed with the sights and smells of Deer Lake; remembering Mrs. Childs' resolute face and steady eyes. "I want to send her something... flowers or something."

Trudie sipped her hot chocolate and eased back in her recliner. "Kristen... I've been thinking. I'm sure Mrs. Childs would love to see you and Mary Ann. It would really give her a lift, I think, if she saw the three of us together again."

Kristen sat back down, shutting her eyes against the sharp sunlight. She heard the squeal of seagulls in the distance. She didn't speak.

Trudie continued. "You both could stay here at the house with me. If you can't come before Thanksgiving, then maybe you both could come in December, sometime before Christmas. It would be fun for us to have a little reunion. Just the three of us. It's been so long."

"Have you talked to Mary Ann about this?" Kristen asked.

"No, not yet. I've been thinking about it since Thursday night."

"Mary Ann lives in California now," Kristen said.

"I knew she left Denver," Trudie said, "but I didn't know where she went."

"Yes... we talked about two months ago. She moved to some little town north of L.A., but I don't remember the name. She's doing graphics works for some local ad agencies. She's also into healing, astrology, meditation and all that kind of stuff. She's living in a little house near the ocean with her two daughters."

"I haven't talked to her in over a year," Trudie said.

Kristen got up again and switched the phone from her right ear to her left. "She called to ask me if I knew a good lawyer out there. She's still having problems with her ex. Child support and alimony. Anyway, I put her in touch with a friend of a friend, and then we caught up on things. We mostly talked about our marriages and our kids. Then, as always, we talked about high school and how we wish we could go back and start all over again. I guess a lot of people do that when their life gets all messy."

Trudie placed her cup of hot chocolate down on a

coaster by the chair. "Do you think you could come, Kristen?"

Kristen paused, thinking. "I don't know if I can get away, Trudie. I just made partner a few months ago. I have a huge caseload and Alan and I are seeing a marriage counselor twice a week. I hope it works. The woman costs a fortune."

"I hope it works, too," Trudie said.

"I hate to say it, but most of our marriage trouble is my fault. Alan's a good father, a good provider and he's a nice guy. He's very thoughtful, he's faithful and all my friends like him. I think even our therapist likes him better than me."

"Okay. So what's the problem then, Kristen?"

Kristen pulled back the sliding door and stepped inside, drifting over to a chair. She sat, tucking her right leg under herself. "I don't know, Trudie. I've just been so unhappy lately. Maybe for a long time. I can't put my finger on it. I've got a good life, a good job, a good husband and a beautiful son. So what's my problem?"

"Maybe you should come for a quick weekend," Trudie said. "It might do us all good to be together again."

Kristen hesitated. "Yeah, it would be fun to see you both again, and to see Mrs. Childs. Do you think… she's going to die soon?"

"I don't know. I don't think so, but she was looking pretty weak."

"Okay, look. Give me Mrs. Childs' number. I want to call her. Then let me look at my calendar and see when the best weekend would be. Meanwhile, why don't you call Mary Ann and see if she can come?"

Kristen gave her Mary Ann's phone number then continued. "We'll do a conference call and try to come up with a couple of days that will work for us. How does that sound?"

Trudie sat up. "It sounds great. I'll call Mary Ann and get back with you."

Kristen spent the rest of Saturday dictating letters and preparing for the deposition on Monday morning. She called her son and her husband and then, after dinner, she took a stroll along the beach, recalling her senior year of high school and that warm spring night by Cotter's Pond, where she and Cole Blackwell had made love beside the water under a drenching moonlight. She blushed with re-gret once again as she remembered their duplicity. For the first time, he had broken his usual Saturday night date with Trudie so they could go out. They'd been meeting in secret nearly once a week for two months, but he'd never before abandoned Trudie on a Saturday night.

"Why don't you just tell Trudie it's over, Cole?" Kris-ten had asked, while they drove back to town.

"I can't. She trusts me. She's in love with me."

"And you're not in love with me!" Kristen had said, hurt and angry.

"Of course I'm in love with you, Kristen. You know that."

"Then why don't you tell her that?"

"Why don't you?" he shot back. "You're her best friend."

He'd turned his eyes back on the road. "I've got to concentrate on school and baseball. We have a big game coming up. All this stuff is distracting me."

The memory was an awful one. Kristen sighed heavily as she found the edge of the tide and waded in, barefoot, her capri pants rolled to her knees. The red sun was sink-ing into the sea and flaming clouds were piled on the distant horizon. *"Silly high school stuff,"* she thought. *"Stupid, silly high school drama."*

But in bed that night, Kristen slept fitfully. Cole finally did tell Trudie about his and Kristen's relationship and she heard all about it from Mary Ann.

"I'm sorry, Trudie, but I've fallen in love with someone else," Cole had told Trudie while they were sharing fries, friction and frowns at Burger King. Trudie tossed her cup of Coke at him and walked out.

Kristen and Cole both attended Ohio U. and dated through their sophomore year, when Cole met someone else. It was Kristen's turn to get dumped. Right after graduation, Cole married Marylyn Cass Harrington, a petit blonde from a wealthy Boston family. Kristen still bristled at the way Marylyn spelled her name. It was so pretentious.

Kristen rolled over on her side, staring into the darkness. *"Stupid high school drama."*

Cole and Marylyn were divorced eight years later. They had a son and a daughter. Cole had called Kristen one night, soon after. He was in New York and wanted to see her.

"You know, I never loved anyone but you. I made a mistake, Kristen. Marylyn came after me, and her father said he'd help my career. I was stupid. It was all a big mistake."

"Go to hell," Kristen had told him, slamming down the phone.

FIVE

It was 73 degrees in southern California and the warm air was moving. Mary Ann O'Brian drove leisurely under the tall palm trees of Carpentaria Avenue. She gazed out at the surf shops, cafes, antique stores and fast food restaurants. There was a relaxed calm about the town, an everlasting quality about the place, as if time had paused for awhile to rest after eons of relentless toil. That's what Mary Ann loved about it. There were no hurried strides; no blaring horns; no tension on the tanned bodies and pleasant faces of the people who lived there.

When she'd first moved to California, she felt a gentle happiness, an instant relaxation and a timeless freedom, as though her life back in Denver and Ohio had happened lifetimes ago.

As the car bumped across some railroad tracks, Mary Ann took in breaths of the soft, intoxicating air and craned her neck, searching for the ocean, just like she always did. And then the sea came into view, as if some stage manager had drawn back a huge white curtain, revealing the natural majesty of ocean and sky.

The impact was astonishing. Mary Ann was surrounded by a horizon of mountains and a glittery endless ocean view, with white rolling waves and a broad tan beach. She removed her sunglasses to see plunging cliffs and, in the distance, the shadowy Channel Islands. Mary Ann slowed down as she took it all in, silent and grateful to be living there.

It hadn't been an easy decision to leave Denver—to leave the familiar—sell the house, pull the girls away from their school and friends—just because she was having a major life crisis and knew a life-change was paramount for her mental and physical health.

When her friend Deb called from California to tell her that a quirky little house was for sale at a reasonable price, and that she'd help Mary Ann find graphic design jobs both online and in the area, Mary Ann jumped at it.

Deb, a social worker and a Reiki practitioner, mentioned that the community was also open to alternative medicine, healing and astrology, all of which Mary Ann had studied and practiced. With the money she'd receive from the sale of her old house, her savings and her husband's erratic child support and alimony checks, they'd make out just fine.

It was Mary Ann's red-haired daughter, 13-year-old Lynn, who gave her the most trouble over the move. She went into screaming fits. They'd argued and fought for days, and several times, Lynn threatened to run away.

Carly, a cool 15 year-old blonde, was the more stoic, simply brooding and not speaking for hours at a time. A week after they moved into the Carpentaria house, she'd refused to speak to anyone. She texted, or used a pad and pen to write questions and answers. Strangely, she also refused to take a shower for six days. It was Lynn who finally told her sister that she stunk and she'd had enough.

A month later, the girls had fallen totally in love with the place. They met boys who were teaching them to surf, they made new friends at school, and most important to them, they had glorious tans. They sent photos of themselves on the beach in two-piece bathing suits, hip-shot, flashing dazzling smiles. They posed with sun-drenched muscular boys on their surfboards, noting in their texts that it was 75 degrees, while in Denver it was 29 degrees and they were about to get another snowstorm.

Mary Ann traveled a two-lane road, taking in the coastline and sprawling houses facing the sea. She was charged with life, her bright eyes eager, her face animated as she scanned the area. "God, this is beautiful," she said, aloud.

She saw surfers bending into curling waves, surfers belly down on their surfboards paddling out to sea, and surfers standing on the edge of the tide studying the waves, their surfboards tucked under their arms. There were swimmers, sunbathers on bright towels, and sailboats leaning into the easy wind.

Mary Ann angled left down a quiet road to her house and parked outside the one-car garage. It was a square stucco house, nearly 3000 square feet, with a mish mosh of twisting, sun-bleached dune fences that enclosed the yard and rambled up toward the upper dunes.

Mary Ann carried the two bags of groceries toward the house, looking back toward the sea. Her daughters, Carly and Lynn, were on the beach with Deb, who lived just a few houses away and frequently spent time with the girls.

Their house was a quirky one. The ceilings were low and the floors covered with a worn brown carpet. The living room had a 1960s nautical maple living room set, and on the coffee table was a large, pink flamingo lamp, hovering over a 13-inch brass statue of Buddha.

A narrow stairway led up to the second floor, to shadowy rooms and kitschy porthole windows. The bathrooms smelled of mold, the showerhead spit staccato streams of mostly cold water, and the kitchen had faded green linoleum. The kitchen walls were yellow, the kitchen table sunshine yellow, and the four matching chairs were upholstered in yellow washable vinyl plastic. But none of that mattered to Mary Ann and the girls. It was quiet and warm, and it was only 300 steps from the beach.

Mary Ann entered the house, took the groceries to the kitchen and set them down. That's when she saw the note from Carly:

Mom:

Dad called. Said he needed to talk. Doesn't he have your cell number?

Mary Ann slid the note aside and began putting the groceries away. Her bright mood shifted to a brooding dread. She didn't want to talk to him. She had nothing else to say to him other than just send the child support checks on time. He was calling because the checks were two months late, and this month's check would probably be late too. The same old pattern. He never changed or tried to change.

Mary Ann heaved out a sigh and wandered into the living room. She stood in the center of the room for a time, her arms folded, her eyes closed, her body rocking gently back and forth, as she took deep breaths and allowed the agitation of her mind to settle. She silently repeated the words *peace, contentment, tranquility.* It was a practice she'd begun almost eight years before, after she'd visited an ashram in Santa Barbara and met a woman, an

43

Indian meditation master. That encounter had changed her life.

With her eyes still closed, she visualized the ashram, a big white oval building, with a glorious panoramic view of the blue ocean. It was surrounded by flower gardens, and quiet stone paths that meandered through trees and acres of rolling, shimmering grass. There was a pond with benches, and an expanse of trees, where meditators sat on little blankets under a cool, protective shade.

Inside the main hall of the ashram, Mary Ann remembered chanting in Sanskrit. The music began with the deep pulsing drone of the tamboura, an Indian musical instrument that resembles a lute. It's used as a drone to accompany singers or instruments. Its deep, vibrating sound represents to the ears the Aum or Om sound of the creative force of the universe. A flute drifted in, and then the light ethereal voice of a female singer. It was a lovely sound, otherworldly and soothing. More singers joined in, layering the chant with rich harmony and vocal improvisations. Finally, the swelling sound of over 400 voices chanting in unison was unexpectedly thrilling and enthralling.

Afterward, her meditation was deep and powerful. Her meeting with the meditation master was a life-changing event. It had helped to get her through the difficult divorce that followed.

Mary Ann opened her eyes and sat down on the carpet, arranging herself into a full lotus position. She still had a residue of acid anger over the divorce and it often threatened her peace. She still awoke some nights in a sweat, shouting at Robert for betraying their marriage—for having a child with another woman while he was still married to her. She still had a pulsing anger over his unreliable and grudging financial support, and too few quality visits with his daughters.

Carly, at 15-years old, kept her hurt inside herself, pretending she didn't care. Lynn, at 13, openly cursed him, refusing to see him the last time he visited. That wasn't good either. Mary Ann didn't want her daughters growing up to hate their father. She was careful not to speak negatively of him or portray him as the selfish bastard she thought he was. For that alone, she felt she was a saint. But who knows what will happen in the future? Their relationship with their father could change for the better. Maybe he'd even grow up someday and take responsibility for the family he helped create.

Mary Ann was struggling for mental calm when her cell phone rang. She ignored it, continuing her relaxation techniques: deep breathing and visualizations. But something inside nudged her to answer it. She unfolded her legs, got up and reached for her phone.

"Mary Ann. It's Trudie."

Mary Ann lit up, her mood instantly brighter. "Trudie! What perfect timing. It's so good to hear from you. How are you?"

"I'm good. Freezing my ass off, but I'm fine. I got your new number from Kristen."

"You talked to her?"

"Yes... just a few minutes ago. She's in San Juan for a deposition."

"How is she?"

"She's good."

"Still married?"

"Yes... Still trying to make it work."

"You were the smart one, Trudie. You stayed single. No heartache. No silly complications that drain away so much of your life force."

After a long silence, Mary Ann said, "Uh-oh…Did you get married, Trudie, since we last talked?"

"No, Mary Ann. I'm still very single. I'm calling because I went to see Mrs. Childs. She had a lumpectomy on her breast."

Mary drifted over to the couch and sat down, her eyes suddenly downcast and sad. "Oh… I hate to hear that. Is she still in the hospital?"

"No, she's at her daughter's house. Her daughter's a nurse and she's looking after her. She asked me to call you and Kristen and say hello."

"I would love to see her again. Can you give me her phone number? I'll call her."

"Sure. But I had a thought. Why don't you come back to Deer Lake for a visit? Kristen's going to try to come for a couple days. You could both stay at the house with me. There's certainly plenty of room."

Mary Ann considered it, the invitation exciting her. "When is Kristen going?"

"She doesn't know yet. She said we should have a conference call and figure out a time."

Mary Ann stood up. "Okay, I like it! I do. The three of us could go see Mrs. Childs and surprise her."

"Yes. Maybe we could even do our old Rockettes' act," Trudie said.

Mary Ann laughed. "Wouldn't that be a hoot? Maybe we could call some of the others who were in the Christmas shows. Are there any still living in town?"

Trudie thought. "Not many. Like your father and brother, most moved away. Even Kristen's parents moved away several years ago."

"Can you reach Kristen now?"

"I think so. Hang on. I'll try her."

Minutes later, Kristen was on the line. They fell into easy conversation, laughing, chatting, sharing old stories and struggling to recall the names of old classmates and teachers.

"Okay," Trudie said. "Let's set a date when you both can come."

"I like Mary Ann's idea about getting some other people together to go see Mrs. Childs," Kristen said. "We could put on a little show for her."

"There aren't that many people around, Kristen," Trudie said. "There's Ray and Connie Baker. That's about it."

"Then let's track the old group down and ask them to come," Mary Ann said.

"Sure, why not," Kristen added.

"Okay, wait a minute," Trudie said. "Wait a minute. I just had an idea. If you two could make a long weekend, let's say sometime in December, maybe we have enough time to call some others and have a kind of Christmas reunion. Maybe we could even put together a small little Christmas show for Mrs. Childs and perform it somewhere. That would cheer her up. And it would be fun. Just like the old days."

"Holy wow!" Mary Ann said. "I like it! I do."

"I love it!" Kristen said. "I absolutely love it! The Christmas Girls together again, putting on a show for Mrs. Childs? It's perfect!"

The three began to brainstorm, their excitement and enthusiasm spreading like a wild fire. They'd call and email old classmates, engage the community to help with publicity and raise money, talk to the high school board about using the high school auditorium. They'd find musicians, hang decorations, build sets, choose music, cater food and help find motels for guests.

"Wait a minute!" Trudie said. "Do we have enough time to do all this? I mean, Thanksgiving is this Thursday. That only leaves us about three weeks. Nobody wants to be away from their family on Christmas."

There was a long, thoughtful silence.

Kristen spoke up. "Okay, look. You're there, Trudie, with Ray. You're both going to have to be the point people, the main contacts, at least initially, until we get there."

"Kristen, do we *have* the time to do this?" Trudie repeated.

"Hell yes, we have the time! Of course we do. We've got to do this for Mrs. Childs."

"And for ourselves," Mary Ann said. "We need to be together again. It's been too long and we can't let this opportunity pass us by. I can make a lot of calls at this end. Who was the 20th reunion coordinator, Trudie?"

"Ray Howard."

"Great, so we'll get emails and phone numbers from Ray. Wait a minute! Better than that, he has them all already, so he could do a mass emailing like he did for the 20th reunion, that didn't happen."

"Great idea. Yeah, and then we can concentrate on the other stuff," Kristen said.

"Then let's come up with a firm date," Trudie said.

They stopped, searching their calendars, as they pondered, whistled and concentrated. Minutes later, they'd decided on the second weekend in December.

Trudie considered that, and then shook her head. "Christmas falls on Thursday, right? So I say, why don't we do the show on Christmas Eve?"

"What?" Kristen said. "No way. Everybody wants to be home for Christmas."

"She's right, Trudie. I'll want to be with my girls. My father's going to my sister's in Florida. We're supposed to meet them."

"Okay, I know everyone won't be able to make it, but some will. Some will like the change and some will love to escape from their families and come here and do the old Christmas show. Anyway, they can bring their families. We'll make it a big Christmas party, with Mrs. Childs as the centerpiece. It will be different, and memorable. We'll hire a photographer to take pictures and movies and then give them away. People will love it."

Kristen looked down at her newly manicured red nails. Mary Ann patted her waist, suddenly nervous that the 20 pounds she'd gained in the last year would make her a topic of whispery disapproval and criticism. Trudie twirled the ends of her hair, feeling the rise of anxiety at the thought of seeing many of her old classmates, especially Cole Blackwell and Jon Ketch. She was also becoming increasingly aware of the enormity of what she herself had proposed. Did she really want to do this?

"Here's what we do," Kristen said. "We'll have Ray send out the emails and ask how many would be willing to come for the Christmas Eve performance and party, and how many would prefer to come a week or so before, for the same performance."

"Sounds good," Mary Ann said.

Trudie took in a breath. "Okay. I'll talk to Ray and get to work on the emails. Before we do anything else though, I need to talk to Mrs. Childs' daughter to see if she thinks Mrs. Childs is strong enough for all this. If she says no, then the whole thing's off. Also, we have to make sure it's all kept quiet, a big secret. If Mrs. Childs finds out, it will spoil the surprise."

The girls agreed and then brainstormed additional ideas and possibilities. They laughed and reminisced, at times growing silent if the memory still had sting. As the possibility of seeing each other again became real, their enthusiasm and excitement took over, and they trampled over each other's words until none could hear what the other was saying.

After Mary Ann hung up, she went to her upstairs bedroom, found her high school yearbook on the top closet shelf and pulled it down. She bounced down on her bed and slowly leafed through it, drawn into memory and emotion.

Twenty minutes later, the girls boiled into the house, laughing and calling for her at the foot of the stairs. Mary Ann was absorbed in the senior class portrait of Oscar Bonds. What had happened to him? They'd met once ten or so years ago at Christmas, before her father had moved from Deer Lake.

She and Oscar had been lovers their senior year in high school. He was the first boy she'd had sex with. She'd told Trudie about it, but not Kristen. Kristen talked too much and was always giving unasked-for advice.

Oscar was a shy boy, but intelligent and genuine, graduating as valedictorian of the class. His lanky, loose-jointed build; his gray eyes; his long, lantern-jawed face; his oddly languorous boyish charm, were all attractive and entertaining. He went to Purdue on a full academic scholarship, majoring in civil engineering. Last she'd heard, he was working in Chicago.

Mary Ann closed the yearbook and lay back on her bed, staring up at the ceiling. She had truly cared for Oscar. Maybe she'd even loved him. She'd even imagined herself married to him and, in private moments, was sure he'd ask her to marry him. He was steady and dependable. He was kind. She'd liked the way he gently made love to her.

She'd persuaded him to participate in the Christmas show. He'd built an elaborate set of Santa's workshop and a faux fireplace, where Mrs. Claus, played by Mrs. Childs, sat knitting in a rocker, reciting *'Twas the Night before Christmas.* Everyone was impressed with his meticulous work and easy manner.

Ten years ago, when they'd both come home for their Christmas visits, they'd met over coffee and sandwiches. Mary Ann had boldly asked him why they'd separated just a month after they'd graduated. She said she never knew what had really happened. She'd thought they were compatible lovers and good friends.

Oscar had gained some weight and seemed more self-assured, but he was still quiet-spoken and thoughtful. He shrugged. "I guess you confused me," he'd said.

"Confused you?" she'd asked, surprised. "How did I confuse you?"

"I guess I thought you were too strange or something. You were always talking about things I didn't understand. I guess it just made me feel kind of uncomfortable."

"What did I talk about?" Mary Ann had asked.

"All that occult stuff about astrology and those tarot cards. That just confused me. I guess I thought we just wouldn't be compatible."

Oscar had married a research scientist. Mary Ann didn't know what kind of research she did, but she supposed they were compatible, even though Oscar said they didn't have any children.

Mary Ann shook her head, still feeling the pain of his words. Robert thought she was too far-out too. "Too

1960s spacey", he'd said more than once. It was true, Robert thought she was a little quirky, but he'd always told her she made him laugh. They certainly weren't laughing by the time of the divorce.

"Mom!" Carly called. "I'm hungry. Let's start dinner."

Mary Ann pushed up on her elbows and sighed. "Yeah, okay. I'll be right down."

She swung her legs to the floor and sat there, amazed that those 18-year-old emotions were still breathing and pacing about inside her gut, alive, as if it had all happened yesterday. Would Oscar and his wife come to the reunion?

Mary Ann closed her eyes and silently repeated: *Peace, contentment, tranquility.*

SIX

On the Saturday after Thanksgiving, Ray Howard dropped by Trudie's house, bringing a spreadsheet with the results of the Christmas reunion email. After ringing the bell, he let himself in, immediately noting the welcoming aromas of freshly baked cookies and percolating coffee. As he took off his coat, a smiling Trudie entered the living room, carrying a large platter of Christmas cookies she'd baked just that morning, her 'first edition batch' as she called them. She placed the platter on the coffee table and returned with two large Santa Claus mugs filled with coffee.

Trudie and Ray sat on the couch, sipping coffee and munching Linzer heart cookies with raspberry jam, almond shortbread cookies, gingerbread men, and Christmas tree butter cookies with colorful sprinkles. Later on, she was going to tackle the berry tarts with lemon cookie crust.

"These are fantastic!" Ray said, mumbling and chewing. "Are you going to eat them all yourself?"

"Yeah, right, like I want to look like Santa on Christmas. I'm not going to gain back those 15 pounds I worked so hard to lose. You'll take some home. I'll take a few to the kids I tutor, and then the rest to the office. It's become a holiday tradition. Dr. Preston would never forgive me if I didn't bring in a big batch of Christmas cookies for everyone, especially him."

Ray looked at her, curiously. "Seems kind of strange, people eating cookies in a dentist's office."

"No one has ever complained. By the way, isn't it time for your six-month cleaning?"

Ray frowned, mid-bite. "Yeah...And I think I have a cavity."

"Don't put it off, Ray. You won't get another set of teeth."

"Yeah, yeah, yeah."

"Oh, whatever. Let me see the printout."

Ray handed her two sheets of paper.

"I emailed the same list to Mary Ann and Kristen, like you said."

Trudie quickly scanned the list, searching for specific names.

Ray sipped coffee and chewed. He was 6'3", about 40 pounds overweight, with heavy jowls and dark intense eyes that seemed to see everything. He projected a courtly manner, a blend of gentle respect and amused observation. His dark brown hair was balding on top.

"Of the 196 graduating seniors on my mailing list," he said, "63 have responded so far. Of the 63, 41 said they could come for the reunion if it were held on the weekend of December 17, 18, or 19, or Thursday through Saturday. Now listen to this. A total of 44 said they'd be willing to come for the Christmas Eve performance, and most want to participate in the show in some way or the other."

Trudie's anxious gaze slid down the list to the YES column. There they were: Jon Ketch and Cole Blackwell.

They were coming. Her eyes stared blankly. She felt a dull ache and dread. There were so many emotions shooting up from some buried place—shooting up like erratic geysers.

Ray continued. "Of course, when it gets down to it, 15 or more in the YES column won't show up. That's the way it always is. There will be some emergency or they'll just change their mind."

"Okay, but still, that's a good number. And I'm assuming more will probably respond in the next few days?"

Ray sipped his coffee and shrugged. "Some, but not many."

Trudie's eyes rested on two names: Bonnie Styles and Herman Bevis. Beside their names Ray had typed DECEASED.

Trudie looked at him in stunned surprise. "Bonnie is dead?"

Ray nodded, sadly. "Yes. Her husband called me. He said she was killed in a boating accident on the Ohio River last summer. He kept her email box. He said when he got the email, he started crying. He sounded so bad, Trudie. I really felt for him."

"I'm so sorry," Trudie said. "What happened to Herman?"

"Heart attack while jogging in Knoxville, also a little over a year ago. He was the pastor at a Baptist church down there. You remember, he always was into his church and the Bible."

Trudie took in a breath. "Bonnie stage-managed the Christmas show our junior year, remember?"

Ray scratched his nose, lifting an eyebrow. "Oh yeah. She was so nice and easy. And then our senior year, Liz Tyree showed up. She was a terror. She even told me my piano playing was all wrong. When I asked her what *wrong* meant, she said 'You're just pounding too much.'"

Trudie lowered her head and laughed a little. "She was good, though. There were no technical mistakes during the show, not one. Liz Tyree is detail-minded and she demanded perfection."

"Well, she's on the list," Ray said, pointing at her name. "She's coming. She lives in Lexington, Kentucky."

Trudie shook her head. "I hope she won't ask to stage manage."

"Of course she will," Ray said. "You know she will. That's probably why she's coming."

Trudie shut her eyes and shook her head. "And so it all begins. The fights, the arguments, the craziness and the headaches."

"Speaking of beginning. Did you call Mrs. Childs' daughter?"

"Yes. She was excited by the idea. She said her mother would love to see the show again, even though she might act otherwise. But we all know that."

Ray cleared his throat, a Linzer cookie poised at his lips. "Do you think Mrs. Childs will be up and around by then?"

Trudie opened her eyes, staring beyond him, thinking. "Well ... If worst comes to worst, you, me, Kristen and Mary Ann will go to the house and perform the show. One way or the other, Mrs. Childs gets a Christmas show. How are your piano skills?"

"I may teach English, but I still play every Sunday at the Methodist church. Not that you know that, since I never see you there, Ms. Parks."

Trudie wrinkled up her nose. "I'll be there for the Christmas service, Ray. Did you keep any music from the old Christmas shows?"

His head slipped to one side, offended she asked. "You know I'm a pack rat. I still have my boy scout uniform, my first GI Joe—let's not go there on that one—and, yes, I still have the entire score—the complete score—of the senior class Christmas show from 20 years ago, including orchestral parts and conductor's notes, all packed neatly away in a trunk in my attic."

Trudie looked at him, admirably. "You are a wonderful piece of work, Raymond Howard."

He batted his eyes, playfully. "Yes, I am. And you should see the attic. My mother has threatened to throw me out of the house unless I throw out some of that glorious junk." He shook his head in mock despair. "Alas, I can't seem to part with any of it. I even have the first piano piece I played at a recital, and the first love letter I received."

"And who was that from?" Trudie asked, riveted.

Ray paused. "Are you ready for this? It was from our good friend, Kristen."

"Kristen!?"

Ray nodded. "Yep. The 7th grade. Kristen was a little vixen even then. You know she always liked the tall guys. Of course she didn't know I was gay, and I'm not sure I did either. Kristen still may not know I'm gay."

Trudie gave him a knowing stare. "Ray... believe me, at this point she knows you're gay. She doesn't care. But we're getting off track here. When are you going to speak to the school board about us using the auditorium for the show?"

"First thing Monday morning."

"Do you foresee a problem?"

"There's one snotty little bi... witch, Marjorie Lyons. She's the new principal and she thinks she owns the school. She's like a little general. She's only five foot one and I swear you'd think she was six foot five the way she marches around barking at people. I'm not sure she likes me very much. My students' test scores are down and she makes an ugly face every time she passes me in the hallway. I'm killing myself trying to get these kids to read so their reading levels go up, but they just don't want to read. It's all video games and texting—misspelled words."

Trudie stood up. "Ray, we need that auditorium. We can't move ahead unless we know we can perform there."

"I know, I know. I'll tackle it on Monday."

"Tell your principal it's for a good cause. Tell her why we're doing this. We're doing it for Mrs. Childs and all the alumni out there in the community. How can she object to that?"

Ray shrugged, reaching for another cookie. "It will cost us."

"Okay, fine. Find out how much and let me know as soon as possible. For now, Kristen's working on a budget, but we'll probably hand it over to Connie in a week or two. We don't have much time."

At the front door, Trudie tied Ray's burgundy scarf about his neck and then handed him a tin box filled with cookies. Ray grew reflective. "It's funny, isn't it? All this reunion business just stirs up old thoughts and memories. I had the weirdest dreams last night, about things and people I hadn't thought about in years. And guess who was right in the middle of everything, barking orders?"

Trudie smiled. "Mrs. Childs."

Ray nodded. "Why do we love her so much? She was a tough woman."

"Not really. She just acted tough. It was her persona. We all knew she cared about us. We all knew she was a dedicated teacher, and not just in drama class. She talked to us like a mother, gave good, solid advice, yelled at us when we were wrong, praised us when we did a good job. And I know she spent some of her own money to mount some of those plays and musicals."

Ray nodded. "And then the school budget was cut and art, music and drama were eliminated. They gave her a perfunctory retirement party and that was it."

"Out with the old and in with the new," Trudie said.

Ray turned toward the bright day. "So life goes. At least we have sun today and no snow is forecasted for tomorrow."

"I really want her to have this party—this Christmas performance, Ray."

He narrowed his determined eyes on her. "And she will. We'll all make it happen."

On Monday evening, under a heavy gray sky and light falling snow, Trudie parked her car near the Courthouse square and hurried toward the library. A few Christmas shoppers passed, their hats and shoulders dusted with snow. A father and his young son shouldered a large Douglas fir Christmas tree, struggling across the street in heavy traffic. Christmas lights blinked on in the shops and restaurants, adding a cheerful quality to the town. She glanced at her phone to see if Ray had texted her about securing the auditorium, but he hadn't.

There was still time for some shopping before she met with the students in the library. The shops were full and bustling; the Christmas carols bouncy and light. She bought a brown turtleneck sweater for her brother, left the shop and approached the redbrick Georgian style library, with its clock tower, Ionic columns and wide staircase.

Trudie had been tutoring math-challenged students for five years. Her father once asked her why she did it.

"Because I like it. It makes me feel useful somehow. I was always good in math and Mrs. Childs said we should try to help the world with the talents we have."

"Why didn't you go into teaching then?" he asked.

"I didn't want to teach all day long. So I tutor one evening a week and I am happy when they understand what an isosceles triangle is."

Her father canted his head to the right, asking. "And what, pray tell, is an isosceles triangle?"

"Textbook def?"

"Any def."

"A triangle with two equal sides. The angles opposite the equal sides are also equal."

"Fascinating," her father had said, returning to his newspaper.

For the next hour, Trudie sat at a heavy mahogany table near three rows of bookshelves, under a vaulted ceiling. She was working on math homework with two 9th grade boys, an 8th grade girl and a 10th grade boy. Both 9th grade boys were distracted by the pretty 8th grade girl named Ashley, who had long blonde hair and a blossoming body.

Trudie saw Ashley erasing the same equation for the third time.

"How is it going?" Trudie asked.

Ashley lifted her soft, discouraged eyes. "I just don't understand word problems. I keep making the same mistakes."

"My father used to say, 'She who does not make mistakes, usually makes nothing.' Let me help you with it."

After working with Ashley, Trudie noticed the antisocial 10th grader was slumped and bored at the far end of the table, texting. She had told him repeatedly to put his phone away and he always obeyed, but only for a minute or so. Then he'd hide it between his legs, eyeing it, pretending he was studying the algebra problem on the notepad before him.

Trudie pushed her chair back, got up and strolled to him, hands clasped behind her back.

"Almost finished, Larry?" she asked.

Larry Watson jumped, unaware she'd materialized. He was an overweight boy, with a moon face and long, black curly hair that fell over his ears and forehead.

"It's all okay," he said, not looking up.

"It's all okay if you have an answer. Do you have the answer, Larry?"

He shrugged. "Ummm... not yet."

"Put the phone in your backpack, Larry. Don't take it out again. If you do, don't come back. Do you understand? You're wasting my time and yours."

Grudgingly, Larry shoved his phone into the side pocket of his canvas backpack and zipped the flap shut. Trudie sat down next to him.

"Okay, let's start again."

"This is like real boring, you know."

"It's boring because you're making it boring. Throw the switch in your head, Larry. Throw the switch from boring to interesting; from 'I'm bored', to 'let's take an adventure and learn something new.'"

He shrugged, his uninterested expression expanding, his eyes blurred on the notepad.

"What do you like to do, Larry?" Trudie asked.

"Just hang out. I don't know."

"Yes, you do know. What do you like to do?"

"I like guitars. I like old guitars, like from the 1950s and 60s. I like to do audio stuff with my brother."

"What kind of audio stuff does your brother do?"

"He sets up audio for rock bands: amplifiers, mics, speakers. Stuff like that. When he's working close by, like in Columbus or Cincinnati, I go help him. I get to play the guitars sometimes."

"Okay. What are some of the names of the guitars you like?"

He shifted in his chair. "I don't know... I like...the Gigilotti GT Custom. And I really like the Gibson ES-125 Electric Archtop."

Trudie took a piece of white paper and a pencil. She scribbled down an algebraic word problem and then slid the paper across the table so Larry could read it.

He studied the page, his curious eyes sliding across it.

Larry wants to get $200,000 for his vintage guitar. An agent charges 20% of the selling price for selling the guitar for Larry.

a) What should the selling price be?

b) What will the agent's commission be?

Larry's eyes opened a little wider. Trudie saw sudden interest in them. "That's a lot for a guitar," he said.

"Doesn't matter what the price is. Work the problem. Let x be the selling price: x - 20%x = 200,000. Go to work on it. Use the tools I gave you last session."

Larry massaged his forehead, and fell into concentration.

Trudie got up and checked on the others while Larry scribbled down some ideas.

Ten minutes later, Trudie went back to Larry. "How's it going?" she asked.

Larry looked up at her. She saw light in his eyes. She saw pride.

"It's still too much for a guitar."

"Did you solve it?"

Larry said, "Okay, so if I used your tools right, I solve for x to find x equals $250,000. So the selling price is $250,000. Then 20% times 250,000 = $50,000. So the agent's commission is $50,000. Right?"

Trudie folded her arms in satisfaction. "Yes, Larry, that is absolutely correct."

"The agent is rippin' the guy off," Larry said. "That's just wrong."

Trudie grinned. "Now go to work on your homework problems, Larry."

After tutoring, Trudie stopped at the Town Market for a half-baked chicken, mashed potatoes, and peas and carrots. She didn't have the energy to cook. As she drove home through light snow, she passed Rusty's Café. She slowed down. She had an idea. She glanced down at her take-out food, made up her mind and turned into Rusty's half-full parking lot. With a slight hesitation, she unbuckled her seatbelt, got out and started for the stairs. She felt hopeful and bold, and a little foolish.

She entered, feeling the warm blast of heat as she scanned the busy café—the burgundy booths and heavy wooden tables and chairs. From the bar, off to the left and behind the restaurant, she heard shouts. There were two TVs broadcasting a football game.

The counter was mostly empty. From overhead speakers, she heard the familiar beats and choruses of cheerful Christmas carols. A Christmas tree by the entrance twinkled with white lights.

Trudie didn't see the guy she was looking for—the guy she'd met the last time she'd eaten there. Conflicted, she was about to turn to leave, when she saw him emerge from the Men's bathroom, striding toward the counter, wearing a white and green ski sweater and jeans. Trudie froze. He saw her and stopped. He lifted his arms in surprise and smiled. He bowed a hello. Trudie smiled, shyly, but started over to him. Then she forgot his name. It simply flew out of her head. She panicked.

"Well, hello again, Trudie," Don said. "I believe that's your name, if memory serves. And most of the time it serves."

Trudie fumbled for any word. "Hello..." then a name flashed into her mind. "...Dan... right?"

He scratched his head and turned about, as if searching for someone beside him. "Dan? Dan? Now where can he be?"

Trudie was mortified. "I'm sorry, that's not your name, is it?"

"Well, Trudie, a Don by any other name is still a Don. Don Rawlings."

"Don! Yes... I'm so sorry. I'm usually very good with names."

"Then I must make a better impression. Are you meeting somebody, or can you join me at the counter?"

"I'm free."

"Would you prefer a booth?"

"No, no, the counter is fine."

Trudie slipped out of her coat and eased down on the stool next to Don's. She saw he'd nearly finished his chicken dinner, and it was again drowned in a lake of ketchup.

He followed her gaze. "Yes, chicken again. I'm in a bit of a rut, I think. I almost went for the meatloaf but then, in the end, the chicken a la ketchup won out."

Trudie breathed in her nerves and when the waitress came for her order, she chose the meatloaf, though she'd lost her appetite.

Don's cologne was musty and sexy, his deep voice entrancing. It had been years since she'd felt this girlish excitement, enjoying the sweet bewilderment of sudden attraction.

Their conversation began with the weather: it was cold, not much snow had melted. She'd heard there was more snow on the way. Christmas shopping? Don had already bought presents for his little niece and nephew, but still had to find something for his parents, who were living in Tucson.

"Have you started your shopping?" Don asked.

"Some. I just buy for my grandparents, my brother and a few friends."

"Parents?"

"They're both deceased," Trudie said.

Don looked over and paused before saying "I'm sorry."

Trudie changed the subject. "You're not from around here, are you?"

"No. Born in Tucson. Went to college in Phoenix."

"What brings you to Deer Lake?" Trudie asked.

Don pushed aside his near-empty plate. "I'm part owner in a tech company. The one just outside of town, *CodeMobile*."

"Yes... I drive by it. It was a big addition to the town. People were talking about it for months. We were all afraid you were going to choose a more attractive town."

"We like it here. The property values are good and we've found a good work force."

"You're involved with internet security, right?"

"Yes, we're a security software company. Internet security is big business these days. We're growing like crazy, which is a good thing, but the business has tentacles shooting out everywhere, and that's a crazy thing to manage. No complaints though. And what about you? What kind of work do you do?"

"I'm a dental hygienist."

Don brightened. "Fantastic. I've been looking for a good dentist. It's been eight months since my teeth have been cleaned."

"Sounds like you're confessing. Shall I absolve you and make you an appointment?"

Don laughed. "Yeah... Let's do that. Let's make an appointment."

Their eyes met, and neither pulled them away. Their attraction was immediate and electric.

The waitress delivered Trudie's meatloaf, just as her cell phone rang.

Trudie pulled her eyes away and glanced down at her phone. She didn't recognize the number, or the area code. Something told her to answer it. Maybe it was someone calling about the Christmas reunion.

"Excuse me," Trudie said, reaching for her phone. "Hello?"

"Trudie Parks from the outlaw town of Deer Lake, Ohio, where gunslingers shoot cowpokes, whiskey bottles and swinging chandeliers, while kissin' feisty singin' dance hall girls, how the hell are you?"

Trudie laughed. She knew who it was, of course. She recognized the voice and she recognized the crazy patter. It was Jon Ketch!

"Jon!? Is that you?"

"Yes, ma'am, Lassie girl, it's me.   I'm a comin' to town, Lady Trudie Parks, and I'll be lookin' for love, adventure and a good barroom fight!"

SEVEN

It's not what Trudie expected. While she was finishing up her call with Jon Ketch, Don paid his check, gave her a half wave, a weak smile and left. *That was abrupt*, she thought. He must have thought Jon was her boyfriend or husband or something. She'd wanted to explain who Jon was and mention the Christmas reunion, but Jon was going on and on about how he wanted to put on an abbreviated version of *A Christmas Carol* at the Christmas show, and he was going to play Scrooge. He was already working on the script, and he wanted to know who was coming so he could cast the parts.

"Hello, Jon," Trudie said, finally interrupting his rapid-fire delivery. "We have not spoken in 15 years," Trudie said, hoping Don would get the message.

"Yeah. So?" he said, not missing a beat, "I want you to be the Ghost of Christmas Past! Or Mrs. Cratchit. I'm not sure yet. I'll know when I see you, and see how you've changed. Have you changed? You were so sexy the last time I saw you."

"That was 15 years ago. Of course I've changed."

"Change is good. I haven't changed a bit. I haven't even aged. Oh, and by the way, I'm delusional. Hey, I have to be. I live in L.A. Everybody's delusional out here."

So Don Rawlings left. With the phone to her ear, Trudie swiveled and watched him go, with disappointment and fascination. He was so very attractive.

Jon rambled on until, finally, he said his agent was calling and he had to go. That was it. He was gone, without another word.

Trudie entered her empty, silent house, flipped on the living room lights and stood there. She felt oddly out of place, almost as if the rooms and the furniture had been moved. The silence seemed alive with possibility. What possibility? It was as if the house had been flung off its foundation, had flown across space and landed in a different land. She even felt a little dizzy. She had the strange feeling that something major in her life was about to shift. Maybe it was already shifting. Maybe she was just getting the jitters about the reunion and seeing everybody again. Maybe she was coming down with something.

She made some hot tea, drew a bath and was about to strip off her robe when her phone rang. It was Ray.

"Dragon lady wants a proposal."

"Your principal?"

"Yep. Mrs. Marjorie Lyons, aka, Dragon Lady."

"Okay... no problem. Can you do it?"

"She wants all the details. How many days on site? How many people in the show? How many sets? How many costumes? Security. You name it."

Trudie sat down on the broad rim of the tub, dipping her free hand into the hot water. "Okay, so at least she didn't say no."

"She wanted to. I could see it in her chilly eyes. I tell you, the woman doesn't like me. Then I pulled out the Mrs. Childs' card, because I genuinely love the woman and want this reunion to be perfect for her. I told Dragon Lady that it was a great big Christmas present for a very sick woman who spent almost 30 years at the school. You may recall, Dragon Lady is from Cleveland and has never heard of Mrs. Childs. Anyway, I told her we'd done a Christmas show two years in a row and the town loved it, and it had become a tradition."

Ray's voice deepened. "Now get this. She said, rather snidely, that two years in a row, 20 years ago, does not constitute a tradition. I smiled, demurely, though I wanted to smack her, and recovered by telling her many alumni were coming and they would be in the show, including the famous actor, Jon Ketch. Well get this: she knows who Jon Ketch is."

"Of course she knows Jon, Ray. He's the most famous thing that has ever happened in this one-horse town."

"Okay, well, anyway. Next, I said we'd invite the entire community and make sure her name was displayed prominently on the program."

"Well, aren't you quite the diplomat, Raymond Howard."

"I heard myself say it, and it made me sick," Ray said. "But, in the end, she was almost, and I say almost, civil to me. But being the controlling person she is, she had to add that she will be, quote 'involved in every aspect of the production, to make sure the school is protected and appropriately represented.' End quote. She wants at least a thousand bucks for the high school. Maybe more, after she reads the proposal."

"So we'll raise the money. Get to work on that proposal."

"Yeah, yeah, yeah. Work, work work. Like I don't have about a million and a half papers to grade."

"I'll help you with the proposal. I'm proud of you, Ray. Kristen will be impressed. She always said you didn't have enough force of will."

"Well that little bitch! She had enough force of will for all of us. See you."

Trudie was chin deep in the tub, feeling the warm water relax her tired muscles, when she got a call from Kristen. Trudie lifted up, quickly dried her hand on a handy towel and grabbed her phone.

"What's up, Kristen?"

Kristen's voice was low and conspiratorial. "Guess who I just hung up with?"

"I'm afraid to ask."

"Cole Blackwell."

"Oh, God. What have we started?"

"He wanted to be sure I was going to the reunion. Get this: he hasn't remarried."

"Kristen, this is so high school. We're doing this for Mrs. Childs, you know, not so we can reconnect with our high school boyfriends."

"I know. I know. But he called. So we talked."

"Why are you whispering?"

"Because I'm in the back room of a fancy East Side restaurant at a boring dinner, with one of Alan's wealthy clients. Anyway, Cole said he was looking forward to seeing all of us Christmas girls together again, although he called us The Christmas Women."

"When can you come?" Trudie asked.

"I'm thinking I'll come… this weekend?"

Trudie stiffened with interest. "Really? This is December... the first week in December, Kristen."

"I know. Don't you want me?"

"Of course I want you to come. I'm just surprised."

"I want to see Mrs. Childs, and I want to get started on this. I called her the other day and we had a great talk. She said I was her favorite, of course."

"She's up to that again," Trudie said. "She said I was her favorite when I saw her."

"I'm excited, Trudie. I haven't been this excited in years. I'm sure you can use my help down there."

"Definitely. Can you come back in two weeks?"

"Of course. I'm a partner, Trudie, and I haven't taken any time off since last summer. The courts are going to slow down anyway before Christmas, and I can do my paperwork down there."

"Have you told your husband?"

"Not yet, but he's got to be away too, in Chicago. Alexander's in school until the 18th. So it's all good."

"Then come on down."

"Cole asked about you, Trudie."

Trudie closed her eyes. She suddenly flashed to the past, to that spring night when Cole called to cancel their date. "I just don't feel so good," he'd said. "It's my stomach... I guess I ate something bad. We've got a big game coming up and I'd better get some sleep."

Days later, after Trudie told Mary Ann about their cancelled date, Mary Ann hesitated, then finally confessed that she'd seen Cole and Kristen driving away from the A&W that night, Kristen's arm around Cole's neck. Mary Ann hadn't been sure what to do, but finally couldn't stand to see Trudie so naïve.

"Move on, Trudie. You can do a whole lot better than Cole Blackwell," she'd added.

Trudie was jarred back to reality when Kristen said, "Trudie, are you there?"

Trudie's eyes popped open. "Yes... I'm here."

"Cole's a shit, but he always did turn me on, especially in his basketball outfit. He owns a medical equipment business. Makes a fortune, or so he says."

Trudie slid down deeper into the water, silent.

Kristen's voice grew softer. "I know you really liked him too, Trudie, and I still feel terrible about what I did. But I was 17..."

"I don't care, Kristen. It was 20 years ago, for God's sake, and I just don't care. Let's just stay focused on the show and Mrs. Childs."

"You sound angry."

"I'm not." She lifted her free hand and then let it drop. It slapped the water and splashed her face. She wiped it. "I don't care. So text me the flight info and I'll pick you up in Columbus, okay?"

"Okay, sister friend. Can't wait to see you."

Later that night, while seated in a recliner near the shimmering fire, Trudie called Julie to check up on Mrs. Childs.

"Mom had a really restless night," Julie confided. "And she's getting very depressed at the prospect of starting another round of chemotherapy."

Julie explained that Kristen was coming to town and asked if they could come by over the weekend. Julie was enthusiastic.

"Yes, of course. Mom loves company, especially her old students. Teaching was her passion, as you know. It always makes her feel better. Yes, come."

After she hung up, Trudie surfed the TV, but found nothing of interest. She picked up a novel, read two pages and laid it aside. She thumbed through old text messages and tossed her phone down. She sat staring into the gleaming fireplace, hearing it crackle and hiss. She folded her arms tightly to her chest, feeling sick and tired of being alone. Of living alone. Of thinking alone. Of making every damned decision about the house alone. It seemed to her that everyone she knew had somebody. Loved somebody. Had children or had had children and families. Once again she'd spent Thanksgiving with her grandparents and their friends, the only person under 75. What the hell was the matter with her? Why didn't she ever find the right guy and get married?

She felt a surge of anger. Anger at Kristen. She had a good husband and a smart, handsome son, and she had the nerve to call and tell her that Cole Blackwell always turned her on. She was 38 years old, for God's sake! She sounded like she was 18 again! Didn't she know what she had? Couldn't she be grateful for all that she had: a successful career and loving family!?

Trudie pushed up, went into the kitchen and searched the cabinet corner, where she always hid chocolate bars. Why the hell was she hiding them? From whom? Nobody cared. Nobody gave a damn whether she ate the chocolate or she didn't eat the chocolate. She peeled back the wrapper from the extra dark chocolate bar and broke off a piece. Why did she struggle to lose those 15 pounds? No one noticed. Her boss, Dr. Preston, didn't even notice or, if he did, he didn't say anything. Didn't he notice? Granted he'd been married for 25 years and had a happy marriage and didn't flirt with other women, but she'd worked for him for 16 years. Couldn't he have at least noticed? Couldn't he have said, "Well, Trudie, look at you. You're looking quite thin these days?" Or "Trudie, have you lost a little weight? You look great!"

And why did Don leave so abruptly back at Rusty's? Was he so insulted just because she got a phone call from some other guy? What was that all about?

Trudie broke off another piece of the chocolate and shoved it into her mouth. She let it melt on her tongue, as her mind grew more agitated, as if storm clouds were rolling in and she wanted to rain out all her dark emotions, bad thoughts and ancient resentments.

And now Kristen was coming. Did she really want to listen to Kristen blabbering on about Cole and her husband, and probably some other guy or guys she's been flirting with in New York?

Trudie broke off another piece of chocolate. She looked at it, shaking her head, and then plopped it into her mouth, thinking back on past dates: one with Peter Hills, an internist in town. He was kind, quiet spoken and respectful. He was 43 and had never been married. They dated four or five times before he kissed her. She felt nothing. Absolutely nothing. He must have felt the same, because he never called again. They'd see each other in town, occasionally, and they'd smile and wave, as if they hardly knew each other. He had once made the comment that she was "Quite attractive."

And then there was Tom Klein, an attorney. He was nice, but not particularly attractive. Their relationship went nowhere.

Carl Stenowski was a car mechanic. He was muscular, fun and smart. She liked him, but he was seeing another woman, who soon snatched him away from Trudie and married him within two months. Now they had two kids and seemed relatively happy. Trudie still saw him now and then, although she avoided taking her car to him. They still had a little spark for each other and she didn't want to pursue it. She might get hurt.

Trudie marched into the den and, once again, pulled down her senior class yearbook. She held it for a time, but didn't open it. What did she hope to see or feel or find? Twenty damned years had passed and she was alone in the same town, doing the same job, while her friends were off having successful careers, adventures and families.

Trudie had been to Florida, St. Thomas, Austen, Texas and Cancun, twice, with Harriett Turner, the woman who cut her hair. On the trip to Austen, a big boisterous car dealership owner told Trudie she was the prettiest thing he'd ever seen. Then he told her he'd been married five times.

Trudie replaced the yearbook and slumped down in the leather desk chair. Her father's desk chair. She swiveled about, wondering why she'd lived the life she'd lived. How could she have changed it? Lived differently? Been more aggressive? Maybe she should have grabbed Carl Stenowski and forced him into marrying her, like that other broad had done. But she didn't. She just wasn't the type.

Her phone rang. She hurried into the living room to answer it.

"Hey, Trudie. It's Mary Ann. I was just thinking about you and remembering how much I've missed you."

Trudie was startled by tears forming in the sides of her eyes. "Oh, God, Mary Ann, it's so good to hear your voice."

"You okay? You sound funny."

"No, no, I'm fine. I'm just moping around feeling sorry for myself. Nothing serious. This whole reunion thing is starting to make me crazy. It's bringing up so much stuff."

"Well, ever since we talked the other day, I've been thinking about how much I want to see you." Mary Ann's soothing voice instantly relaxed Trudie, just as it always had.

"Ditto that, girl. It's been way too long."

"Guess who I got an email from?"

Trudie eased down into the recliner. "Oh God, don't tell me. Oscar?"

"Yep. The one and only Oscar. He said he got my email address from Ray."

"And he wants to know if you're going to the reunion?" Trudie asked.

"He never remarried."

"I didn't know he was divorced."

"Not divorced, Trudie. His wife died."

"Oh God, really? Wasn't she young? What did she die of?"

"Leukemia. Oscar said she'd been exposed to high levels of radiation doing her lab research."

"How did he sound?"

"Okay. It happened two years ago. She was older than Oscar. She was 44."

"So he's coming?" Trudie asked, pulling up her legs and tucking them under herself.

"He said he'd like to see me. He said it would be fun to work on the Christmas show again."

"Mrs. Childs will be so happy to see everyone."

"I called her," Mary Ann said. "We had a great talk. Of course she told me I was her favorite."

Trudie laughed. "Of course."

There was a pause. "It will be so good to see you again, Mary Ann. Kristen's coming this weekend. Any chance you could come?"

"I don't have the money, and the girls are still in school. But I'll be there in two weeks. Nothing can stop me."

"God help us," Trudie said. "Jon Ketch will be here."

"Crazy, wonderful Jon. The *big* Hollywood star. I was so in love with him."

"Weren't we all?"

Later that night, as Trudie lay in bed drifting off to sleep, she wondered if Jon Ketch would still find her attractive. It was a silly thought, really, but he *had* written something to remember in her yearbook.

I have been in love with you since we were in the 7th Grade. Hey, I can say that, now that we're graduating and I'm going off to college. Remember me sometimes, when I'm famous. And yes, I was always jealous of Cole! Why the hell didn't you love me?

Trudie's last thought before she fell asleep was, "I did love you."

EIGHT

Late Friday afternoon, pulling her black leather carry-on, Kristen exited the airway tunnel and strode purpose-fully into the terminal, searching for Trudie. She was dressed in designer jeans and a burgundy sweater over a white blouse. With her chic ponytail, sultry lips and star-let figure, she drew men's eyes and women's curiosity.

Trudie spotted her. Was it possible, she thought? Was it possible that Kristen Anderson Lloyd was even sexier and more attractive than the last time she'd seen her? Much more attractive at 38 than she had been at 18 or 28!?

Kristen saw Trudie in the crowd and she lit up, wav-ing. They closed the distance between them, falling into an embrace. They held each other at shoulder's distance, their faces animated and bright, and then they hugged again.

"You look so svelte, girl!" Kristen said, looking Trudie over. "Wow, skinny girl!"

Trudie was so grateful that somebody finally noticed her weight loss that she grabbed Kristen and hugged her again. "And you look fantastic, Kristen! Hollywood gorgeous!"

"Yoga, yoga, yoga and swimming twice a week!"

They started off arm in arm toward the exit.

They left the expressway near Deer Lake and traveled along a dark asphalt highway bisecting a white winter plain. The sun was already beginning its descent over bare trees against a bleak winter sky, where a V formation of geese was lazily beating south.

Since leaving the airport, the girls had caught up on families, old friends and Deer Lake's many changes.

"When can we see Mrs. Childs?" Kristen finally asked.

"I thought we'd go tomorrow. She's strongest in the morning, according to her daughter."

"I bought her some earrings from Tiffany's," Kristen said. "I hope she doesn't think I'm trying to impress her. They weren't that expensive and they reminded me of her. They're sterling silver Greek drama masks."

"She'll love them."

Trudie turned off the highway onto a side road. As the horizon became rosy, the view over white sloping fields to a distant forest was sublimely beautiful.

"And I brought you something." Kristen said, reaching into her purse and drawing out a beautifully wrapped box.

"You always were too generous. I've just started Christmas shopping."

"It's nothing really. But you have to open it right away."

"I'm tearing into it as soon as we get to the house."

Trudie turned into the driveway, stopping at the garage entrance.

"Do you have a tree yet?" Kristen asked.

"Not yet."

"Good. Tonight let's get a tree and decorate it."

"Great idea. I'll bake some more Christmas cookies."

Kristen clapped, enthusiastically. "I love your Christmas cookies. I'll buy the champagne. But first, after I unpack, I'm taking you to dinner."

"You don't have to do that."

"Of course I do. You're putting me up for the weekend. Let's go to the most expensive restaurant in Deer Lake."

Trudie gave her a doubtful, sideways glance. "That won't be hard."

An hour later, they were sitting in a booth at the Olive Garden, near the new mall that Kristen had never seen but had eyed lustily as they drove by. "We have to go shopping tomorrow," Kristen said.

Trudie ordered the Grilled Chicken Toscana and Kristen the Parmesan Crusted Tilapia. They took in the Christmas tree, the poinsettias and the soft muted lighting, as they sipped red wine. Trudie untied the ribbon on her Christmas present from Kristen. She lifted the lid from the Tiffany blue box and found a little flannel bag. She released the draw strings and shook out a dazzling, 3-inch snowflake ornament. Trudie stared in wonder, as she held it up to the light. It turned and sparkled.

"This is stunning, Kristen. Sterling silver?"

"It's no big thing. I got a deal on it. See why I want us to get the tree tonight?"

"This will be the first ornament I hang on it. Thank you, Kristen. It really is beautiful."

Kristen took her friend's hand, looking at her earnestly. "I'm so glad to be here, Trudie. It just feels so good and right to be together again. I can't wait to see Mary Ann and talk and laugh the way we used to. I want us to have the best Christmas ever. I want us to sing and dance and go ice skating like we used to. I want to make up for all the time that has passed. I want Mrs. Childs to recover. I want to see her barking out orders again, laughing and bossing us around. On the plane coming down here, I thought, why haven't we all three stayed in touch? Why did it take Mrs. Childs getting sick before we all came together again?"

Trudie turned serious. "I hope she doesn't get worse before the performance. The other day, she looked awfully frail."

Kristen patted her hand. "She'll be fine. When she sees the three of us together again, she'll feel better and get stronger. I know it."

Just as the waiter deposited their dinners, Trudie looked up and saw Don enter the restaurant with another man—an older man. Trudie's eyes widened with surprise. Kristen noticed.

"What's the matter?"

Trudie blinked away her nerves, snatching up her fork. "Nothing... I just saw somebody I know."

Kristen looked about. "Who?"

"Nobody."

"Trudie, you said it was somebody you know."

To Trudie's dismay, the hostess led the two men toward their booth. Trudie cut into her chicken and took a bite, her eyes focused on her plate. Then she heard Don's deep voice.

"Trudie!"

Trudie glanced up, faking surprise, chewing. She grinned and nodded, covering her mouth with her hand. "Oh, hello."

Don was dressed in a dark suit and powder blue shirt. His masculine presence drew Kristen to attention. Her interested eyes darted across Don's handsome face.

"We're always meeting in restaurants," Don said.

Trudie swallowed. "Yes. I guess we're always hungry," was all she could manage, and as soon as it left her mouth, she wanted it back.

Don laughed. "Yeah. Oh, excuse me," Don said, turning toward his companion. "Trudie this is Zack Prior. Zack, Trudie Parks."

Kristen flashed a sexy smile, as she lifted a feminine hand with perfectly manicured red nails. "I'm Kristen."

Don smiled down at her and took her hand. "Don," he said, studying her.

Trudie felt a sharp rise of jealousy.

Trudie shook Zack's hand. He was in his 50's, with iron gray hair and steady blue eyes. She saw lusty interest in those eyes.

"Nice to meet you, Trudie," he said.

"Trudie and I are old friends," Kristen said. "Are you and Trudie old friends, Don?"

Don glanced over at Trudie. He considered Kristen's question. "I hope Trudie and I will soon be old friends. Certainly good friends, anyway."

Kristen's eyebrows lifted.

Trudie tensed up, alive with new attraction.

Don smiled.

Zack, seeing Trudie was taken, now focused on Kristen. He smiled, revealing very white teeth. Trudie thought, *he's had his teeth whitened.* She also thought, *From the look in his eye, he'd like to sink those white teeth into Kristen's gorgeous neck.*

"Zack and I have some business to take care of. But afterwards, in 30 minutes or so, we'd love to have you join us."

Trudie hesitated.

Kristen didn't. "We'd love to. For dessert?"

"Yes. Good. Meanwhile," Don said, "I'll send you over two more glasses of wine."

After they were gone, Kristen sat staring at Trudie, as if she didn't quite know her old friend as well as she thought she did.

Trudie ignored her and kept eating.

"Well, Don is awfully easy to look at, isn't he, Trudie?"

Trudie looked up. "We just met a few days ago. We've never been out. I don't know anything about him, except that he's partial owner of the new tech company where the underwear factory used to be."

"This town has certainly changed since I was here last. Trudie, darling, he really likes you. I saw it in his eyes. If you have something going with him this weekend, don't let me get in the way."

"We don't have anything going... at least not yet. Anyway, you and I have a lot to do this weekend, and every weekend until this Christmas show is over."

Kristen took out her laptop and they began brainstorming logistics and a budget for the show. As always, Trudie was impressed with Kristen's ability to nail down details and come up with solutions. She was all action and focus, asking questions, making notes and thinking a problem through from the beginning to its logical end.

Thirty minutes later, Don reappeared and invited them over. The ladies reached for their wine glasses and joined the two men at their corner booth. They ordered dessert and coffee and drifted into easy conversation about the weather, their professions and, oddly enough, old Christmas movies.

It was Kristen who finally brought up the Christmas show, its background, some history and Mrs. Childs' condition. Trudie saw compassion on Don's face, as he listened quietly, without moving.

Zack stared into his phone, checking his messages, glancing up occasionally with a vacant smile, obviously preoccupied and not particularly interested in what Kristen was saying.

"I want to be a part of this," Don said, abruptly. "What can I do?"

Trudie looked at Kristen, who stared back at her, indicating with her eyes that she should respond.

Trudie spoke up. "Well... Don. What did you have in mind?"

"I have nothing in mind. I just think it's a thoughtful and wonderful thing to do and I'd like to get involved in some way. Do you need some financial backing?"

"Yes," Kristen said. "We have a kind of working wobbly budget, but we figure it will cost between four and seven thousand dollars, including advertising, sets, costumes and the rental space."

Zack laid his phone aside. "I'm sorry, I have to leave. Some business things have just come up. It's been a real pleasure, ladies."

Trudie slid out of the booth and let Zack up. He made his apologies, told Don he'd be in touch in the morning, and then he retreated.

Trudie sat back down, aware that Don was deep in thought.

"Make the budget ten thousand," Don said, emphatically. "Ten thousand is an easy round number that most people can grab on to. I'll contact some business people around town and see what I can do. Who do you have doing promo?"

"An old classmate of ours, Ray Howard. He lives in town."

"Good, good. Publicity will cost the most, I think. But I think once you get this out people will jump at it."

Kristen sat up, energized by his generosity. "Yes, I'm sure the whole town will get behind it. Our high school Christmas show used to be one of the biggest events of the year. People loved it."

"Yeah, it's a fantastic idea," Don said, rubbing his hands together. "And it will be an honor for me to be a part of it."

Trudie looked at Don in admiration. Kristen sat back, smiling, sipping her coffee.

"That's awfully nice of you, Don," Trudie said. "I'm sure many of our classmates will donate as well. We've had a huge response so far."

"That's so cool," Don said. "I'll help raise what I can and you all can continue raising money on your end. Things always cost more than you think and, it seems to me, we want to do this right. I'm assuming this is all a big secret."

"Yes," Kristen said. "It's going to be a big surprise, so we'll have to target the publicity carefully."

"What did you say your former teacher's name is?"

"Mrs. Childs," Trudie said. "Mrs. Myrna Childs."

Don flashed a broad grin, while forking a piece of the white chocolate raspberry cheesecake. "Eat up, ladies, there's more tiramisu and lemon cream cake. Did you know that I can play a mean tenor sax? Well, of course you didn't know. I once played a solo in our high school Christmas show. I played *Rudolph the Red Nose Reindeer.*"

Trudie and Kristen laughed, and Don looked at them in mock offense. "Hey, don't laugh. I wasn't bad. There were two guys behind me dressed as reindeer dancing around. One guy was kinda fat and the other guy was huge and clumsy. They were football players, so you can imagine what kind of a dance they were doing."

The girls laughed harder, holding their stomachs.

Don laughed too. "It wasn't as bad as it sounds. The crowd loved it. We got a standing ovation. Hey, do you think you can find a spot for me in the show? Maybe we can find a couple of reindeer outfits?"

The girls doubled over, laughing, drawing the curious eyes of diners nearby.

Outside in the parking lot, Don told them he'd be out of town for over a week, on business trips to New York and California. He said he'd stay in touch with his assistant, and if they needed to reach him they could reach him through her. They exchanged numbers and good-byes. He shook Kristen's hand and drew Trudie in close, kissing her cheek. "I'm excited, ladies. I mean, I am really excited. I'll start putting this into motion. As soon as I get back, I'll be able to jump in with both feet."

In the car on route to buy the Christmas tree, Kristen turned to Trudie. "If you're not interested in that guy, then let me know, because he's a winner."

"And *you're* married."

"Doesn't mean I can't flirt."

Trudie turned, sharply. "Not with him!"

"Ha, ha! So you are struck, sister girl?"

Trudie grinned. "Yes... you could say that. I *am* struck. I like him very much."

"I say we put him, and his two reindeer, in the show. What do you think?"

Trudie laughed again, seeing the performance clearly in her mind. "Oh, yes. That's a definite yes. I definitely want him around."

NINE

Trudie came slowly down the stairs, one hand on the rail, the other making a fist against a deep yawn. She was still in pajamas and bathrobe, wearing her white terry slippers. She heard Kristen's perky voice coming from the kitchen. *Oh, that's right,* Trudie thought, *Kristen is always perky in the morning, but perky even after wine at dinner, and a bottle of champagne while they decorated the tree and ate cookies?*

Trudie shuffled into the kitchen, still nursing a slight headache. She'd never been much of a drinker and last night she'd drunk more than she had in years.

Kristen was leaning back against the counter, makeup on and fully dressed, cell phone to her ear, coffee mug beside her. She waved, looking vibrant and refreshed. Trudie managed a half-hearted greeting as she trudged to the coffee pot. She poured a mug full and left the kitchen for the living room.

Kristen had already switched on the Christmas tree lights, and the stately Fraser fir stood in gleaming elegance near the picture window. Its gold and red globes reflected the white lights, instantly lifting Trudie's lethargic state. Kristen's Tiffany snowflake ornament glittered and beckoned, so Trudie stepped over and touched it.

How thoughtful Kristen is, she thought. *And so fun to be with... just not in the morning.*

Trudie slumped down into the recliner and took a generous gulp of coffee. Her eyes closed in grateful satisfaction as the warm liquid warmed her chest.

Minutes later, Kristen bustled in with her usual eager restlessness. "Good morning, Trudie. A little snow fell last night. It's so beautiful. I took a run/walk around the neighborhood."

Trudie's eyes opened in astonishment. "How long have you been up?"

"Six-thirty."

"It's after eight. How much sleep did you get? We went to bed after one in the morning," Trudie said.

"If I sleep five hours, that's a good night. You know I never did sleep very much. Oh, and I love the four poster bed and the rose color scheme, and that gorgeous and warm down quilt. When did you have the house redecorated? It looks fantastic."

"Just after Dad died."

Trudie yawned again, barely able to take in Kristen's rapid-fire conversation.

Kristen stepped over to the tree, fingering the snowflake ornament. "So I talked to Alexander and he's second in his class in math. I'm so proud of him. He stinks in English, go figure. But he loves science and math and he says he wants to be an aeronautical engineer. Wow! That surprises me. I also spoke with Alan. He said it's snowing like crazy in Chicago and he hopes his flight isn't delayed or cancelled. He sends you a hello."

Trudie nodded, massaging her forehead.

Kristen turned, ready eyes sparkling. "So, what time can we go see Mrs. Childs? Also, I called Ray and he said we should meet him for breakfast at Rusty's. Now I know it's Saturday, but Ray said the high school is open and we can go over and take a look around. Oh, and he said he emailed you the proposal he's going to send to Dragon Lady. He said we could go over the whole thing during breakfast."

Trudie's blurry vision struggled to focus. She felt Kristen's relentless energy fill the room like buzzing bees. She had boundless energy, and she had to be busy doing something, accomplishing something, talking about something, thinking about something or preparing something, every minute of every day.

Mary Ann had always been the buffer. She balanced the three of them. Her energy was measured, easy and light.

Trudie held up her hand. "I just need to wake up, Kristen. Last night was a lot of fun, but I feel like I've been kicked in the head. I just need a little recovery time."

Kristen nodded several times. "No worries. I've got some letters to dictate anyway. You get yourself together and let me know when you're ready to move."

At 10 o'clock they met Ray at Rusty's. Kristen and Ray hugged and caught up while Trudie drank more coffee and checked her phone. To her surprise, she had texts from both Jon Ketch and Don Rawlings.

While Ray and Kristen chattered and laughed, Trudie read the texts, Jon's first.

Hola Hot Girl: I'm anxious for your first kiss. Make it a slobbery one! **A Christmas Carol** *script is done and I've decided not to cast you as the First Ghost. You'll be too busy. Ray sent me the list of alumni coming. I've already got the play cast. 45 minutes, tops, for the play. Flying in on the 21st. Look out! Call for extra security!*

Trudie chuckled, scrolling to Don's text.

Great fun last night. Still excited. Called some local people. Tell Ray to get me promo ASAP. Need something tangible to show. See you!

Trudie slumped a little. She'd hoped for something a little more personable from Don. Was he hiding something? Maybe he was married or engaged. Maybe he had a girlfriend? Why would a handsome single man like that not have a girlfriend?

Over breakfast, Kristen examined Ray's proposal and made some insightful suggestions. They rewrote it on her laptop, while Trudie answered emails and texts from old friends, who had questions about the show and the accommodations. Then she called Julie to see if the three of them could visit Mrs. Childs that morning.

A little before noon, Ray, Kristen and Trudie entered Mrs. Childs' house. They found her sitting in the living room in a deep comfortable chair by the fire, and covered by a quilted blanket. Although she had a bad cold, she expanded in happiness and health when she saw them before her. As they took her hand and kissed her cheek, her pallid face took on vibrant color.

Kristen was nervously effusive around her old teacher, something only Trudie noticed because she knew Kristen so well. Kristen had difficulty editing her feelings and emotions, and Trudie had noted the mild shock and sudden concern on Kristen's face when she saw Mrs. Childs' thin frame and drawn cheeks. Trudie even thought she saw the start of tears, but Kristen quickly recovered, presenting a radiant smile and the aqua Tiffany's box with white ribbon.

Mrs. Childs held it, noticeably moved. She shook it and gave Kristen a kindly smile. "Can I open this now or do I have to wait until Christmas?"

"Now, of course," Kristen said, with amused authority.

Very carefully, Mrs. Childs removed the ribbon and lifted the lid. When she parted the tissue, her weak eyes opened in surprise. "Oh, my... look at those. Greek theatre masks. Just look at them," she said, happily. "I just love them!"

Kristen helped her put them on, while Julie brought a mirror and held it up. Mrs. Childs stared, turning her head, glowing with appreciation. She took Kristen's hand and kissed it. "Thank you, Kristen. So thoughtful and so appropriate."

Then Ray was all hand patting and gossip, filling Mrs. Childs in on the latest high school news and information about former students. Trudie was impressed by his ability to give details about their classmates without divulging any plans for the Christmas show.

After Julie brought glasses of eggnog, they toasted the Christmas season. And then Mrs. Childs' eyes narrowed on Kristen.

"I bet you are a good attorney, Kristen. You always loved to argue with me, over the smallest little things."

Kristen made a little gesture with her glass. "I was only offering suggestions, Mrs. Childs."

"No, Kristen, you were arguing. Not that I always minded. Sometimes I liked your suggestions."

"Which suggestions did you like? Do you remember?"

"Of course I remember. I still have my brain, you know. You once made the suggestion that you, Mary Ann and Trudie should sing *Jingle Bells* like the Andrews Sisters did. You had me listen to the record three times.

I said, none of the people in this town will know who the Andrews Sisters were. They were popular back in the 1940's. But you insisted, saying, 'What is education for, Mrs. Childs? Aren't we supposed to enlighten, inform and instruct?' Well, what could I say to that?"

Kristen lowered her head in pretend embarrassment. "Was I that obnoxious?"

"Yes, Kristen, you were. And the way you flirted with the guys. Oh, my..."

Ray spoke up. "She still does flirt, Mrs. Childs. She was flirting with our waiter this morning at Rusty's. He was about 19 years old."

Kristen slapped him in the arm. "I did not!"

"Yes, you did," Trudie said. "He blushed when you told him the girls in New York City would fall all over him."

"So they would," Kristen defended. "He was handsome. Did you see those beautiful eyes, his thick neck and his long, curly, reddish-blond hair?"

Mrs. Childs laughed, her whole body shaking. "Okay, I rest my case," she said. And then she suddenly broke into a painful hacking cough. She bent forward, her hand covering her mouth, her face pinched in pain, flushing scarlet. Julie stepped in and held her, offering a tissue. Mrs. Childs took it, covering her mouth. Finally, the attack gradually subsided.

"I'll be glad when she gets over that cold," Julie said, troubled.

The three former students looked on, concerned and distressed.

They left the house fifteen minutes later, silent and cheerless. Ray drove away in his car, promising to meet them at 3 p.m. to take a tour of the high school auditorium. In the meantime, he had errands to do.

Trudie took the long way back to the house to let the emotion settle and to show Kristen the new housing divisions, the farm-to-table market, and the brand new Quad movie theatre.

Kristen sat quietly, with the expression of someone who has just discovered a sadness she had no idea was inside her.

"Are you okay, Kristen?"

Kristen sat with folded arms, staring out the window at the gray overcast day. Snow flurries drifted over the rolling, white fields.

"I hated seeing Mrs. Childs like that. I just hated it. She was so strong. Strong and filled with life. That's one thing I always loved about her. People shouldn't have to gradually shrivel up like that. She was so dignified."

"She's still dignified, Kristen. You can see it in her eyes."

"She was so embarrassed, coughing like that in front of us. She never showed us weakness. Always strength. That's another thing I learned from her. Always show strength, even when you're scared to death. Even when you know you're losing... an old lover...a legal case... a marriage."

Trudie glanced over. "Are you losing your marriage, Kristen?"

Kristen didn't look at her friend. Her voice was quiet; she spoke at a near whisper. "I don't know. Maybe. Maybe... because I screwed up. I wish I were a better person, Trudie. I wish I were good and true like you always were."

Trudie braked at a red light, her eyes flitting about, seeking an answer. "Kristen... don't go there. I'm no one to admire. I'm just trying to figure it all out just like everybody else is."

"But you were always solid and honest. I loved that about you. I hung around you hoping some of that would rub off on me."

Trudie tried to speak but nothing came.

Minutes later they were passing the courthouse square, viewing the manger scene and the grand 20 foot fir tree on the village green. Children were building a snowman and throwing snowballs.

"I'd forgotten how lovely this town is during Christmas," Kristen said. "It feels so good to be back here, and to spend time with you again. Keep driving, Trudie. Let's just keep driving around. This is so much fun. Then let's go to the mall and shop a little before we meet Ray. Shopping always makes me feel better."

Twenty minutes later they'd parked at the mall parking lot. Trudie killed the engine and they sat in a chilly silence, not moving.

"Cole called me again," Kristen said. "He said he'd never stopped loving me. I've been thinking about that. I've been thinking that I'd like to see him again. Hell, I want to see him again. What does that say about me?"

Trudie looked away.

"Don't judge me, Trudie. Please. Not now. I'm all screwed up and confused. Alan and I are like strangers, and not easy strangers. We don't even sleep together anymore. I think he has a girlfriend. I don't know for sure, but I think so."

Trudie listened, and then looked at Kristen uneasily.

Kristen continued. "Alan makes a ton of money, travels all the time and... I don't know. I think he travels because he wants to get away from me. I look at myself in the mirror sometimes and I say, hey, who the hell are you, girl? I don't know you anymore. And I'm getting older. The lines are coming. The gray hair is here."

Trudie stared ahead, watching shoppers pass, clutching bags, talking on cell phones.

"Kristen, why don't you bring Alan to the reunion? It might do you both good to get away from everything and spend some time together in a different place. Bring Alexander too. Make it a family thing. A lot of the alumni are bringing their kids."

Kristen sat thinking about it, turning it over in her head. "I don't know. Do I want him here? It might spoil everything. It's nice being away from all that. It's nice having an escape into the past before everything got all messed up."

"Do you hear yourself, Kristen? Spoil everything? What does that mean? You can't go back into the past, Kristen. You know that."

"Maybe going back into the past is just what I need. The more I think about it, I think it's *just* what I need."

Trudie pulled the keys from the ignition and dropped them into her purse, almost losing her patience. "Has Alan ever been to Deer Lake?"

"Once... for just a couple of nights, before my parents moved away. He wasn't thrilled. He called it the 'back end of a hole in the wall', whatever that means. And anyway, he and Alexander want to go skiing in Colorado. We have a house in Breckenridge. He wants me to fly out on Christmas day and join them."

Inside the mall, they didn't talk while they browsed the aisles of the first store they saw and picked through a few racks of clothes, hearing familiar Christmas songs wherever they went. Trudie had never seen Kristen look so despondent. It wasn't like her. Trudie nudged them over to a Starbucks and bought them both a sandwich and a cappuccino.

While they sat staring out into the broad corridor at the shoppers, Trudie entertained Kristen with stories of her patients: the woman who wouldn't stop talking even with the suction tube in her mouth; the business man who texted continuously while she struggled to clean his teeth; and the elderly man who kept a silver flask of whiskey in his hip pocket.

They finally left, empty-handed, and drove to the high school, arriving before 3. Ray met them in the parking lot, and they mounted the front stairs and entered the school together. Inside the quiet hallways, they heard the soft echo of their footsteps, and Kristen remarked on how little it had changed in 20 years.

When Ray opened the double auditorium doors, they entered into silence, stepping forward and gazing in absorbed wonder at the spacious hall, the dimly lit rows of seats, the deep shadows in the balcony and the wide proscenium stage, with its impressive burgundy velvet curtain. Memories flooded back—the echo of conversation, fragments of music and the drum of dance steps.

Kristen flashed back, imagining Mrs. Childs marching about the stage shouting orders; hearing the mellow trumpets and chorus singing *Deck the Halls*; seeing, in slow motion, the three of them, The Christmas Girls, all dazzle and smiles, kicking high with swinging Rockette precision to *Jingle Bells*.

Kristen turned, meeting Trudie's gaze. The moment felt privately sacred, and they smiled under the spell of the past. Kristen linked her arm in Trudie's and drew her close.

"This is going to be so much fun, isn't it? I am so excited."

Kristen's phone buzzed. She glanced down at it, startled. "Oh God, it's Cole. I've got to take this."

Ray and Trudie strolled down the aisle together, while Kristen drifted into shadows in the back of the house.

"What's that all about?" Ray asked.

Trudie turned away. "Don't ask."

TEN

At Trudie's house on Sunday, Ray and Kristen worked on promo ideas while Trudie called the motels around town negotiating lower rates for the confirmed 48 people and their families who'd be staying 2 to 3 days. Then she called three restaurants for availability and catering costs for the Christmas Eve party after the show. The only one available, with space large enough for 70 to 100 people, was good old Rusty's Café. Next, she discussed the hours, menu and liquor costs. It wouldn't be cheap, but at this late date it would have to do.

Ray emailed a flyer and promotion materials, along with some firm budget numbers, to Don Rawlings and alumni who'd pledged financial support. At three o'clock, Kristen was packed and ready to leave for a six o'clock flight back to New York, leaving from Columbus. She and Ray had a final hug, promising to stay in touch. Kristen lingered in the doorway to ask him a question.

"Are you involved with anyone, Ray?"

"I wondered when you were going to ask."

Kristen's expression turned apologetic. "I should have, Ray. I'm sorry."

"Oh stop it. I was seeing a guy in Columbus for awhile. He moved to Washington, D.C. He's heavy into politics. I go there sometimes. He comes here sometimes. We're close, but... Well, it ain't perfect, but then, what is?"

Kristen nodded. "Yep... what is?"

"Enough, you two," Trudie said. "You're depressing me, and I refuse to be depressed during the holidays."

As they were approaching the Port Columbus International Airport, Kristen broke a long silence. "We accomplished a lot this weekend."

"There's still a lot to do,"

"I called Mrs. Childs while I was packing," Kristen said. "She sounded better."

"Good. I'll call her tonight."

"Mary Ann sounded good last night, didn't she?"

"Yes."

Traffic was fast and erratic, drivers sliding in and out of lanes, horns blaring. Trudie took a couple of breaths and slowed down, adjusting her rearview mirror.

"Can't wait to see Mary Ann... and her daughters."

"Me too."

"Are you disappointed in me, Trudie?"

Trudie glanced over. "What?"

"You know. You've been avoiding me."

"I have not."

"You have..."

"Kristen, you're a grown woman. You've got to live your life the way you have to live it. What else can I say?"

Kristen stared ahead, seeing the signs to the airport. "This silly reunion is bringing up a lot of shit. It's like I'm 17 or 18 years old again."

"We're not 18 years old, Kristen. We're all grown up, or so we're supposed to be, anyway."

Kristen looked at Trudie, curiously. "Why haven't you gotten married? I mean, you're smart and pretty..."

Trudie felt the rise of a swift, trapped anger. It was a question she'd had to answer too many times.

"It's what happened, okay!? It's life." She tried to control her anger, but it was seething inside her, pushing its way out. "Nothing ever seems to go the way you think it should. Do you think I want to be alone in that empty house—that I wanted to live alone with my father? No, I didn't. It just didn't happen, okay? I had some serious relationships. I was asked a couple of times...actually, three times. I guess I didn't love them—any of them. The whole thing scared me. I mean, I look around at everybody and I think, maybe I don't want to get married, because who stays married and who is happy anyway?" Trudie threw up a helpless hand. "Oh, the hell with it. It doesn't matter."

But in the deep silence, anger continued to roll out of her. "I thought Cole and I would get married once. I thought I loved him. Well, guess what? That didn't happen. He lied to me and went off with you! I guess he's been in love with you ever since. Okay, so now you can both hook up again and pick up where you left off. So fine. So let's drop the whole thing, okay?"

Kristen spoke up. "Trudie, I didn't mean..."

Trudie cut her off. "I don't care, Kristen. I just don't care anymore."

Trudie whipped the car into the right lane, laying on her horn when a car in front slowed down. Then she jerked the car into the exit lane and sped off to the airport.

Trudie lowered her voice, struggling to control her emotions. "It all happened a hundred years ago, Kristen. None of it matters now. I didn't get married because I never found the right person. It's that simple. Things just didn't work out for me that way. Maybe they never will."

They arrived at the terminal and Trudie parked at the curb. They sat in an icy silence, feeling blunted and hurt. Kristen sat dead still, her eyes locked ahead.

Trudie felt awful, wishing she'd kept her mouth shut. Finally, she opened her door and pushed out. She opened the trunk and heaved out Kristen's travel bag, as Kristen came around to retrieve it.

Without speaking they hugged. They avoided each other's eyes.

"You'll stay in touch?" Trudie said.

"Of course..."

They stood, staring at the pavement.

"Do we really want to go through with this whole re-union thing?" Kristen asked. "It's starting to hurt."

"Yes, we are going through with it for Mrs. Childs, and for all the other alumni who are coming. We've set this whole thing into motion, so now we have to go through with it."

Kristen nodded, hugged her friend again and started off. She turned before she pushed through the glass doors. "Thanks for the weekend, sister girl. It was fun. See you on the 21st."

Trudie waved, managing a smile. "Have a good flight home."

Before leaving the airport, Trudie texted Kristen: *Sorry about the outburst. I'm a bit nervous about everything. Call when you can. Love ya.*

As Trudie was sending her text, she received one from Kristen. *I'm such a bitch sometimes. Forgive me. Are we having a midlife crisis? So much fun with you. Love ya.*

That night, back at the house, Trudie sat on the couch and re-read her texts, stopping on Jon Ketch's. She was excited at the thought of seeing him again. He was the most famous person she'd ever known, and she knew he would be a big draw for the community. Ray and Kristen had placed his name on the flyer that was to be passed around town at the library, local businesses, restaurants, and malls.

COME ONE! COME ALL!
20-YEAR REUNION ALUMNI CHRISTMAS SHOW
AT THE DEER LAKE HIGH SCHOOL AUDITORIUM!
FEATURING HOMETOWN BOY AND
HOLLYWOOD ACTOR
JON KETCH
AS EBENEZER SCROOGE IN
"A CHRISTMAS CAROL!"
ALSO FEATURING
THE CHRISTMAS WOMEN,
LIVE ORCHESTRA, DANCERS, SINGERS
AND SING-ALONG CHRISTMAS CAROLS!

The house was quiet after Kristen left and Trudie wandered into the study and sat in her father's leather desk chair, staring out the windows into the darkness. She read Jon's text again. "A big slobbery kiss." She smiled.

She and Jon had dated a number of times, although he'd always pretended that she had turned him down whenever he'd asked her out.

But how could she ignore that bright autumn day during their senior year, when they'd picnicked under the trees near the school? They had skipped Ms. Dillon's social studies class, which of course didn't matter, because Trudie would get an "A" anyway, and Jon would get a predicable "D", for which he was proud.

"A 'D' is nothing to be ashamed of, Trudie" he said, chewing vigorously on some French fries, his mouth open. "Getting a 'D' means that I have earned the devilishly DEElicious DEEstinction of DEEliberately DEEciding to DEEclare to the DEEhumanizing delegates of the dumb DEEpartment of education at Deer Lake High, that I, Jon DEE Ketch, DEEtest them and don't give a big rat's ass what grade they give me! They can all kiss my DEElectable arse!"

Trudie laughed wildly. His rakish cleverness had always entertained her. He was a character from right out of Shakespeare, a Puck or The Fool in *King Lear* or a young Falstaff. He was a Ferris Bueller.

They munched on Whoppers, fries and a large soda with two straws. They had stolen a towel from the gym locker room and had spread it out on the grass near a splashing stream, under the shade of shining autumn trees, from which they had an unobstructed view of the school. They lay there, staring up into the infinite blue sky, feeling the cool wind and burnt autumn smells. The sunlight dappled their faces.

"I once went to New York City and had a Whopper on 5th Avenue," Jon said, chewing, "And you know what I called it?"

"The 5th Avenue Whopper?" Trudie asked, giggling.

He pointed to Trudie. "You are clever, Lady Trudie Parks. It was the best Whopper I've ever eaten. Hands down. The best!"

"Why was it the best? Give me details," she asked.

"Because it was a 5th Avenue Whopper, of course!" he said, lifting his chin imperiously. "It had class. It had attitude. It had the rich flavor of privilege and East Side breeding. It was a pompous Whopper...A stuck-up-your-ass Whopper."

"Was it a wealthy Whopper? A well-educated, well-bred Whopper?"

"It was all that and much more, Lady Parks of Deer Lake."

"What more did it have?" she asked, enjoying this game, this play-acting. She pulled phrases from roles she'd memorized in Mrs. Childs' class. "Give me more, you rascal you. You rogue, you rescuer of women, although I am still only 17 years old and would not call myself as such, that is, a woman."

Jon arched a startled eyebrow, looking her up and down. "Oh, but you are a woman, my Lady. Oh yes, when you lift that little skirt of yours, I can see, without any compunction or hesitation, that you are definitely a woman... Oh yes."

Trudie batted her eyes. "So tell me about this big, big Whopper."

"It was a Whopper unsurpassed in its ability to demand that one eat it with a special kind of style and grace."

Trudie laughed again, and then, quite suddenly—just like that—she was caught! She was sexually turned on and she was sure Jon saw it in her eyes. "Wow! I want that Whopper," she said, with a sexy wink and sneer.

John dropped down to the blanket and quickly kissed her, pinning her shoulders with his strong arms. Trudie reached for him, pulled him down and kissed him deeply.

Maybe Jon scared her. He was wily, shocking and unpredictable. She didn't feel secure around him, but he thrilled her; excited her; turned her on.

Trudie's father didn't like him. Most of the teachers

didn't like him. In fact, her history teacher, Mrs. Wallingford, pulled Trudie aside one day. "Jon Ketch is a rebel, Trudie," she said. "Be careful. He'll probably wind up in a prison cell some day."

A week after that picnic, Trudie went on her first date with Cole Blackwell. Jon didn't speak to her for weeks.

Trudie gently rocked the desk chair, twirling the ends of her hair. She'd conveniently forgotten about that, or maybe she'd just shoved the guilty memory in a drawer someplace in the back of her mind. Jon wouldn't look at her in the hallway and avoided her in social studies class. He grew brooding and quiet. Yes, she had forgotten that.

Jon was a crazy fun guy, but he didn't have the tall, aloof and graceful sophistication of Cole Blackwell, whose family had just recently moved to Deer Lake from Lansing, Michigan. Trudie had fallen hard for him. He was so popular, quickly becoming the top basketball star. She melted into his arms when he kissed her. She got weak in the knees when he spoke her name. She fell in love with him without understanding it. All she knew was that she felt lucky to be the chosen one. Out of all the girls, he had chosen her.

Even now, when she recalled Cole, she felt a warm stirring across her skin. A gentle increased heartbeat and expectation, as if he were just outside her bedroom, ready to enter and make love to her.

Trudie lowered her head, embarrassed by her adolescent memories. She was amazed by her body's passionate recall after so many years. Twenty years meant nothing to the body or the mind, so it seemed. To them there was no time, just refurbished old sensation and the reawakening of a suppressed passion for a man who probably hadn't given her much thought in 20 years. *His* passionate memory, his one desire, had been Kristen Anderson.

Obviously, Kristen had been the love of his life. Maybe Cole was Kristen's. Who was to say?

Trudie strolled into the living room and stood staring into the dark, unlit fireplace. Maybe the old memories remained potently alive because she hadn't been involved in a passionate relationship since. Why? She didn't know. Too independent? Too scared? Too set in her ways? Too choosy?

Trudie was eating in front of the TV when her phone rang. It was Julie.

"Is this a good time?" Julie asked.

"Of course. Is everything all right?"

"I'm at the hospital with Mom. She was coughing and had a fever. I didn't want to take any chances. I checked her in so she could be monitored."

Trudie switched off the TV, worried. "Do you need me to come over? You must be tired."

"That's so nice of you. My brother, Nick, is coming on Tuesday, so that will help." She paused. "I hate to impose, but do you think you could spend some time with her tomorrow evening? Would that be convenient?"

"Of course. I'll come right after work. I can be there by 6:15. Is she at St. Mary's Hospital?"

"Yes. I really appreciate it, Trudie. Thank you."

As Trudie was loading the dishwasher, the inevitable awful thought arose: what would they do if Mrs. Childs was too sick to attend the Christmas performance, or if she died? It was all being planned for her—to honor, up-lift and entertain her. Should they make alternative plans just in case? Should she call the others and get their opinions? No. She would wait until she saw Mrs. Childs tomorrow night. She'd make the decision then.

Trudie lay in bed until 2 a.m., wide awake, mind spinning. She finally threw back the quilt, slipped on her robe and went downstairs to make hot chocolate. Leaning against the counter, gently stirring the milk and chocolate syrup, she shivered a little. The temperature outside was in the single digits, 6 or 8 degrees. Another quiet and lonely night.

She sat at the kitchen table sipping the hot chocolate. Soon the whole house would be in motion, with Kristen, Mary Ann and her two daughters romping, talking, and filling all the quiet spaces. Within two weeks, Trudie's life would be hectic and unpredictable, boiling with activity, emotion and responsibility. The past would come alive again with old faces, old stories and new possibilities. It was an exciting and scary thought.

Trudie stood by the sink and rinsed her cup, allowing her mind to settle on Mrs. Childs. She had supported and inspired them all. Her class had been challenging, fun and controversial, even 20 years ago.

"Don't just walk through life and complain about its constant challenges," Mrs. Childs often said. "Be a lion. Roar at life. Be courageous and, most of all, learn how to be happy. If you don't know how? Make it up. Pretend, just like you do on that stage up there. Just act and pretend until, finally, one day, it becomes part of you."

Back in bed, Trudie prayed for her old teacher. She prayed for her renewed health and well-being. She thanked God for Mrs. Childs' strong and good influence, and then Trudie selfishly prayed that God would give her teacher the health and strength to rise up and attend the Christmas show.

At that same moment, two doctors were summoned to Mrs. Myrna Childs' hospital room. She had developed pneumonia; she was fighting for her life.

ELEVEN

Mary Ann O'Brian pulled her daughters out of school two days early and flew to Columbus, Ohio on Wednesday December 17th, arriving at 2:30 in the afternoon. An excited Trudie met them at the exit gate, embracing Mary Ann warmly and offering Lynn and Carly hugs. Lynn, being the friendlier, hugged back, while Carly stood aloof and distracted, her half-hooded eyes focused on a handsome boy who had been on the same plane and now strolled by.

Trudie quickly perceived that Mary Ann had added pounds and hair since the last time she'd seen her. She'd always kept her curly red hair relatively short, and had always been full-figured, even voluptuous, with full breasts and broad hips. The new weight rounded her breasts and expanded her hips, giving her an "earth mother" appearance. Her now long, red hair was pulled back, with just a few wispy strands coming loose from a clip that rested at the back of her head. That one feature added an arty, sexy quality. The easy smile was the same, the laughing eyes and the relaxed manner, the same, and so Trudie responded as she always had to her good friend, with relaxed pleasure at being in her company.

Lynn was built like her mother, with dancing eyes that took in everything. Carly was a tall, California blonde, with lots of attitude, and a thumb that could text faster than anyone else Trudie had ever seen.

Driving to Deer Lake, Trudie tried to engage the girls in conversation about their new lives in California, their new house and their new school. She received simple phrases or one word answers, while the girls glared into their phones.

Mary Ann gave Trudie a side-long glance, her expression both resigned and annoyed. Then she whispered, "When you want to be proud of them, they always embarrass you."

Mary Ann twisted around to face them. "Ladies, please put your phones away and look out the window or something. There are other things to do besides play with your phones."

Carly made an ugly face as she lowered her phone. Lynn obeyed, staring out into the snowy landscape with sudden wide-eyed bewilderment, as if she'd just noticed it.

"It's looks so cold out there," she said.

"Duh. It *is* cold," Carly responded, bluntly. "It's Ohio in December."

Mary Ann turned to Trudie. "They've become such warm weather snobs ever since we moved to California."

"I love the snow in December," Trudie said. "It wouldn't be Christmas without snow and cold weather. Now, January and February, that's different. Give me Southern California."

"You'll have to come and visit, Trudie. You'll love it. We're close to the beach. You can hear the ocean as you drift off to sleep at night."

"I'll come," Trudie said. "You won't have to ask me twice."

"It's been too long," Mary Ann said. "We have to stay in touch more."

Trudie agreed as she turned right, and they traveled down a winding road, under a moving white winter sky. "I'm so glad you came early. Things have really gotten hectic. The town's response has been overwhelming. Ray and Connie Baker..." Trudie paused, looking over. "You remember Connie?"

"Sure, voted most friendly. Cheerleader. Married Bud somebody?"

"Yes, she and Ray and I have been inundated with emails and calls. So Ray, Connie and I got together and we decided, why not charge for the show? We could pay for the expenses and then use what ever is left over to start a college scholarship fund in Mrs. Childs' name. Connie has a degree in Business. She agreed to handle the banking and the ticketing, as well as the details of setting up the scholarship."

Mary Ann's eyes filled with delight. "What a great idea!"

"Everything has been moving so fast. Ray and I have been struggling to think everything through. He's been coordinating logistics and then following up with me. There are so many details, and one thing snowballs into the other."

"How much are you charging for the tickets?" Mary Ann asked, energized, oblivious to her daughters, who were once again texting, surfing and playing games.

"Connie decided on fifteen dollars. The auditorium is already sold out."

"I had no idea it would take off like that," Mary Ann said, amazed, staring past Trudie into the distance as she thought about it. Her eyes were shining, thrilled by the possibilities. "If I remember right, the auditorium seats about eight hundred. That's somewhere around twelve thousand dollars!"

"Yes. We thought that was a fair price, but now Ray thinks we should have charged more, because people are upset that they can't get in."

Mary Ann was seized by an idea. "So why not have two shows? One at say 5 p.m. and one at 8 o'clock?"

Trudie was gripping the steering wheel so tightly that her fingers hurt. She released it, one hand at a time and, opening and closing her fingers, she felt her heart race.

"We thought about that... but we have to clear it with the principal of the school and with all the others: the performers, musicians. Oh, and Molly Cahill has just emailed to say she's coming. She'll do the choreography."

"I love Molly. She'll be a great choreographer. She can get all of us looking good up there if anybody can."

"She owns a yoga studio in Louisville, Kentucky and teaches dance to kids. Anyway, we'd have to redo the programs and print more. It's becoming a logistics nightmare. And we're not going to have a lot of time for rehearsals."

Mary Ann twisted her lips up in thought, readjusting her legs. "Where will the rehearsals be?"

"In the basement of the Methodist church where Ray plays the piano on Sundays."

"Sugar Hill Methodist?" Mary Ann asked.

"Yes, you remember?"

"Of course. Oscar and I went there when we were dating. I went because my mother wanted me to. Of course we never listened to the sermon. We sat in the back, touching and making love eyes."

The land leveled out. Trudie sat back in her seat and tried to relax. The sky was lowering and appeared heavy with snow. "Has Oscar contacted you again?"

Mary Ann lowered her voice. "Yes... but I'm not really looking forward to... well, you know. It was a long time ago. We were high school kids. I'm sure we've both changed a lot."

"I liked Oscar. He was always thoughtful and respectful."

Mary Ann turned serious. "How is Mrs. Childs?"

"Julie brought her home a couple days ago. I spoke to her briefly this morning. She's better, but still weak. Thank God they caught the pneumonia right away. That could have killed her."

"I want to see her," Mary Ann said. "When do you think we can go?"

"I'll call Julie."

Mary Ann glanced back at her daughters, checking on their phone status. They dropped the phones into their laps and swiftly faced the windows, faking interest.

Mary Ann turned back to Trudie. "Did you spend much time at the hospital with her?"

"I went three times, twice to relieve Julie and Nick. Mrs. Childs didn't talk much. She just took my hand and squeezed it. She blinked and smiled and I sat with her while she slept."

Mary Ann looked at Trudie, pointedly. "I definitely want to spend some time alone with her. Do you think Julie will mind?"

"No, I don't think so."

Mary Ann paused, considering her words. "I'm a healer," she said.

Trudie glanced over. "A healer?"

"I don't mean I'm any kind of a miracle worker or anything, but I can help people feel better. Sometimes, wonderful things happen. I've been practicing for almost eight years now."

"I didn't know," Trudie said, as she took the exit off the expressway, slowing down.

"I don't talk about it. People think you're crazy if you talk about it. Not so much in Southern California, but... well, anyway," she concluded, leaving it hanging. "I just want to spend some time alone with her."

"You always were interested in the occult," Trudie said. "What kind of healing do you do?"

"A combination of techniques I've learned and practiced. One is Reiki. Ever hear of it?"

"Yes. There's a woman in town that does it, I think. One of my patients told me about her. I don't really know what it is though."

Trudie glanced into her rearview mirror and noticed the girls were on their phones again. She stayed mute. They were driving past a new car lot and some fast food restaurants, the same scenery one could see in nearly every town in America.

Mary Ann continued. "Reiki is a Japanese healing technique for stress reduction and relaxation that helps promote healing. It's based on the idea that an unseen 'life force energy' flows through all of us and that is what gives us life. If the life force energy is low, we are more likely to get sick or stressed. If it's high, we are likely to be happy and healthy."

"Sounds like we could all use some of that," Trudie said, approaching the turn off to her street.

"I'll give you a free session," Mary Ann said.

"Next, you'll be teaching us how to levitate," Trudie said, lightly.

"Why not?"

They laughed.

Minutes later, Trudie drove up the driveway to her garage.

Inside the house, Mary Ann got reacquainted with the house she'd spent so much time in during high school. She loved the new color schemes, the new furniture and the modern kitchen. Then they argued about who would sleep in what bedroom. Trudie insisted that Mary Ann take her bedroom and the girls move into the bedroom across the hall. Kristen would stay in the back bedroom at the end of the hall. Mary Ann protested, saying she'd sleep in the den.

"No, Mary Ann. I've got the whole thing figured out. The queen sleeper sofa in the den is comfortable and the room is very quiet. No questions or arguments."

Carly and Lynn wandered the house with renewed interest. They explored the rooms and found the unexpected back oak staircase that spiraled up to the second floor. Then Trudie led the way as Mary Ann and the girls ascended the pull-down attic ladder to the vast remodeled attic, with polished wood floors and bay windows.

Trudie opened boxes of old clothes and hats and the girls delighted in trying some on, posing before a full-length mirror. Lynn was absorbed by a large box of straw and feathered hats with veils, while Carly turned to an old trunk. Inside, she found a vintage dress that belonged to Trudie's mother in the 1950s. Her soft blue eyes filled with excitement and imagination. She looked at her mother and then to Trudie for permission. Mary Ann shook her head. Trudie nodded. "Go ahead, Carly. Take it out."

Carly slowly reached down into the oak trunk and carefully removed the acid free tissue. She gently lifted the lacy chiffon dress, fascinated, lost in a dream. She studied the special stitching, the beads and sequins and pearls, allowing her fingers to touch them and explore the cool, soft fabric.

Mary Ann and Trudie exchanged inquiring glances. Mary Ann shrugged, watching as Carly meticulously unraveled the light yellow dress and held it up next to her chin, examining herself in the mirror. It was full length and elegant; it would be a perfect fit. Carly was entranced, her imagination carrying her off to a glamorous party, where a handsome man in a tuxedo drifted over and offered her a chilled martini, with a glowing green olive. Not that she'd ever drunk a martini, but that didn't matter. It was the dress that created the magic, the mood and the romance.

"I love this," she said, softly, turning with the dress, moving to the sound of distant music.

Lynn studied her. "Wow! Look at you. That dress is awesome."

Trudie stepped to the side of the mirror, watching Carly, who was romantically medicated by her inner movie.

"Would you like to wear the dress to the Christmas show, Carly?" Trudie asked.

Carly whirled, bursting with excitement. "Can I?"

Mary Ann inched forward, apprehensive. "Trudie... that's an heirloom."

Carly's pretty face was glowing. "Oh, yes... Can I?"

Trudie nodded. "Yes. You'll look gorgeous in it."

Carly reached, giving Trudie a one-armed hug. "Thank you. Thank you so much."

Lynn, lifting the veil on the black feathered hat she had on, turned to Trudie, frowning. "Is there something in that trunk I could wear with this hat?"

Mary Ann blew out a sigh. "Girls... please."

Trudie indicated toward the trunk. "Take a look. You

might find something."

The girls stayed in the attic while Mary Ann and Trudie went to the kitchen to prepare dinner.

"You're too generous, Trudie," Mary Ann said. "That is a stunning dress and yes, Carly will look fabulous in it, but what if she rips it or spills something on it?"

"So be it. It's better to be worn by a pretty young girl who appreciates it, than it is to lie in that old, musty trunk rotting away. To tell you the truth, I'd forgotten all about it."

When Trudie's phone rang, she glanced over to see who it was. It was Don Rawlings. She stared at the phone with a certain nervous reluctance. Finally, she answered.

"Hi, Trudie, it's Don. Is this a good time?"

"Yes. Fine, Don. How are you?"

"Good. Got back late yesterday. I just talked to Ray and he told me things are really moving along with the Christmas show."

"Yes. It's a little overwhelming."

"I was thinking... I know it's short notice, but if you're free, would you like to have dinner with me tonight?"

Trudie swallowed. She'd like nothing more. "Well, actually, I have guests staying with me. An old high school friend and her two daughters."

Mary Ann looked over and waved her hand as if to say, go ahead.

"Oh, right. I guess people are already coming into town."

"Yes... Don, can you hold a minute?"

Trudie covered the phone with her hand. "This is a guy I met. He's helping to raise money for the show."

Mary Ann was peeling potatoes. "Invite him over.

Why not?"

Trudie shrugged and uncovered the phone. "Don, why don't you come over for dinner? Believe it or not, we're having chicken, and I have lots of ketchup."

He laughed. "I don't want to intrude. Why don't we make it another time?"

"You won't be intruding. Really."

"I'd better stay home and practice my saxophone. Ray tells me he's found two reindeer costumes. But thanks."

After Trudie hung up, she raked her fingers through her hair, struggling to appear at ease. She felt a strong drumming in her chest.

Mary Ann kept working, giving Trudie a sidelong glance. "Is he coming?"

"No...," Trudie said, hiding her disappointment.

"Is he good-looking?"

Trudie nodded. "Yep. Square jawed, tall, with a deep voice. Just my type."

"It's a shame he's not coming. I haven't had dinner with a handsome man in a long time."

TWELVE

Myrna Childs was lying in bed, covers up to her chin, feeling weaker than she'd ever felt in her entire life. Her body was heavy and unresponsive, like a big block of stone—even though she—her spirit—still felt young and light. Inside, she did not feel like an old woman of 76, but outside, her body was becoming a weary old friend.

She was still having some difficulty breathing, each inhalation a struggle, but it wasn't as painful as it had been in the hospital. She had begged Julie to get her out of that God-forsaken place and take her home. If she was to improve—or if she was to die—she wanted to be home in her own bed, even if that home and bed were in Julie's house.

The house she and Curt had lived in for almost 30 years was being rented by a newly married couple and their 1-year old child. They were a nice couple from Virginia, who moved to town after the husband took a job at that new tech company just outside town. He told Mrs. Childs what his job was, but she had not understood. She was not tech-savvy and she was proud of it.

Myrna remembered the autumn day she'd abandoned her home to move in with Julie. Since Julie was divorced and her only son had just started graduate school in California, she'd convinced her mother that they might as well enjoy each other's company. As they drove away, Mrs. Childs watched the last of the pale yellow willow leaves weep down, then drift and sail, and finally come to rest on the stairs and edge of the porch. It was the closing of another chapter of her life.

Even then, Myrna was losing strength, forgetting where she'd put things, feeling overwhelmed by the day-to-day obligations of running a big house. And it was so empty after Curt's death. He'd filled the large spaces with his cheerful industry and quiet manner.

They had been such opposites. He quiet and practical, she loud and theatrical, unable to understand the simplest mechanical concepts. Curt had always kept the house in peak condition, making his rounds on the weekends, tweaking this or that. He could do anything: plumbing, electrical, painting and tiling. And he had been a good, responsive father. He had been a better father than she had been mother, not that she was jealous of him. She was grateful and loved him all the more.

Though he owned a bustling hardware store, and she was a drama queen who seldom set foot in that store, they were great friends and good lovers. They seldom argued, and when Ruby, her mother, came to visit, Curt was the perfect gentleman, even when Ruby insulted his store or his home. The only time he stood up to her was when she insulted his wife in front of him. "That's enough, Ruby," he said sharply, and Ruby never again expressed her feelings about her daughter's wasted life in front of him.

Myrna thought of Curt every day, and missed his solid support and protection of her. She missed his warmth, and she missed his love.

In the hospital, when the doctors had rushed in because she was having difficulty breathing, Mrs. Childs thought it might be the end. But once again, the doctors had brought her back. Julie told her mother that she'd given them all quite a scare.

"Don't do that again, Mother. Don't try to leave me like that."

"Julie, dear," she responded, "the day will come. We all know that."

Myrna believed that when the fates, the Grim Reaper, or God himself made an entrance—after waiting in the theatre wings with infinite patience to lead you away—you had to leave the stage and hope that your performance had been a good and meaningful one.

She was in the last act of her life. It was nearly her time. So be it. The chemo, the surgery, the radiation and then the pneumonia had all been too much for her. Myrna had never been one to ignore reality or get sentimental over things. As the Bible says, there is a season for everything, a time to be born and a time to die. Myrna wasn't sad about dying. She'd had a full life. She'd been a wife, a mother, a grandmother, and the best teacher she knew how to be. She'd led a good life, a worthy life, she hoped.

The light in her room was dim. It was quiet in the house. So she wouldn't miss the sweetness of Christmas, Julie had placed a miniature balsam Christmas tree on the chest of drawers, in clear view from the bed. Its steady white lights and cool evergreen scent were heavenly, and heavenly was the right word. Mrs. Childs would probably be dropping into that Promised Land soon.

Myrna took a slow breath and closed her eyes, feeling her head sink deeply into the soft pillow. She *did* want to live to celebrate another Christmas though. She'd loved Christmas, ever since she was a little girl growing up in

New York's Upper West side of Manhattan, on Amsterdam Avenue. Her father owned a drugstore there. It had lots of wood paneling, wooden drawers, and tall shelves, and two sliding wooden ladders. She loved the hex tile floor with its colorful pattern that zigzagged around the store. It was so much fun to hop-scotch across it. Her father never minded, even if customers were in the store. He'd just laugh and say "That's my girl!"

A jumbo malted milk cost only 7 cents. At the Tip-Top Luncheonette, around the corner, the breakfast special was 12 cents, and you had a choice of a doughnut, roll or bagel.

At Christmas, her father always brought her little gifts from the drugstore: red and black licorice whip candies, lipstick, Christmas ornaments and face creams.

Myrna's mother, Ruby, had been an aspiring singer, dancer and actress and, by the time Myrna (who was named after the famous actress, Myrna Loy) was four years old, her mother was dragging her to theatre and nightclub auditions. Myrna would wait on wooden benches with the other performers when her mother was called in to audition. One time Ruby had managed to land a job, performing in a floorshow at The Latin Quarter Night Club in 1944.

Myrna's father, Eddie Lewis, disapproved of his wife's theatre ambitions. He waited up one night, sneaking peeks out the window. He saw her being escorted home by the night club manager. He flew into a rage and threatened to kill her. They'd had frequent arguments and slapping fights, but that one was the worst. He demanded she "Stay home and take care of our daughter, and your husband!"

Myrna's parents finally split up when Myrna was 12 years old. In 1950, she and her mother left New York to live with her grandparents in Cincinnati, Ohio. It would be years before Myrna returned to New York. The two times she saw her father, he drove to Ohio to see her. He promised he'd pay for her to visit him in New York when she was 16, but he died of a heart attack in 1953, when Myrna was just 15.

When Ruby Lewis left Manhattan, she knew she'd never achieve her goal of becoming a professional actress, but for a while, she did try to find theatre work in Ohio. She managed to perform in an amateur production of *Show Boat* before she finally gave up her dream and accepted a permanent role as a secretary for McAlpin's Department Store in downtown Cincinnati. As the years passed, she gained weight and lost her girlish figure and face.

But for Myrna, those first magical Christmases in New York were etched in her memory. At Christmas, her parents made an extra effort to get along, for their daughter's sake. They took her to Carnegie Hall to hear the great *Messiah*, to local churches for Christmas caroling, and to Radio City Music Hall to see the Christmas show with the Rockettes and the living nativity, complete with camel and sheep. They took her to Macy's to see Santa; they walked from 34th Street to Rockefeller Center to view the window displays at all the stores along Fifth Avenue from Lord & Taylor to Saks Fifth Avenue. And on Christmas Eve, they attended the Lessons and Carols service at one of the churches in the area, and then went home for hot chocolate and cinnamon raisin toast with lots of butter.

Myrna fell in love with the music, drama and pageantry of Christmas. She loved the carols and the choruses singing Bach and Handel. She joined in the sing-a-longs, feeling the joy and peace of the season. Christmas music uplifted her; it cheered and sustained her, and whenever her parents fell into their inevitable combative arguments or her mother grew depressed as soon as Christmas was over, Myrna would close her eyes and recapture the majesty and glory of the Christmas season.

"You will be a great actress someday, Myrna," her mother often told her. It became a kind of mantra. "You'll be the great star I never was. You will, won't you, my darling?"

What could Myrna say? She never wanted to disappoint her mother, a tall imposing woman with dyed auburn hair and a big soprano voice, who did everything with a dramatic flair, from wearing big, sweeping hairstyles to sporting gaudy jewelry. She had a big booming voice and grand gestures, as if, truly, all the world *were* her stage. She dressed in dramatic and revealing outfits, with low-cut blouses or slim skirts or sleeveless dresses with crinoline ruffles. She wore halter tops that revealed too much midriff. She changed her hairdo and bought new costume jewelry nearly every week, making frequent use of her employees' discount. Her outfits were not always appreciated by her bosses at the department store.

Myrna opened her eyes, staring up at the ceiling, using its soft surface as a screen to reminisce—to watch, as if they were a movie, the old images flickering across the surface...old faces, old scenes, old conversations.

Despite her mother's objections, Myrna studied for a degree in education at the University of Cincinnati, saying she wanted a profession to fall back on in case, like her mother, she did not succeed in New York. But she minored in theatre and had a successful run as Laurie in a 2-week production of *Oklahoma* her senior year. All those years of singing, drama and dance lessons that Ruby had insisted upon had paid off.

"It is the way I tithe," Ruby would say. "Some people give 10 percent of their salary to the church. Well, I give 10 percent for your lessons, Myrna, because I worship the church of the theatre," she'd said with an imperious air. "You *will* be a big star someday."

After graduating, Myrna did what was expected of her and moved to New York. It was an exciting time to be in New York, and an exciting time for the theatre. She auditioned for *Bye Bye Birdie*, but didn't make the chorus. She also auditioned for *The Unsinkable Molly Brown, Wildcat* and *Do Re Mi*. Again, she was cut in the final singing audition. She didn't have her mother's voice. Hers was heavy in the lower register and a bit strident in the upper.

But there were good days. Like many, she worked as a waitress. She snuck into plays at half-time with fellow thespians. She got boisterous and drunk after auditions, singing on the side streets with other actors. She often ate at the 6th Avenue Deli with an older, still-struggling actress, who told her many stories about actors who had made it. One story was about the not-yet-famous star, James Dean. She'd watched him cross the street and fall in front of a taxi cab on his knees, as a joke. It was shocking. People were stunned. They pointed and stared. The cab driver screeched to a halt, just missing him. He leaned out the window, angry and shaken, shouting, "You son of a bitch!"

James Dean got up laughing, brushed himself off and hurried along.

Myrna's first break was a part in the chorus of *Subways Are for Sleeping*. It played over 200 performances. After that, she found work in other short-running shows, but only in the chorus or as an understudy. In late 1962, she played the second lead in an Off-Broadway show, but her performance didn't win the excitement of the critics.

One critic wrote "*Myrna Lewis never seems to rise much beyond mediocrity, when so much more is asked for.*" Another wrote "*Ms. Lewis doesn't elicit much sympathy for a young, abandoned wife. I personally felt the husband was justified in leaving her.*"

The best review she ever received was not from a critic, but from the famous actor, Jason Robards, who'd received rave reviews for his performance in Eugene O'Neil's *The Ice Man Cometh*.

After he saw Myrna in an Off-Broadway performance of *The Bed You Lie In*, he found his way to her closet of a dressing room and told her, in his rich baritone voice, "You moved me, Myrna Lewis. You moved me to tears. Well done."

Myrna's acting career fizzled and Ruby Lewis grew progressively pushier and more irritable at her daughter's lack of success, finally declaring, "If you had my talent, you'd be a star by now. You just don't have it."

During Myrna's last year in New York, she grew increasingly more interested in analyzing the craft of acting, as well as in directing. She attended rehearsals of fellow actors and took notes on their performances. Her friends found her observations helpful and insightful. She began directing scenes in acting classes and was praised by her fellow students as well as by her teachers, who suggested she consider a career as a director. They said she had a real eye for directing, a real talent for bringing out the best in an actor and in a scene.

Myrna was thrilled. She'd finally found her life path, her true calling. That's when a friend of her mother's called to say that Ruby had collapsed at work. After years of battling alcoholism, she was too sick to live alone.

Myrna returned home to find her mother in the hospital, rail thin, malnourished and diagnosed with high blood pressure and cirrhosis of the liver. Myrna knew her mother drank, but she didn't know it had gotten so out of hand.

She stood over her pale, bony-faced, hollow-eyed mother and told her, "You have to stop drinking, Mother. Now. Or you will kill yourself."

Her mother looked at her, with disdain. "What are you doing here? You should be auditioning, working. You don't have the talent I had. I would have made it if it hadn't been for your father. You have to work, work, work at it, Myrna. I don't want you here. Get out!"

Myrna did not leave her mother. She found a job teaching drama at Norwood High School, a small town within Cincinnati, Ohio, and she slowly nursed her mother back to health. A year later, Myrna met Curt Childs, a German American who owned a hardware store in Deer Lake, Ohio. Curt's grandfather, Martin Kind, had changed his surname from Kind to Childs, since "kind" in German meant "child." He had added the "s" so that no one would ever have an excuse to say, in jest, "the Children family."

Curt and Myrna married in 1964. They settled in Deer Lake and Myrna became the drama teacher at the high school two years later.

In 1970, Myrna's mother died in her sleep. Ruby hadn't taken a drink in seven years, but she remained bitter and accusing. The mother and daughter relationship remained strained and distant to the last, and the week before Ruby passed, she attacked her daughter yet again with the usual questions: "Why did you marry that man and throw your life away? Your father owned a drugstore and he owns a hardware store. Why did you have to repeat your past? Why did you come back here and throw your career away?"

Myrna did not answer. She stood proudly erect before

a woman whose cold eyes had persistently pronounced her a failure. Myrna did not take that in. She had made peace with her life. She had her teaching job, and her students, and a profession she loved.

The bedroom door opened and Julie entered quietly, creeping toward the bed.

"I'm awake," Myrna said.

"How are you feeling, Mother?"

"Not bad. I've been looking back. Taking stock, you might say. I'd forgotten some things. So many memories."

"There are more to be made, Mother."

Myrna swallowed. She looked earnestly at her daughter and smiled. "You have been the best of daughters, Julie. Have I ever told you that?"

Julie sat down, brushing back a loose strand of hair that had fallen across her mother's forehead. "Not in so many words, Mother. But I always knew you loved Nick and me."

Myrna rolled her head away, thinking. "Maybe I left you both alone too much. Maybe it was because my mother was always in my face, pushing me. I didn't want to repeat that. Maybe I went too far the other way. I don't know."

Myrna turned back to her daughter, enjoying her daughter's pleasant face and kind eyes. "Was I a good mother, Julie?"

"Yes, Mother. You were, and not just to me. You were a good mother to your students. You must have been. Look how they remember you and come to see you."

Myrna shut her eyes, and again she saw her students' many faces flit by. She saw them so clearly.

Julie stood. "You sleep now, Mother. I'll check in on you in a little while."

After Julie left, Myrna opened her eyes, wondering and struggling with doubt. What mother, what teacher, doesn't have doubts? Had she really been a good and loving mother? Had she really made a difference in her students' lives? Had she been too harsh or brusque with them? Too unkind, too unforgiving of their insecurities? Not complimentary enough? Had she been too pushy and strident, like her mother had been?

In the final analysis, and this *was* her final analysis, did she really help her students prepare for a life of challenges, setbacks and triumphs? Had she really taught her students anything?

Myrna's attention was drawn to familiar music drifting in from the living room. *Silent Night.* She smiled. Julie, too, grew up loving Christmas music. Every year on December 1st, she took out the dozens of Christmas CDs she'd collected through the years and started playing them, always starting with Nat King Cole. Then came *The Messiah.* Christmas in various cathedrals. The Boston Pops, Tony Bennett, jazz and pop singers, New Wave versions of the classics, and even an old Bing Crosby rendition of *Jingle Bells.* Julie didn't like to sing, which was for the best, because she couldn't carry a tune. Mrs. Childs folded her hands on her chest and tried to sing. She produced only a squeaky, breathy struggle of a sound that caught in her throat. Nonetheless, she sang on.

During the Christmas show at the high school, they'd always ended the program with *Silent Night.* The lights were dimmed, and the ushers distributed little white tapered candles. One lighted candle was lit by another and another, until the entire auditorium was a mass of flickering candles. It was heavenly to experience the entire auditorium filled with people gently swaying and singing, their glorious voices filling the vast space with a divine, soaring peace. It had always brought tears to her eyes, although she'd never let anyone see her cry. She'd retreat into the shadows, thankful that God had placed her in the perfect job with the perfect people at the perfect time.

"Was I a failure?" Myrna asked, whispering to herself.

Mrs. Childs lay in her bed, remembering, smelling the vanilla and evergreen scent, hearing the swelling voices of *Silent Night*, as if the singers were standing in her room, surrounding her. She sang along with them, until her eyes closed and she drifted off into a deep sleep.

THIRTEEN

The alumni performers began arriving on the afternoon of Friday, December 19. After checking into various motels and Bed & Breakfasts, they called or texted Ray or Trudie for the latest plans. Most eventually made their way to Rusty's, where they crowded around the circular mahogany bar, slapping backs, swapping old stories and catching up with their lives. Some were heavier, some balder, some even more youthful than at the last high school reunion, probably because of line-erasing fillers. Perlane and Botox were the unacknowledged makeup artists.

Of the women who'd put on pounds, only Betsy Oaker wasn't self-conscious. She'd been a thin high school cheerleader who was now 60 pounds heavier and she didn't apologize for it. "Being thin is over-rated," she said. "It just takes too much work to maintain." She liked her body and it liked her. Her face looked youthful and plump, without fillers.

The thinner women swapped diets, discussed yoga classes, and adjusted tight clothes. Dana Richards wore a low-cut blouse to show off her breast implants. The men struggled not to stare, but failed repeatedly. They turned away only when imagination overwhelmed them or their wives gave them a raised eyebrow.

The more prosperous men wore blazers and slacks. Others wore jeans, ball caps and T-shirts.

In the café, children and teenagers were introduced to their parents' old classmates, who'd never seen them except on *Facebook*. Most kids seemed dazed or bored by the spectacle, staying glued to their phones or tablets, looking up only long enough to reach for a soda, a slice of pizza or a chicken wing. Some discovered the old electronic pinball machine in the corner. They charged and circled it, becoming swiftly engrossed by the steel ball bouncing off bumpers and targets as they worked the flippers, thrilled by the "dinging" bell.

Trudie left work at 5 p.m., picked up Mary Ann and her daughters, and they arrived at Rusty's around the same time Ray did. Both were surprised by the swarm of people who met them, cheering them when they entered. They pushed into the crowd, shaking hands, receiving kisses, being handed a beer or a glass of wine.

The locals, well aware of the coming events, joined in, hefting pitchers of beer and filling empty mugs. A fat Christmas tree blazed with red and white lights, couples twirled to *Santa Claus is Comin' to Town* from a juke box, and the celebration became high and loud.

On Saturday afternoon, Trudie and Mary Ann struggled to complete the calendar of events and schedules, pinning down who would be rehearsing when, and where, and finalizing what costumes and props they would need. They answered waves of phone calls, emails and texts. They had already met with the high school board members to assure them that the safety of high school property was a top priority. The principal, Mrs. Lyons, remained unpleasant and irritating, firing question after question, many of which had been answered several times before. Trudie was beginning to wonder if the woman had a learning disability.

But Mary Ann's calm energy and approach finally smoothed the principal's ruffled feathers, assuring her that there would be no consumption of alcohol and no borrowing of stage sets, although she had agreed to let them use a few costumes and props. And yes, they would hire extra security, as had already been agreed upon several times.

There was a tidal wave of things to complete, and both Trudie and Mary Ann kept glancing at the racing clock, keenly aware that Kristen, John Ketch, Oscar Bonds and Cole Blackwell would all be arriving that evening. And they'd heard from Julie. Mrs. Childs was not doing well. If she didn't improve by Sunday, Julie was afraid she'd have to take her back to the hospital.

"I wish I could work with her today," Mary Ann said. She'd managed to have only one healing session with her, on Thursday afternoon, the day after she'd arrived in Deer Lake. When Mary Ann had first entered Mrs. Childs' bedroom, Myrna had taken Mary Ann's hand, held it close to her cheek, thanked her for coming and then uttered the expected words: "You were always my favorite."

"And you were definitely my favorite teacher," Mary Ann said. They talked about the past and present, about Mary Ann's daughters and her life in California, and then Mary Ann told Myrna about her work as a healer, explaining how Reiki often helps people who are in pain.

"Would you be willing to give me a session?" Myrna asked. "I'm open to anything that will help fight this thing," she added.

Mary Ann called Julie in and explained that they would need at least 30 minutes alone. Julie folded her arms and frowned. "Are you sure it won't tire her out?"

"Julie, I trust Mary Ann," Myrna said firmly. "I want to do this."

Afterwards, Mrs. Childs told them both that she felt better. "I feel stronger, Mary Ann. Truly, I do. I feel more peaceful."

Mary Ann could tell that Julie was still skeptical. She had hoped to work with Mrs. Childs every day until the show. "But Julie doesn't seem all that open to it," she told Trudie. "She believes in traditional medicine. I think she thinks I'm a flake or something."

Mary Ann had seen it before, and she didn't insist on returning the following day, but she sincerely hoped Julie would allow her to go again soon.

By Saturday evening, more alumni arrived and, once again, Rusty's was the official meeting place and party spot. During this party, Ray, Trudie and Mary Ann circled the room, passing out the calendar of events, schedules and rehearsal times. The first general meeting would be held at the church at one o'clock Sunday afternoon. Rehearsals, theatre staff assignments, costume, prop, and decoration committees and set building would begin immediately after.

For two days, there had been an unspoken anticipation in the air at Rusty's, a rising expectation among all the alumni as they waited for the appearance of John Ketch, clearly the most famous and controversial of them all. Jon had stayed in touch with only a few and, typical of Jon, had refused to let anyone know what hour or what day he would arrive. Also true to form, Jon had emailed his chosen cast of *A Christmas Carol* their parts, demanding that they be "letter perfect," all parts memorized, by the first rehearsal on Monday morning, December 22nd.

At a little after 9 p.m., Rusty's Bar and Café was alive with music, talk and celebration. Suddenly, the side EXIT door was flung open and a burst of cold wind swept in. At first, only a handful of people close to the door noticed him. Jon Ketch, dressed in an old faded bomber jacket, jeans and red sneakers, stood dramatically, legs apart, fists on his hips. His brown and gray hair was exploding out from his head like Einstein's.

He broke for the bar. Chuck Miles, the bald bartender with snake tattoos on his neck and right arm, saw him approach as he was drawing down two mugs of beer. Jon sliced through the stunned crowd to the edge of the bar. He hoisted himself up on a stool, hopped onto the bar, and strutted back and forth like Mick Jagger, doing hip-shots and shoulder rolls, narrowly missing half-filled martini glasses and mugs of beer.

The room surged, reeled, pointed and found Jon Ketch. Then Gavin Phillips, Rusty's owner, switched off the jukebox, just as he and Jon had previously arranged he'd do.

Jon Ketch stood strafing the group with his accusing eyes, his compact physique imposing. Then he flashed a hint of the sarcastic grin every classmate knew so well. He flung his arms wide, reaching, sweeping the crowd, as if addressing thousands. The room gathered into a buzzing hush.

Jon's booming theatrical voice filled the room. "Thespians, wastrels and polygamists, lend me your ears!"

The room exploded into applause, many playing along, shouting, "Hear! Hear!"

Jon held up his hands to quiet them, and then continued, as if reciting lines from Shakespeare's *Julius Caesar*.

"I come to bury the past, not to praise it! For what is the past but a collection of half-remembered lies about old girlfriends, old boyfriends, unseemly deeds and regrettable actions? It is a history badly told by us fools, who can barely remember what the hell we ate for breakfast this morning."

There was laughter and ragged cheers, as beer mugs and wine glasses were raised.

"And, dear friends, if you are shocked by my aged appearance, then get your sorry-looking asses into the bathroom and look at yourselves in that unfortunate broken mirror. None of you look any better than I and, I dare say, most of you look even worse! You've put on pounds, paunch and pretense! Whoa be unto you, you rakish heathens of Rusty's!"

The crowd shattered into laugher, drumming their feet on the floor.

Jon reached out to the bartender. "Bartender, a club soda and cranberry juice, if you please, Sire!"

Chuck did as commanded and Jon thrust the glass high, ready for a toast.

"Here's to you all who can still drink wine.

I do not, I simply decline.

But that still leaves me with women and song

And that's why I'm wearing a bright red thong!"

There was the thunder of stamping and feet, laughter and applause.

"And now, my dear friends, no autographs, please! Only hugs and kisses, but not by any of these ugly old guys I see here before me. Only the women, the beautiful, the adoring, oh, all the women may kiss me, and tell me lies, and send me down the road to sweet, sweet perdition!"

Jon leapt off the bar, hitting the floor with a thud. In

seconds he was surrounded and smothered by kisses, hugs and handshakes.

At that moment, Kristen entered Rusty's, having driven herself in a rented car from the airport. She'd gotten lost, driving thirty minutes out of her way, angry at herself for taking a shortcut she thought she remembered, but didn't. She was looking forward to a glass of wine. Mary Ann saw her first. She yelled out, waved and picked her way through the crowd until they met and fell into an embrace.

Trudie was on the periphery of the crowd when Jon spotted her. He lifted a playful eyebrow, pointed at her and, with a lowered chin and steely eyes, he went to her in a rush. He was bear-hugging her before she could speak. With his hands on her shoulders, he examined her carefully. She was still trying to catch her breath and gather herself.

"Hot damn, Trudie! You have gone and gotten skinnier, prettier and sexier. Brace yourself."

Jon planted a big kiss on both cheeks and then grabbed her, tipped her down to the right, bracing her with his arm, and kissed her long and deep.

The group circled them, shouting, whistling and applauding.

A minute before, Don Rawlings had just entered Rusty's, and that kiss was the first thing he saw. It didn't disturb him, but he was mad at himself for not doing it himself when he'd had the chance. Okay, maybe not so demonstratively, but he regretted not accepting Trudie's dinner invitation the other night. That had been a mistake. But then, he'd just been dumped by a woman the month before, and he was a little hesitant to begin another relationship.

Jon released Trudie, who was still reeling from the

sexy kiss. He probed the room, the edge of his hand at his eyebrows shading the light, searching, his head moving slowly from left to right. "Where are they?"

And then he saw them. "Kristen Anderson! Mary Ann O'Brian! Get your beautiful faces over here!"

They met near the bar. Jon flung an arm around each of their shoulders, pulled them close and kissed them firmly on the mouth. After they'd disengaged, Jon gestured for Trudie to join them.

The three women stood linked arm in arm, Trudie in the center, staring down at the floor, shyly, Mary Ann grinning warmly, and Kristen poised and confident, her red lips glistening.

"Ladies and gentlemen, I give you the ladies who made all this possible. The ladies who got us all together, once again, so we can perform our Christmas show and honor our wonderful drama teacher, Mrs. Myrna Childs. I give you The Christmas Women!"

There was a loud round of applause, whistles and feet drumming.

Ray Howard stood in the back near the EXIT door, hands behind his back, quiet and withdrawn.

Amidst the applause, Trudie craned her neck, looking for him. When she spotted him, she caught his eye and motioned for him to join them. He shook his head vigorously, held up a hand like a stop sign and mouthed the word, "No." He wasn't comfortable in the limelight, and never had been.

After the applause subsided, Trudie mustered her courage and held up a hand to quiet the group.

"I also want to add that, without Ray Howard, we never would have gotten this thing off the ground. He has been working non-stop for weeks."

She turned to Ray and led the crowd in loud applause.

Ray backed away against the wall, blushing, as his old classmates honored him. He was embarrassed, but pleased.

The party roared on until after 11 o'clock. The teens and kids were taken back to their motels, while husbands or wives involved in the show remained at Rusty's, formed groups at tables, and ran their lines with Jon, or reviewed arrangements and dance steps with Ray and Molly. Mary Ann waited for Oscar to show up and, when he didn't, she asked Trudie to drive her and the girls back to the house. Trudie then returned to Rusty's, sure that Cole Blackwell would make an appearance.

Trudie wasn't aware that Don Rawlings was sitting at the counter eating his usual fried chicken dinner. He hadn't wanted to intrude. It was their night—the reunion for Deer Lake High School—and he didn't want to distract from that. And, anyway, it looked as though the famous actor Jon Ketch had a thing for Trudie. Their kiss was no ordinary kiss. Afterwards, Trudie had seemed dazed, while Jon seemed aroused and wanting more. How could he, Don Rawlings, compete with the famous Jon Ketch? So Don ate his dinner and was gone by 8:30.

A little after 10 o'clock, Cole Blackwell appeared, now the tallest person in the place. Trudie saw him first. Kristen was at the bar hanging on Jon's arm, sipping wine, recounting the time Jon upstaged her act during the last Christmas show. During her solo, *Let it Snow, Let it Snow, Let it Snow,* Jon had swung across the stage like Tarzan, dressed in a Santa Claus suit. The audience shattered with laughter and applause. Mrs. Childs was so angry at him that she gave him a D for the class. (She later changed it to a B.)

"'D is for drama,' I told her," Jon said, laughing.

"Then she said I was a self-absorbed blockhead."

"I said... 'Yes, ma'am. I thought you knew that.'"

"Now get this," Jon said, entrancing the group around him. "Then Mrs. Childs said, 'Jon you are an impertinent little shit!'"

Kristen doubled over with laughter.

Trudie stood behind a crowd, sizing up Cole. He had aged, appearing older than forty, but he was still tall, distinguished, wearing gray slacks, a blue blazer and a white Oxford shirt. She noticed that he was graying at the temples and wore the somber expression of someone who'd mislaid happiness. Before stepping into the bar, he paused, glancing about with a certain misgiving and reluctance, his hands pushed deeply into his pockets. Oddly, none of the old crowd had noticed him. Were they still expecting and hypnotized by the youthful star basketball player Cole, unable to see the mature man?

Trudie didn't move, stunned by excitement and sudden fear. Jon's kiss had awakened her body to sexual possibility for the first time in a long time. But now, seeing Cole standing there, she was filled with dread and confusion. How would he respond to her when he saw her? Would he kiss her? Would he ask her to join him so they could catch up on old times? Did she care?

At that moment Kristen followed Jon's eyes and twisted around to see Cole. When he saw her, his face swiftly changed from frowning discontent to sudden delight. Kristen took him in slowly, with warm, peering eyes. She set her wine glass down on the bar, pushed away and strolled over to him. They stood staring at each other for a moment, their eyes glowing with memory, expectation and desire. They embraced.

Jon studied them, a curious eyebrow lifted, as he turned to see Trudie's reaction. She was a statue, her face a blank page, revealing nothing. But her eyes flashed bitterness.

"Well, what do you know about that?" Jon said. "Kristen and Cole are still in love, and after all these years."

Five minutes later, Kristen grabbed her coat and purse. She said her goodbyes, not seeing Trudie and not wanting to. She and Cole left Rusty's together.

FOURTEEN

Early Sunday morning, Trudie, Kristen, Mary Ann and her daughters were all seated around the oak dining room table, eating breakfast. Trudie avoided Kristen's eyes, and Kristen, at the far end of the table, was uncharacteristically quiet and preoccupied with her troubled thoughts.

The night before, Trudie had kept the door to the den slightly ajar. At 2 a.m., she heard Kristen rattle the front door key and let herself in. She didn't get up to talk to her. She slept fitfully after that.

Mary Ann was eating oatmeal, wide awake, meticulously going over the rehearsal schedule, while Trudie's slitted eyes struggled to focus on her scrambled eggs. She was sipping a glass of orange juice when her phone rang. She glanced down at it. It was Julie. Trudie's heart sank.

"It's Julie," Trudie said to the others, just before she answered.

Kristen and Mary Ann looked up with sudden alarm.

"Trudie... Mom's back in the hospital," Julie said, her voice low and hoarse from lack of sleep. "She got up last night and fainted in the bathroom, fell over into the tub. Luckily I was sleeping lightly and heard her cry out. I called an ambulance ... she got to the hospital about 2 o'clock this morning. I think she just fractured a rib, but they're doing all sorts of tests."

Mary Ann and Kristen saw the alarm in Trudie's face.

"I can come over if you need me," Trudie said.

"I don't know, Trudie. She's getting weaker instead of stronger. The oncologist says we just have to wait until she's ready, until she's over the pneumonia completely. But Mom keeps saying she won't have any more chemo. Maybe it's too late by now anyway. Maybe they didn't get all the cancer. Maybe it has already started to metastasize."

Trudie fought for calm. "I can be there in an hour. You should go home, eat and get some rest. Is she awake?"

"In and out... Trudie..." Julie hesitated, and Trudie waited. "Trudie, Mom has been asking for Jon. I can't tell if she's completely lucid or not. She keeps asking for Jon Ketch... you know, the actor."

Trudie lowered her head, smiling. Mrs. Childs and Jon had always had a complicated relationship. Sometimes love/hate, but mostly love/love. Mrs. Childs had nurtured Jon's talent and encouraged his ambitions, even when his parents had tried to kill them. More than once, Jon had told Trudie about confrontations between Mrs. Childs and his father. Mrs. Childs had stood up for Jon's right to pursue his own life, had defended his acting and his participation in her class.

Trudie shook off the memories as she returned to the present, startled by Julie's anxious voice. "Trudie... is Jon around?"

"Yes... Julie. Jon is in town. He's here for the reunion."

"I thought so. I saw it in the news this morning. Trudie... Mom's not going to be able to attend your

Christmas show. I'm so sorry. She would have loved it, but she's just too weak."

The silence lengthened. Mary Ann and Kristen were still and silent, waiting. They saw the disappointment and sorrow on Trudie's face.

"I understand, Julie," Trudie said, at a near whisper. "Do you want me to call Jon and ask him to come with me to the hospital?"

Julie sighed into the phone, making a little whooshing sound. "It can't hurt. She's so proud of you all. In her mind, I guess she wants some kind of closure."

"We could all come: Kristen, Mary Ann and Jon, if you don't think it would tire her out too much."

"At this point, it could only help. I know she'd love to see you all, and there may not be many more opportunities."

A few hours later, a little after eleven, The Christmas Women arrived at the hospital and met Julie, who looked weary and nervous. She thanked them for coming and told them the doctor was with her mother. It might be awhile before they could see her. She might have to be taken for more tests.

Trudie suggested Julie go home and get some rest. They'd call her if there was any change. Julie hesitated for a moment, and then finally left.

The girls had stopped at the mall and purchased a huge bouquet of flowers in a light pink vase. While Trudie went to the ladies' room to add water and re-arrange the flowers, Kristen and Mary Ann found the waiting lounge. Kristen extracted another artfully wrapped present for Mrs. Childs, and when Mary Ann asked her what it was, Kristen just shook her head, her face pale and private.

Trudie arrived with the vase of flowers and placed them on a blue plastic chair. The girls sat waiting, Kristen staring blankly, at nothing. Mary Ann sat upright, hands placed on her knees, eyes shut. She began to meditate.

Trudie scrolled through her many email messages, responding to the important ones, many from Ray. Trudie texted him where they were and what was going on. He texted back, alarmed and concerned. He was sitting in church, listening distractedly to a sermon about *The Real Meaning of Christmas.*

None of the girls wanted to approach the topic of Mrs. Childs not attending the Christmas show. It was too painful and depressing.

Jon texted that he was on his way.

Finally, Trudie shut her eyes to rest them and help clear her scattered thoughts. She heard muffled voices and a ringing phone. She smelled disinfectant when a cleaning cart rattled past.

Jon arrived about twenty minutes later, carrying a shopping bag. He was instantly spotted by the staff, as they huddled near the elevator or peeked out from rooms, discretely whispering as they watched him stride to the Nurses Station. He waved and wished them a "Happy Sunday."

He found the girls in the lounge. His hair was smoothed back and his neon blue eyes were alive with unease. The three ladies were stunned to see him wearing dress shoes, pressed grey slacks, a white shirt and a blue patterned tie under his bomber jacket.

"How is she?" he asked.

The girls stood. "We don't know," Trudie said. "Her doctor's with her. They said we have to wait."

Jon looked pointedly at Mary Ann. "I hear you do healing stuff."

"Healing stuff?" Mary Ann asked, almost at a laugh.

"Yeah. Hey, I looked at your website. It's cool. Can you heal Teach?"

Kristen sat back down, listless and depressed. Trudie found a pair of reading glasses in her purse, slipped them on and stared into her phone, as new emails popped up.

Jon turned to her. "Wow, look at you in glasses."

"I just need them for reading sometimes," Trudie said, a little defensively. "My eyes are tired. I didn't sleep much last night."

Jon studied the glasses. "I like the red rectangular shape. They're similar to a pair my second ex-wife used to wear. She always ripped them off before she took a swing at me."

Jon swung his attention back to Mary Ann. "Can you heal Teach?"

Mary Ann picked imaginary lint off her long gray sweater dress. "I'm not a miracle worker, Jon. I don't have great mystical powers or anything."

Jon considered her answer. "Okay... so what the hell kind of healing do you do? Can you help her or not?"

Before Mary Ann could answer, he looked down at Kristen, who was still somber, lost in thoughts. "Kristen, what's the matter with you?"

She didn't look at him. "Nothing."

"Did you and Cole have fun last night?"

All three girls tensed up.

Kristen threw him a hard glance. "That's none of your business!"

He held up his hands, as if to pat down her sudden anger. "Hey, be cool, Kristen. I'm harmless."

"You have never been harmless, Jon. Never. You have always been inappropriate."

Jon chuckled. "Inappropriate? Me? No way. And,

anyway, where did you learn that big word, inappropriate? In law school?"

"Go to hell, Jon!" Kristen snapped. "You're such an asshole. I don't care if you are a big Hollywood actor."

"Touchy..." Jon said, turning his attention back to Trudie. "I really do like those glasses, Trudie. I think you look sexy as hell in them."

Trudie blushed a little, keeping her eyes glued to her phone. "Thank you."

His attention swung back to Mary Ann. "So can you help Teach, Mary Ann?"

Mary Ann's calm eyes patiently focused on him. "I want to try to help her feel better. More peaceful. Maybe I can help alleviate some of the pain."

Jon was preoccupied as he half-listened. "Mary Ann, I'd say you've gained about 20 pounds. Right?"

Mary Ann sucked in a sharp breath. She closed her eyes, counting to five before reopening them. "Yes, Jon. I've gain 20 pounds. I overeat sometimes and I don't always exercise as much as I should."

Jon nodded, thoughtfully. "I see... I see. Well, that's not so bad, Mary Ann, when you think about it. Since high school, you've only gained one pound per year. And you know what?" he said, placing a finger at the side of his nose, examining her from top to bottom. "I like it. I like the weight. Yes, I do, and I like your long red hair. Yes. You look earthy and wise. How about that?"

Kristen spoke up, sarcastically. "Thank God the great Jon Ketch approves. What would we do if he didn't? Well, we'd all have to throw ourselves under a train like Anna Karenina, wouldn't we?"

Jon arched an eyebrow. "Now that's a nasty thing to say, Kristen. And you've always been such a kind, unselfish and thoughtful little bitch."

Kristen shot up, ready to fight.

"Enough!" Trudie said, hand up. "We're here to see Mrs. Childs, not insult each other like we did in high school."

Jon grinned, shoving his hands into his bomber jacket. "Always the sensible one. Trudie. Old safe, sensible and cautious Trudie. That's why we all love you so much. You keep your head on, when maybe it would be good if you lost it sometimes. Yep, just..." Jon made a sweeping move of his hand, as if swinging a sword across her throat. "Swap! Off with the head. Yep. Lose that scared, reclusive but very pretty head."

Mary Ann looked away and down. Kristen barked a laugh. Trudie glowered.

A thin, fresh-faced nurse entered, her adoring eyes fixed on Jon. "You can see Mrs. Childs now, Mr. Ketch."

"Mr. Ketch!" he exclaimed, a dramatic hand covering his heart. "Oh, my, dear child of the healing arts, please call me Mr. Strange or Mr. Short, because I am only 5 feet seven inches tall, or even call me Mr. Daft, but never, please never, my dear girl, call me Mr. Ketch. It is like a swift dart, striking me in my poor, ole, loving heart."

The young nurse stood stationary, speechless.

The three girls exchanged exasperated glances. Kristen rolled her eyes. Mary Ann shook her head and Trudie shrugged.

The women entered Mrs. Childs' private room first, with Jon bringing up the rear. A nurse stood beside the bed, and Mrs. Childs lay with her eyes closed. The four former students stood in a semicircle at the foot of the bed, staring, waiting. Trudie placed the flowers on the broad window sill and returned to the others. A ray of sunlight lit up the yellow roses and white carnations.

Jon spoke first. "Hello, Teach."

Mrs. Childs' eyelids fluttered and slowly opened. Jon set his shopping bag down and nodded once, a short, abrupt downward slash of his head. Then he snapped a crisp military salute.

"Captain Jon Ketch reporting for duty, Teach."

A flash of confusion crossed Mrs. Childs' face and then, as if clouds were parting to reveal a sunny blue sky, Mrs. Childs lit up with a smile. "Jon? Is that you?"

Jon held the salute. "Yes, Ma'am, and I have brought you presents from distant, exotic lands."

The ladies looked at the shopping bag as Jon picked it up and stepped to the right side of her bed.

Mrs. Childs reached out a trembling hand. Jon took it. "Jon Ketch... You always were my favorite."

The girls grinned at each other.

Jon made a sour face. "Teach, you know that's not true. I was never anyone's favorite anything—not even to my two ex-wives and three daughters. Well, okay one of my daughters thinks I'm okay, but she's still young and impressionable. Give her another year and she'll hate me too."

"I was just thinking about you, Jon. I think I had a dream about you," Mrs. Childs said.

"Goodness, gracious! Doctors have pills to help you with nightmares like me," Jon said. "Those big blue pills can make me just, poof! Disappear. I'll talk to the head Doc and take care of it."

Mrs. Childs' head slowly turned toward the girls. Her smile broadened with pleasure. Her small eyes danced. "Oh, my, how lucky I am to have you all here with me! Come over here."

The three ladies did, taking her hand, kissing her cheek or forehead. "You...all of you are here. How nice."

Jon indicated toward the flowers. "The ladies brought you even more flowers. Aren't they beautiful, Teach? The Christmas Women."

She turned to see them, pleased. "Oh, yes. I do love fresh flowers. Thank you, ladies. And look at you. You are such pretty, intelligent and classy ladies, aren't you?"

Jon gave his old teacher a doubtful look. "Teach... your eyesight is failing you. These dolls may be good to look at, but classy? Good heavens, no! Low-class hussies, every one!"

Mrs. Childs managed a weak laugh. "Oh, Jon, you are such a scoundrel."

He bowed. "Thank you, my Lady."

Kristen edged forward, presenting her wrapped gift. "Another present for you, Mrs. Childs."

Mrs. Childs stared with surprise and interest. "Another present? You already gave me those precious earrings."

"I saw this in a little shop near our brownstone. I thought of you so I bought it," Kristen said, handing her the present.

Mrs. Childs shakily tugged off the bow and gently removed the shiny red paper, revealing a white box. She opened the lid, lifted the white tissue paper and peered in. Her face opened with pleasure.

"Oh, my, look at this!" she exclaimed, startled by its beauty. She held it up for all to see. It was a gleaming 14k gold drop pendant, with peacock gray and white freshwater pearls, descending from a diamond-accented bale.

Mrs. Childs was overwhelmed, unable to pull her eyes from the piece. "It's absolutely beautiful! It must have cost a fortune."

Kristen crossed her arms, pleased. "It wasn't a fortune. I got a deal. Let me help you with it."

Kristen took the necklace, gently draped it about her teacher's neck and fastened it. Mrs. Childs beamed. "I feel so special in it. So regal. Thank you, Kristen. Thank you for your thoughtfulness and generosity."

Jon reached into the shopping bag. "Okay, now it's my turn, Teach. Everybody step back and give me room! These gifts are one-of-a kind and you won't find them anywhere else in the entire world! Are you ready? Your first exotic present from distant shores is…" Jon drew it out and held it high. "Soap on a Rope!"

Everyone laughed, as he laid it on her bed.

"No more reaching for that soap that slips from your little fingers, Teach. Hey, it will make a nice necklace too. Much nicer than Kristen's."

Mrs. Childs laughed.

"Next!" Jon yanked out the next gift. "A power bar! Extra protein to fight off those germs… and those probing, meddling doctors!"

There was more laughter.

"Next! Voila! Sani Flush, the greatest of the toilet bowl cleaners! Dissolves stains with bubbling action!"

Mrs. Childs' body shook with laughter. Even the nurse laughed.

"And finally, but not the least."

Jon swept the faces with his bold eyes. He drew out an artfully wrapped 11x7 gift. He gently handed it to Mrs. Childs. She examined it, shaking it.

"What's this, Jon?"

"Open it, Teach. It's something I've kept for 20 years. Go ahead, open it."

The room gathered into curious silence.

The nurse helped Mrs. Childs sit up, her back against two pillows. She slowly nudged off the red bow, slipped a finger under the taped seam and released it. With a final questioning glance at Jon, she peeled back the paper.

When she saw it, she gasped. Tears formed in the corners of her eyes. The girls moved closer to get a better look.

Mrs. Childs was so overcome, she couldn't speak. She stared at it, enthralled, before passing it to Trudie.

Trudie held it up for all to see. Their faces softened; their eyes grew misty. It was a gold-framed photograph, taken on the Deer Lake High School stage during the final night of the Christmas show twenty years ago. Mrs. Childs stood in the center with her four students. On one side stood Jon and Trudie. On the other, were Kristen and Mary Ann.

Mrs. Childs wore an emerald green dress with a red scarf, tied elegantly about her neck. Her expression was that of a serious director: firm, focused and confident. Jon had a squinty smile, and was wearing his bright green elf costume, complete with pointed ears and shoes.

The Christmas Girls wore short, tight red dresses, with white faux fur hats and 3-inch red heels. Trudie looked stiff and constrained by her prettiness, her smile only half formed. Kristen seemed to purr in her snug red outfit, her expression a coquettish invitation. Mary Ann's warm smile and lifted chin revealed her mystery and unpredictable charm.

Mrs. Childs' grateful eyes slowly lifted, focusing on her former students through blurry vision. The nurse handed her a tissue and Mrs. Childs gently dabbed at her eyes.

She nodded several times. "Well... here you are, and I'm feeling so sentimental. I want to write an autobiography and say hearts and flowers about you all..."

She wiped her eyes again, while the emotion subsided. "I wish we could do that Christmas show again. It was so much fun."

FIFTEEN

Mary Ann insisted on staying with Mrs. Childs until Julie arrived. Meanwhile, Trudie and Kristen drove to the house to collect the girls and drive over to the Sugar Hill Methodist Church to prepare for their 1 o'clock rehearsal. Jon decided to stay behind with Mary Ann. He told Trudie to have somebody else read the part of Scrooge until he got there.

After the nurse left Mrs. Childs' room, Mary Ann sat down next to her, while Jon remained standing at the foot of the bed, his arms folded, watching with keen interest.

"Mrs. Childs," Mary Ann said, "are you comfortable if I work with you the way I did the last time? I may touch your arm, or your head, and maybe the area around your heart. Is that okay with you?"

Mrs. Childs had grown noticeable weary. Her face had drained from the earlier pink. Jon looked on, apprehensive.

"Yes, Mary Ann. But if you don't mind, I'm just going to close my eyes and sleep for a little bit. I'm suddenly very tired."

"Yes, you just sleep, Mrs. Childs. Just relax and go to sleep."

Mary Ann stood and placed a gentle hand on Mrs. Childs' forehead. Jon watched her, carefully, as Mary Ann closed her eyes. Her mouth moved ever-so-slightly, as if she were saying a prayer or repeating some kind of mantra. This was not foreign to Jon, whose first wife had had Reiki sessions to relieve migraine headaches. Throughout his adult life, Jon had visited ashrams in California and New York, a Zen monastery in Japan and an ashram in Mumbai, India, where he'd met a holy man—a man said to be enlightened. Jon did not talk about this or discuss his daily meditation practice with anyone. It was deeply personal; he kept it a secret.

He watched Mary Ann carefully as she spread her hands slightly above Mrs. Childs' chest, repeating silent prayers. Twice, she stroked her teacher's hair and blew softly across her face. She went to the foot of the bed and lovingly held Mrs. Childs feet, while taking in deep breaths, and then letting them out slowly.

Jon continued watching in admiration, as Mary Ann worked. Within minutes, Jon become aware of a deep silence enveloping the room—an ineffable live thing that seemed to pulse. This quiet helped ease his restless thoughts and relax his nervous energy.

Time seemed to stand still as Mary Ann moved to the opposite side of the bed, repeating certain movements, again touching Mrs. Childs on the forehead and stroking her hair.

Jon witnessed his old teacher's breathing deepen, her body grow still and peaceful. He closed his eyes and drifted into an unutterable peace—a soft velvety peace that he'd felt only one other time in his life. When he was in India, sitting cross-legged at the feet of that holy man.

Julie arrived a little after three. She found Jon seated

on one side of her mother and Mary Ann seated on the other. Both had their eyes closed. Julie was startled by the quiet of the room. It had the calm, healing energy of a cathedral after mass, or a temple after a service. She found it a little unnerving.

Mary Ann opened her eyes and got up. Jon did the same.

"Is everything alright?" Julie asked, her eyes sliding from Mary Ann to Jon.

"Yes, fine," Mary Ann said. "She's been sleeping."

Jon didn't speak.

In Jon's car on the way to the rehearsal, he glanced over at Mary Ann. "What did you do back there?"

Mary Ann's eyes were closed. She looked tired. "That was special. Mrs. Childs has a very soft and sweet energy."

"What did you do?" Jon persisted. "I felt it. I felt something."

Mary Ann opened her eyes and looked over. "If anything happened, it had nothing to do with me. If anything, I just try to get out of the way of the healing energy. It doesn't always happen, but I felt something very special happen back there."

Jon kept passing her glances as he drove along quiet suburban streets, past a park where kids were swinging, squealing and building a snowman that was leaning far to the right.

Jon leaned a little, looking at Mary Ann differently. "Where did you learn to do that?"

"A woman. A very special woman. Over a period of about eight years she taught me some techniques and practices. She was a gifted healer, but she didn't want any publicity. She healed and she always asked her patients to remain silent about her. She wanted to be anonymous."

"And who is this woman?"

"She was a meditation master I met in Santa Barbara."

Jon drove on slowly. Theirs was one of only three cars on the road on a sunny Sunday afternoon. Jon slipped on sunglasses when the glare off the snow stabbed his eyes.

"Did you heal Teach?"

"I don't know, Jon. Like I said, I'm not a miracle worker."

Jon nodded, staring grimly. "I want her to have her princess-at-the ball moment, Mary Ann."

"I know, Jon. We all do."

Mary Ann and Jon found the back door to the Sugar Hill Church basement and entered. They saw Ray at the piano, conducting a 24-person chorus as they belted out *It's the Most Wonderful Time of the Year*. The sound reverberated, bounced and echoed off the concrete block walls, giving the impression of a choir twice its size.

Jon found the side room where *A Christmas Carol* rehearsals were in progress, and Mary Ann searched for her daughters. When she didn't see them, she texted them. They didn't text back. She continued down the short hallway, ducking into a Sunday school room, where Trudie and Kristen were seated at a long, low table, on little wooden chairs, working on laptops. On the walls were pictures of Bible stories, along with children's color-by-number drawings of baby Jesus, Mary, Joseph and the Wise Men.

Both girls glanced up when Mary Ann entered.

"How is she?" Trudie asked.

"Sleeping." Mary Ann shrugged. "I don't know. She looked better when we left. Have you told the group she may not be able to come to the show?"

Trudie sat back and stretched. "No. I'm still hoping. At the group meeting at one o'clock, Ray told everyone that two shows are confirmed, and the second show is nearly sold out. The first show will begin at 5:00 and the second at 8:00. Each show will be an hour and forty-five minutes, maybe longer because of Jon's play."

"Have you seen Carly and Lynn?" Mary Ann asked.

Trudie stood, working the kinks out of her neck. "I sent them into the play rehearsals. I hope you don't mind. They've been watching my DVDs of Jon's movies. They are quite taken with him. I didn't let them see *Killers Crossing,* though. It's pretty violent. Carly's in love with Jon, I think."

"God help her," Kristen said.

Mary Ann laughed. "You should see the pictures of him they've been sending to their friends. They were all over him at Rusty's the other night, snapping photos. He was so patient and kind."

"They wanted to be in the play, so I sent them in," Trudie said. "Jon will find something for them."

Kristen lowered her laptop screen. "Liz Tyree is here."

"Liz Tyree!? The stage manager?"

"Yep," Kristen said. "She's marching around like she owns the place, just like she did 20 years ago. The more things change, the more they stay the same. She's the one who says the show shouldn't be more that an hour and a half, including Jon's play."

Mary Ann sat down in a little wooden chair, and it made her look small. "What did Jon say?"

Trudie grinned. "You know Jon. Jon will do what Jon wants to do. He'll tell Liz forty-five minutes, and then he'll make the thing as long as he wants."

"Have you heard from Oscar?" Mary Ann asked, somewhat guarded.

Trudie spoke up. "Oh, yes, I was going to tell you. He's coming in this afternoon."

"We desperately need him to start on the sets," Kristen said.

"Cole hasn't shown up yet today," Trudie said, ignoring Kristen's look of concern. "Jon said if Cole doesn't come to rehearsals today, he's getting someone else to play The Ghost of Christmas Future."

At that same moment, Don Rawlings stuck his head in. "Hello, ladies. Ray sent me here to talk to you about my Rudolph act."

Mary Ann spun around. Kristen straightened, and Trudie shot up. "Oh, well, hello, Don! Come in."

Don stepped in, cradling a saxophone case. He noticed the tired look on Trudie's face and wondered if she'd been with Jon Ketch the night before. If so, his chances with her were probably over. He struggled to think of something funny to say, wanting to see her face light up as it had in the bar, but he drew a blank.

"I guess I need two dancers who will fit into the two Rudolph suits."

Mary Ann stood, offering her hand. "I'm Mary Ann."

Don shook it. "I'm Don Rawlings."

"Oh, I'm sorry," Trudie said. "I forgot you two haven't met."

"I saw you in Rusty's last night," Don said, "when Jon Ketch made his dramatic appearance."

"I didn't know you were there," Trudie said. "You should have come over."

"I didn't want to intrude."

"Don," Kristen said, crisply, "sometimes a girl wants you to intrude, don't they, Trudie?"

Trudie fidgeted with her hair, noticing Don studying her face. "I've been thinking about those two reindeer dancers. Kristen and I think Carly and Lynn would be the perfect dancers for Don's little act. He'll play Rudolph *The Red Nose Reindeer* on his saxophone and the girls will dance. Do you think they'll do it?"

"Are you kidding!? They'd love it," Mary Ann said.

Trudie stepped around the table to Don. "Why don't we find a side room for you and I'll find Carly and Lynn and introduce you. Do you have the reindeer outfits?"

"Yes, right outside."

Rehearsals concluded at 5:30. Afterwards, the excited and energized cast of 41 gathered around the piano and Connie Baker told them that both shows were sold out. There was thunderous applause. She also briefed them on the progress of the scholarship fund.

"Thanks to Don Rawlings, many of the local businesses have contributed generously. Currently, we have over $10,000 in the Myrna Childs' Scholarship Fund and I'm sure more money will be coming in as others hear about it."

There was more spirited applause.

Connie continued. "This scholarship will be presented to a Deer Lake High School student who excels in academics. But... the student must also be interested in drama, and either perform in or direct a play during senior year. We're hoping to raise enough money that we can invest it and use only the interest as the actual scholarship money."

Ray stepped forward. He said that the local TV station wanted to highlight the show and do some interviews. He looked at Jon, who stood in the back of the room, reading glasses on, writing notes in the margin of his script.

"Jon... they want to interview you, of course."

Jon lifted a hand, not taking his eyes from the script. "I'll do it for Teach. I'll do it for the show. Say, yes, as long as they don't ask me why my last movie got trashed by the critics." He shouted. "Because it sucked!"

Everyone laughed.

"Jon," Ray continued. "I also got a call from *Entertainment Tonight*. I have no idea how they found out about all this."

Jon's head snapped up in alarm. He yanked off his glasses. "What!?"

"I'm saying this in front of everybody, because I want everyone to know what's going on. We don't have any secrets here."

Jon raked a hand through his hair. "This is bullshit, Ray. We don't want national TV in on this. They'll turn this town into a zoo and do some stupid-ass bio on Mrs. Childs. They'll highlight her career, bring up the cancer and make us all out to be saints or something. Meanwhile, Teach will be humiliated. You know that. Don't even think about letting them come here and do this. Say no."

The crowd grew quiet, some staring down at their shoes, some staring at Jon, worried.

Ray held up a placating hand. "I *did* say no, Jon. I feel the same way you do. But will that stop them? If they've heard you're here and why you're here, won't other entertainment shows want to do some kind of Christmas special and interview?"

Jon shook his head, fighting irritation. He closed his eyes and pinched the bridge of his nose. He looked up. "Where are The Christmas Women?"

Trudie, Kristen and Mary Ann came forward, standing

by Ray.

Jon marched forward, planting his two feet in the center of the room. His voice took on an edge, his blue eyes fierce. "I do not want this show to be about me! I do not want Teach humiliated. If this thing gets out of control, and if I start seeing mobile TV trucks and camera crews rolling down Main Street, then I'm outta here, okay? I don't like reporters or photographers. They don't give a damn about anything or anyone except their own silly careers. Now you three are in charge. You are the producers, just like you were 20 years ago. All right, produce! Stop this circus from happening. I don't care how you stop it, but stop it. Okay!?"

Jon spun around, stormed off to the rear Exit door, jerked it open and left, slamming it behind him, leaving the room in stunned silence.

Trudie looked at Mary Ann and Kristen, and whispered, "Well, that was dramatic."

As the alumni gathered up their bags, coats and purses, Don spoke up.

"Hey, everybody. If you've got nothing to do tonight, I'm inviting everyone over to my place for a casual dinner. Nothing fancy: hamburgers, hotdogs, pizza, poached salmon, salad and lots of Christmas cookies from the local bakery. The party starts at 8 o'clock and all kids are welcome. Christmas garb of some sort is required! Here's my address."

Cole Blackwell strolled up to Kristen, whispering. She turned away. Cole kept whispering and, finally, Kristen nodded, a smile forming on her lips.

Trudie wandered over to Don, who was shouldering into his dark blue parka.

"That's a nice thing to do," she said.

"I think it will be fun. Are you coming?"

Trudie nodded, looking directly into his eyes. "Yes. Yes, I'm coming."

Out of the corner of her eye she saw Oscar Bonds enter the back door and glance about. He was a little stooped, wearing black-rimmed glasses and looking like a middle-aged version of Harry Potter. Oscar saw Mary Ann at about the same time she saw him. They both went rigid, their eyes locked, as memory and anticipation captured them.

Don followed Trudie's eyes. "Who's that?"

"Oscar Bonds was valedictorian of our class. He and Mary Ann dated for awhile. I think it was serious... at least Mary Ann thought it was."

Don zipped up his coat. "I don't know. I may not go to my twentieth year high school reunion. Something tells me we never really grow up that much. Do we really move on?"

Trudie boldly held his warm eyes, feeling the same invitation she'd felt when she met him that first night at Rusty's.

"I don't know," she said. "On the other hand, I'm ready to move on. I want to move on."

Don lingered, his probing eyes taking her in. He reached out and touched her cheek.

Trudie shivered a little. A rush of sexual energy rattled her, but she couldn't pull her eyes from his handsome face.

"I'm glad to hear you want to move on, Trudie," Don said, intimately. "Moving on is a good thing."

SIXTEEN

By 9 o'clock, Don's party was loud with Christmas music, laughter, impromptu dancing and singing. His Christmas punch—a mixture of fresh fruit juices, clove, cinnamon and lots of Rum—had helped all the adults relax right away, and they continued to drink it with cheerful celebration and ease. There were sodas and juice for the kids.

As the guests arrived, they were greeted by Don's "guards," Molly and Connie, who ensured they were decked out for the season. Everyone had to be wearing something: a Christmas sweater, a red shirt or a green blouse, a Christmas tree pin, red sneakers or a Santa Claus hat. If they weren't wearing red or green, they were handed some red ribbon to put around their necks. Once they had passed inspection, they were ushered into the living room, where Don's two 7-foot trees gave off scent and light; the fireplace blazed; and all the tables and window sills were decorated with votive candles and bright poinsettias.

No one had had trouble finding Don's sprawling ranch-style house, with all the Christmas lights strung in the trees and under the eves of the house; the enormous wreath lit up on the oak door; and the tall, plastic Santa on the front porch. The house lay at the end of a quiet, tree-lined road, nestled near the base of a cliff. The circular drive was bloated with cars, and more cars were parked around the Dead End sign which sat above an icy stream.

Don was busy in the kitchen, grilling burgers and hot dogs, directing Carly and Lynn to fill dishes and replenish the salad, the salmon and the side dishes.

Trudie made her way around the room, sipping on punch, playing hostess and picking up discarded plastic and paper plates. When she noticed Mary Ann and Oscar hiding in the shadows, she left them alone, although she burned to know what they were discussing so intensely. Meanwhile, Kristen and Cole occupied a busy corner, wrapped in conversation, she animated, he listening with unmistakably affectionate eyes.

Trudie almost resisted being judgmental, but ultimately failed.

She returned to the kitchen, just as Don placed the last two hamburgers on plates and beckoned for her to sit down at the kitchen table. Then he opened the refrigerator and spun around with a bottle of ketchup in his hand. "For us!" he said, holding it over her hamburger like a bottle of wine. They laughed and sat down to eat together.

By 10:30, the party was showing no signs of winding down. They joined the others in the living room for karaoke carol singing. For a time, they sat cross-legged near the fire, listening to old high school stories and new stories about kids and wives.

As she listened, Trudie felt that old creeping anxiety return—that she'd missed out on most of the pleasant

166

and challenging things in life. Once again, the old theme of her life returned: her life was speeding by and she had nothing to show for it. She got up and went to the bathroom to escape.

As she strolled back toward the living room, she noticed a text from Ray. *I'm at Rusty's with Jon. He's throwing back Jack Daniels. Help! Can you come?*

Trudie sighed. She wanted to stay with Don! This was the beginning of their relationship and it seemed to be going well. He was the first man in a very long time that she felt strongly attracted to and comfortable with at the same time. He seemed to feel the same way.

But she knew Jon was a loose cannon. Twenty years had changed nothing in him. Maybe he was even worse. Always volatile and unpredictable, Jon had to be managed. She'd read enough news articles about him to know this. She couldn't let him go spiraling out of control.

Cursing Jon, she texted back, *I'm on my way.*

"There's a problem about the show," she told a disappointed Don. "I'm sorry, I have to leave."

He walked her to the door and helped her into her coat.

"I hope we can have some time alone together when this is all over," Don said. "I guess until this show is over you're going to be preoccupied."

Trudie wanted him to kiss her. And then, to her wonderful surprise, he did, a soft warm kiss that startled her with desire. She wanted more of it, and more of him. She wanted to touch his body, his arms, his legs. She wanted to run her hands through his thick mane of hair and press her chest against his. She longed to explore him, fall into him, lose herself in him. It had been so long, so very long, and she felt her body begin to awaken with passion.

But Don backed away. "Thanks for the help tonight. Careful driving."

Trudie was too moved to speak. She could only nod, trembling. She turned and left.

As Trudie drove through the night, tears suddenly began to stream down her cheeks. She angrily flicked them away. She didn't want them. She didn't know why she was crying, and she didn't want to think about why she was crying. Okay, she knew why she was crying. She wanted and needed a life change. She was tired of being careful and guarded. Tired of second-guessing every relationship she'd ever had. Tired of always feeling she had to justify her life.

Did Kristen second-guess her relationships? Did Mary Ann? They were both back at the house having a good time. Kristen and Cole would probably sleep together. Maybe Kristen would get a divorce and marry Cole. *Well, whoop-dee-doo for them!*

Maybe Mary Ann and Oscar would get married. Maybe they'd sleep together tonight or the next night, or any damned night!

By the time Trudie whipped the steering wheel right and drove into Rusty's crowded parking lot, she was shaking. She found the last parking space, parked and killed the engine.

She rested her head on the top rim of the steering wheel, struggling to corral her stampeding emotions. God, what was the matter with her? Was she cracking up? Kristen said she was taking some kind of anti-depressant, because she was so miserable all the time. Maybe it was time Trudie asked her doctor for a tranquilizer or an anti-depressant. Why not?

She shoved the car door open and stepped out, feeling

the liquid cool air wash across her face. At the side door to the bar, standing under the yellow neon BAR light, she heard pounding rock music and the hum of voices inside. As she grasped the cold door handle, her whirling, frustrated thoughts swiftly settled when she thought of Mrs. Childs. How was she? Would she be able to attend the Christmas show? Trudie shut her eyes for a moment, and whispered a silent prayer. When she opened them, she felt calmer, ready to handle Jon and whatever else she had to handle.

Inside, she found Ray and Jon at a back wooden booth, Ray nursing a beer, a sullen-looking Jon hovering over a shot of Jack Daniels. She heard the distant crack of pool balls being scattered, and saw a couple of porky-looking dudes with leather jackets and tattoos at the bar, glancing her way with sudden winking interest. Yeah, right. That's all she needed!

Jon lit up when he saw her. "Holy Trudie Parks!" He slapped the bench next to him. "Come sit with me and have a drink or something!"

She sat. "Are you drunk, Jon?"

"I'm on the way, but the road is long and narrow and there ain't a lot of light."

Trudie looked at Ray. "How many has he had?"

"Four... and two beers."

"Jon, you've had enough. Why don't I drive you to your motel?"

"Will you come in with me? Will you soothe this savage beast, and heal my wounded heart, beating love for you in this jail of rib and bone? Will you soothe this beast who has loved you ever since he was in the 7th grade?"

Trudie gave him a hard, unsympathetic stare. "I'll drive you to your motel and put *you* to bed."

Jon yelled out, pumping his fist. "YES! Now that's what I'm talkin' 'bout, girl!"

"Okay, let's go, Jon," Trudie said, reaching for his arm to help him up.

He stopped, suddenly remembering something. "Hey, what kind of a jerk am I? I haven't even bought you a drink."

"I don't need a drink, Jon. I drank a little at Don Rawlings' party."

Jon gave her a swift look, boring into her eyes, seeking an answer. "Don Rawlings is it? Well, now, let's see. Does Trudie Parks have a beau? A Bo-friend?"

Trudie sighed, grabbing his arm, tugging at it. "Come on, Jon. Let's get out of here."

Ray glanced around, noticing that people were staring at them. But then they had been staring at them ever since he and Jon had arrived. People in town knew Ray was homosexual, and there he was, sitting with the famous movie actor, Jon Ketch. Of course they were staring, and speculating, and whispering, and sometimes snickering. Ray hated being looked at. He despised being trapped like he was. He started to get up.

"Sit down, Ray!" Jon said, slapping the table with the flat of his hand. "You're the only guy in this town who would have a drink with me! You're my only real friend. Hell, come to think of it, you always *were* my only real friend. Let's have one more drink."

"No, Jon. You've had enough. Let's go," Trudie said.

Jon folded his arms across his chest, leaning back, obstinate. He shook his head. "No! Not until you have one drink with me."

He pushed her. "Let me out. Come on. Get out of the way. I'll go get us all one more."

Resigned, Trudie got up and let Jon slide out. He

wandered off to the bar.

Trudie leaned toward Ray. "What's the matter with him? Why is he getting so drunk?"

Ray shrugged. "Mrs. Childs, his kids, his ex-wives, his career. He said loving you was the best thing he ever felt. He's gone through the whole cycle."

"I've got to get him out of here," Trudie said, suddenly noticing that the two dudes at the bar were ambling over. Her shoulders sank. "Oh, God, not this."

By then, the heavier of the two men was standing over the table, beer mug in hand. He had a hard, stony face, glassy eyes and a crooked gash of a grin.

"Hey there, pretty lady. Can I buy you a drink?"

Trudie kept her eyes locked forward. Ray stared down into the table. "No thanks," Trudie said. "My friend is getting me one."

The big guy glanced over at the bar, indicating with his half-full mug of amber ale. "You mean that little runt?"

The skinnier guy behind him said, "I keep tellin' you, Big Frank, that's the movie star guy. That's Jon Ketch."

"Big deal. So he makes stupid movies. I've seen one or two. They all suck. He ain't no better than me."

About that time, Jon was making his way back to the table, a shot tucked under his chin, carrying a mug of beer in one hand and a glass of white wine in the other. He by-passed the shorter guy and skirted around Big Frank.

Nervous, and his hand trembling, Ray took the mug from Jon, as Jon handed the wine glass to Trudie. Jon didn't sit.

"You didn't say what you wanted, so I got you Chardonnay," Jon said. "Most women like Chardonnay, don't you think so?" Jon said, as he turned his steely attention to Big Frank.

Jon pulled the shot from his chin. "Can I help you

two gentlemen?"

"We want to buy the lady a drink."

Jon grinned, but there was a threat in it. "Really? Well, why the hell not?"

Jon looked at Trudie. "Trudie, these fine gentlemen want to buy you a drink."

Trudie ignored them all and sipped the wine. "I have a drink."

Jon lifted a hand. "Well, there you have it, gentlemen. The lady has a drink. We thank you and wish you well as you make your way back to the bar."

Big Frank's eyes darkened. "You her puppet master or something?"

Jon laughed. "Hey, I like that. You have a touch of the poet in you. What did you say your name was?"

"I didn't. But I'm Big Frank."

Jon looked him up and down. "You are big, Frank, and I see you haven't missed many meals in your long and illustrious life."

"That ain't funny."

Jon shrugged. "No, you're not."

"I want the lady to tell me to my face that she doesn't want a drink," Big Frank persisted.

Jon's eyes lowered. He held the tip of the shot glass to his lips and threw it back, gulping it down. He slammed the shot glass down on the table so hard that both Ray and Trudie flinched. Big Frank didn't.

Jon turned his full attention to Big Frank. "The lady said no, Big Frank. That means no. Now you're spoiling my party and you weren't invited. Please be the gentlemen I know you are and leave us alone." Jon bowed a little. "Thank you, gentlemen."

The short man turned to leave. "Come on, Big Frank."

Big Frank didn't budge. He glared at Jon. "So you're some big actor from Hollywood who thinks he's hot shit. You're with this faggot and pretty girl and you think you're better than everybody else here. I say you're just a short little asshole who makes shitty movies and likes to hang out with faggots."

Jon stared back, eyes cool and narrowed, a touch of laughing menace in them. Jon held up two fingers, a tiny space apart. "Now I'm about that far away from kicking your bigoted, ignorant fat ass back to the bar. So please, just get the hell away from me."

Ray's head flopped forward in disbelief and fear.

Trudie made a start to get up. "Jon, let's get out of here. Now. Stop this."

"Sit down, Trudie," Jon commanded.

Big Frank barked out a harsh laugh. "You're gonna kick my ass?" he asked, incredulous. His laugh was deep and raspy.

Jon placed his hands on his hips. "I'll meet you outside, Big Frank, and kick your ass all over the parking lot if that's what you want. I'm not going to mess up my friend, Gavin's, barroom. That wouldn't be nice."

Trudie struggled again to get to her feet, but Jon shoved her down. "No. Stay here. Me and Big Frank have something to settle. No stupid asshole is going to insult my friends."

Big Frank grinned, broadly. "Kicking your movie star ass is going to make me a star, you prissy little faggot-lover."

Big Frank slammed his mug down on the table and Jon marched off, leading the way through the side door and out into the parking lot. Many patrons were watching the altercation, anxious and tense. Some were already texting. They shot up and filed out the door behind Jon and Big Frank, their eyes alive with anticipation.

Jon strode aggressively to a space where an overhead parking light flooded the pavement, spotlighting him. Big Frank followed, coming out of his leather jacket and slinging it away. Under the harsh white light, Big Frank looked tough, coarse and intimidating.

The two men stood five feet apart, each sizing up the other. Big Frank was at least 5 inches taller than Jon, and he had at least 60 pounds on him.

Jon's face was passive, eyes dead calm and narrowed. He held his fists low and he stayed pretty much in the same place. "Come on, Big Frank. You scared of me?"

Big Frank grinned, confidently. He started for Jon, his big square fists up near his chin. Jon stood calmly, waiting, calculating size and distance.

"Big Frank, did anybody ever tell you what a sweet little face you have? Well I could just kiss those pink little cheeks all night. Such a sweet little baby face. And your skin looks as smooth and clean as a baby's ass."

The crowd around them laughed. That provoked Big Frank.

He threw a swift right that caught Jon on the left lower jaw. Jon spun around, wavered, spit out some blood, then came up smiling, shaking off the punch.

"Well, Big Frank. Not bad. But I think a baby-ass face guy like you can do better than that."

Trudie and Ray pushed out the door just in time to see Big Frank slug Jon in the jaw. Trudie reached for her phone. Should she call the police? Then she stopped. No! It would hit the national news and be all over *Twitter* and the internet in hours.

The two men paired off, eyes cautious, bodies taut. Jon still kept his hands low, waiting, standing loose, daring Big Frank with his unblinking eyes and wintry smile.

"You gonna dance around all night, Baby Face, with that big fat ass of yours?"

Big Frank threw a hard right. Jon swept it away.

"Jesus, Big Frank, I saw that one comin' last Friday."

Big Frank threw swift jabs and Jon dodged all of them. Big Frank danced about heavily, like a dancing bear, with great energy and purpose, searching for an opening to pop Jon in the body and face.

"Come on, Baby Face, you can do better than that."

Big Frank charged, swinging his left up and into Jon's stomach. Jon bent over a little and just as Big Frank came in for a right, Jon stepped aside, grabbing for Big Frank's right wrist. He twisted it around and up in an arm lock and, using Big Frank's own momentum, Jon ran him into the back of a car. Big Frank bounced off, yelling out in shock and pain.

Jon stood back, shaking his head, sorrowfully, shaking out his cold hands. "Come on, Baby Face, I'm a short, mediocre actor with bad knees. The doctor just told me I have high blood pressure and I have to watch my cholesterol. A big guy like you should be able to kick my little skinny ass."

Big Frank was enraged. "I'm gonna kill you, asshole!"

Jon nodded, his dark smile widening, his eyes filled with malice. Jon beckoned him with wiggling fingers. "Then come on in, Baby Face, so I can kiss those pink little cheeks."

Big Frank lurched toward Jon. He swung his fists wildly and Jon side-stepped the punches easily. Big Frank stumbled away, off balance. He pivoted clumsily, and charged again. He threw desperate jabs at Jon's eyes. Jon blocked them.

Trudie and Ray exchanged startled glances. The crowd roared.

Big Frank stopped, perplexed, his nose puffing out white vapor like a weary bull. He wiped his nose, panic rising on his face. He tried again. He threw a hard right that Jon knocked away, spinning Big Frank left. With his right foot, Jon kicked Big Frank in the ass, sending him sprawling into the back of the car a second time.

More people burst out the side door, spilling into the lot, pointing and rushing toward the fight. They encircled the fighters, curious and buzzing. Some held cameras, snapping photos, others held their phones aloft and shot a movie.

"Come on, Big Frank, hit him!" his skinny, frustrated partner yelled. "Hit him, kick his ass!"

"You heard the rabble, Big Frank. Come on and kick my ass," Jon taunted.

Infuriated, Big Frank charged Jon again. He swung. Jon deflected the mighty fist and shoved Big Frank backwards. Big Frank staggered, nearly losing his balance.

"Hey, Baby Face, I'm getting tired of playing with you."

With renewed rage, Big Frank charged, his energies scattered and chaotic. Jon moved away, anchored himself, waited for Big Frank's next attack and moved into place. He threw short but hard hooks to the side of Big Frank's head. Big Frank teetered, eyes wide and disoriented. Jon kept it up, jabbing and hooking, his face hard, eyes fierce. Blood spattered Big Frank's face and poured from his nose. He threw his hands up to protect his face, as Jon drummed his fists into Big Frank's face and belly, driving him back, stumbling, his rubbery legs about to buckle.

In desperation, Big Frank struggled to plant his feet. He took one final wild-west, roundhouse swing. Jon ducked and punched Big Frank hard in the stomach. The wind exploded from his body. He doubled over, hands grasping his stomach. Jon seized both sides of his head and shoved him back, violently. Big Frank crashed to the ground, rolling onto his side, barely conscious. He curled into a fetal position, moaning in pain.

Jon was lost in a fury. He strafed the crowd with his burning eyes. There was a paralyzing silence as the group stared back at him, faces fixed in shock and admiration.

"Anybody else ever insult my friends, I'll break their neck. You all got that!? I'll break their damned neck!"

The crowd cheered and applauded. Big Frank's buddy scurried over to help him, as Big Frank sat up, dazed and disoriented.

Jon slowly begin to shed his fury, his taut face relaxing, white clouds puffing from his mouth as he gasped for breath. He staggered a little. The crowd sustained their praise and sharp applause.

Jon slowly recovered, shaking the pain out of his fists. His face opened into a wide toothy grin, and Trudie watched in utter astonishment as Jon took a sweeping, theatrical bow. His face glowed with grace and drama; an actor taking a final curtain call during a standing ovation.

"Thank you, good Lords and Ladies of Castle Deer Lake. Once again, good has triumphed over evil, right over might, David over Goliath! I am, and shall always remain, your humble and obedient knight of the charging windmills, Jon Quixote Ketch of la Mancha!"

Carrying Jon's bomber jacket, Trudie worked her way through the crowd over to Jon, thrusting him the coat.

"You're shivering. Put this on and let's get out of here, before the police show up."

Jon beamed with new pleasure. "Lady Trudie! My dear Lady Trudie has come to whisk me off to safety to her glorious castle on a high chaparral."

"Come on, Jon," Trudie said, as she snatched Jon's arm, tugging him toward the front parking lot.

Jon wrenched away, waving broadly at the retreating crowd. "Merry Christmas to all, and to all a good night!"

Trudie seized his arm again, yanking him toward her car. Ray stood in back of the crowd, watching his old classmates retreat. With beer mug in hand, he privately toasted Jon, even as he heard the scream of an approaching police siren and saw the sweep of a blue dome light.

SEVENTEEN

Kristen and Cole were on a hill sitting on a flat rock, overlooking the town of Deer Lake. They were staring down at the flickering lights, hearing the distant wobble of a siren and the soft hiss of a stream. It was after 11 o'clock. They were wrapped in winter coats, scarves and hats, crouched together beneath a cold, winter sky that held a white three-quarter moon and a mass of close stars.

It had been 20 years since their last visit to this private spot, so pregnant with memory and regret. Neither spoke, not wanting to shatter the night music and the gentle, soothing privacy.

"When I was a little girl," Kristen said, staring sky-ward, "my father told me that Deer Lake, Ohio was one of Santa Claus' favorite towns to visit. When I asked him why, he said because I was here."

She turned to Cole. "Wasn't that a nice thing to say?"

Cole nodded. "Yes, it was. I liked your father. He was always nice to me."

"He didn't like you," Kristen said, with amusement.

Cole turned sharply. "Really? Why not?"

Kristen shrugged. "He knew I was crazy about you. He knew I was impulsive and overly romantic. He knew we had sex. I don't know how he knew, but he knew."

Cole pulled his knees up to his chest, breathing out a white vapor sigh. "I'm going to get paid back soon for all the dumb things I did when I was young. My daughter is very pretty. She's turning 15 in a couple of months and she's already had three boyfriends."

"What's she like?"

"More like her mother than me. A bit of a snob, I think."

"Well, Cole, you were always a bit of a snob."

"You never give me a break, do you, Kristen?"

"Why should I? Did you ever give me one?"

They both turned away, regretting their remarks.

Kristen softened her voice and shifted her weight. "I hope Alexander finds a nice girl. He's a good kid... a little aloof and withholding, but what kid isn't at 13 or 14?"

"My son, Ryan, is 13. He's a jock. Loves soccer and football."

Kristen turned to him. "Do your children get along with their mother?"

"Oh, yes... Yes, they do. They went through an angry period, after the divorce. And they blamed me for awhile. Maybe they still do."

"Why just you?"

He shrugged. "I don't know. It's not like Marylyn was an affectionate mother. A practical one, yes, but not terribly affectionate. But she had... has class."

Kristen lowered her head. "And why haven't you re-married?"

"You've already asked me that."

"And you haven't answered."

He spoke at a near whisper. "You know why. I've told you why."

"Because you're still in love with me?"

Cole was quiet.

"Have you talked to Trudie?"

"Oh, we've been polite to each other. She's chilly toward me, but then I always did find her a kind of cold person."

"She's not cold," Kristen said, defensively. "Trudie is one of the nicest people in this world. She's thoughtful and generous and good. I wish I had one thimbleful of her goodness."

Cole was surprised by Kristen's rigorous defense. "And you're so bad, Kristen?"

Kristen just shook her head.

"Are you so kind when it comes to Mary Ann?"

"Mary Ann is a sweet girl, but I just don't get all the occult stuff—all the New Age business she's into. It's just too far out for me. But I love her. How can you not love Mary Ann?"

"But you don't like yourself?"

"I've been in therapy for five years. I know myself. My strengths and limitations. I know that I never seem to be satisfied with things the way they are. I always want something newer or better or... I don't know, maybe nobody really likes himself—herself—very much."

Cole stretched his legs out, pulling his ski cap over his ears. "You and I are a lot alike, Kristen. You're aggressive and willful. I'm ambitious and steady. Does that make us bad? That's just who we are. I broke up with you 17 or 18 years ago because I was afraid we'd wind up beating each other up or something."

"You just didn't believe in us, Cole."

"I'm not sure about that. We were just kids."

"So now that we're all grown up, how has it changed?"

"You're still married."

"And if I wasn't?"

Cole stood up, slapping his shoulders to keep warm. He looked down at her. "Kristen... I have loved you for a long time. I made a mistake. I've told you that. You know what I want now. I want us to forget the past and have the fun of falling in love all over again. I want us to have the life we didn't have."

"Because you dumped me."

"Okay. Okay! But now is now. Get over it, Kristen. What do we do now?"

Kristen pushed up, stamping her cold feet. "So you want me to throw away my marriage, and completely re-arrange my life because we had a thing in high school twenty years ago and maybe we could pick up where we left off?"

"Let me ask you this. Are you happy, Kristen?" Cole said, firmly. "Can you stand there and tell me that you're happy with your life the way it is? Maybe a change is exactly what you need. Maybe our love is still alive, waiting for us to act on it. Maybe it's time we both made ourselves and each other happy."

Kristen looked at him for a moment, pocketed her hands and turned away. "And maybe we're just fools. Maybe we should just make crazy love for a few days, get it out of our systems, and then go on with our lives."

"Is that what you really want?"

Kristen spun around. "I don't know what the hell I want! I wish I'd never come back here. I wish I'd never seen you again. I don't need this in my life. I don't! I have a husband who loves me, a wonderful son who I'd die for, and a good, successful career. I don't need this."

Cole reached for her, pulled her into him and kissed her. Kristen did not resist. She stood on tiptoes, wrapped her arms around his neck, and kissed him back, long and deep.

After Don's party, Oscar drove Mary Ann and the girls back to Trudie's house. When she told the girls to go on inside and get ready for bed, they gave her a quizzical look, but obeyed.

Mary Ann and Oscar sat in silence.

"Nice girls," Oscar finally said.

Mary Ann watched the girls wrestle with the key, shove the door open and enter. "Yes, they are. They're so excited about being in the show. Jon gave Carly the part of the Ghost of Christmas Present and he made Lynn his script assistant."

"Jon is as wild as ever, maybe even more so. He's a loose cannon."

Mary Ann chuckled. "He is that, all right."

"You're lucky to have your girls," Oscar said.

"Why didn't you and your wife have kids?" Mary Ann asked.

Oscar frowned at the thought. "We talked about it." He laughed, a little embarrassed. "Well, we tried for awhile but..." His voice trailed away into silence. "But then, I guess we were both so engrossed in our work. Amy was a very gifted and dedicated scientist. She won a couple of prestigious awards, you know."

"And you still miss her, don't you, Oscar?"

Oscar turned to look out the window into the darkness. "I miss the rhythm of our lives and our marriage; the tacit understanding we shared. I miss the deep respect we had for each other. I miss our conversations. I miss the sound of her quiet, precise voice. The house has so many empty rooms in it now."

Oscar was suddenly anxious. "Am I talking too much, Mary Ann?"

"Talk away. I've always enjoyed listening and it's good to catch up after all these years."

"I'm sorry. Here I am with you and I keep talking about Amy."

"It's okay, Oscar. Really."

Oscar placed his hands on the steering wheel, staring ahead, allowing the memories to rise and fall and then fade. "Were you lonely after your divorce?"

"No, not at all. I was glad to be out of it. Robert, my husband, loved flying airplanes and he loved chasing women around in those airplanes, and later on, in hotel rooms. I got it all first-hand from a stewardess who wanted revenge after he'd dumped her. "

Oscar scratched his head. "I don't understand."

Mary Ann released the top button on her coat. "Robert is a commercial airline pilot."

"Oh, yes, I see. Of course. Stewardess."

"And he had a girl in nearly every town, or so I learned. Thinking back on it, I don't know why we got married. I suppose I thought he was exciting and so different from me. I thought I should be with somebody different from me. And maybe, for awhile, I was in love with him. I don't know what he saw in me. And then he started calling me his little 'Air Head' because I was reading astrological charts and developing a clientele. And then I studied healing and out-of-body projection and became a part of that community."

Mary Ann gave Oscar a swift glance to gauge his reaction. She saw his eyebrow lift in mild astonishment.

She continued on, unfazed, but smiling at his reaction. Mary Ann was long past caring what people thought of her and her eccentric life.

"Robert thought calling me 'my little Air Head' was cute. Or 'Astro Girl', that was another one of his nicknames for me. It was so demeaning. That's around the time I knew I'd made a big mistake when I married him. Now, I think I *must* have been an air head to have married him. But anyway, I came face-to-face with the old, old story. We had two daughters. I didn't want to break up our home. I didn't want my girls to lose their father."

Oscar listened with interest, not moving. "But you did divorce him."

"Yes... I couldn't take it any longer. It was making me physically ill to be around him, knowing what I knew. I sat down and told my girls that Robert and I were divorcing. I didn't tell them everything, of course, but I told them we were splitting up, but that we were still good friends—even though it hurts to even say that, because we are not good friends at all. But I'd never say anything bad about Robert to my daughters. I want them to have their own relationship with him."

A motor scooter sputtered by and a dog down the street began yapping at it, shattering the quiet.

"Would you like to take a little walk?" Oscar asked.

Mary Ann nodded.

Outside, they strolled leisurely along the sidewalk, past a snowy lawn and an illuminated plastic Santa sled with reindeer. Christmas trees and candelabras lit up the windows of nearby houses, and the low murmur of distant traffic was amplified in the tranquil silence.

"Do you know what astrological sign I am?" Oscar asked.

"You don't believe in astrology, Oscar. Remember? You never did."

"Maybe I could learn to believe in it, if you were around to teach me. Maybe I could learn a lot of things. Maybe I could learn to be more open to things. That wouldn't be a bad thing, would it?"

Mary Ann was gently startled by his obvious overture. She didn't speak.

"I've thought about you a lot, Mary Ann, in the last few months. So many old memories came back and I recalled the oddest details. The way you walked, as if you were never in a hurry to get to the next place or to the next thing. You took good, solid, and sure steps. I remembered your voice, so feminine, and comforting and assured. And I remembered your gentleness."

Mary Ann looked over, uneasy. She was quiet, listening, marveling at Oscar's compliments—maybe not the most romantic of compliments, but surely heartfelt.

Oscar continued. "It's odd, isn't it, that after Amy passed away, within a week or so, memories of you came back into my mind. I found you on the internet... saw your website. I almost sent you an email but then I guess I just got nervous about it and decided not to."

"You're a Virgo, Oscar. You're a Virgo with Capricorn rising. This is what it means: You do what is expected, and then some. You're a calm, cool, and collected business-type. You're very dependable, always ready to help out by rolling up your sleeves and lending a hand, because you're a loyal team player. Success in life is nearly always guaranteed. You are considered indispensable at home and at work. You love being able to sit down in your easy chair at the end of a day and enjoy that "job well done" feeling. It is easy for you to become a workaholic. You can be overly serious and somewhat detached and you may have a limited view of life."

Oscar drew a breath and blew it out toward the sky. He stopped walking, and Mary Ann paused beside him. He looked at her, pocketing his hands.

"I didn't know you knew me so well. I sound so boring."

"I'm sure your wife didn't think you were boring."

"But you think I am?"

"I didn't think you were in high school, Oscar. I truly cared for you. You were smart, well-read and kind to me. I sense you are still a kind, sincere man."

Oscar worked on a thought. Mary Ann saw he was wrestling with it.

"What about relationships, Mary Ann? What about love?"

Mary Ann resumed walking, and Oscar followed.

"I think you're capable of great love, Oscar. It sounds like you loved your wife very deeply."

"Yes, I did. I loved her more than I thought was possible."

"I suspect you still do love her."

Oscar slowed to a stop again, deep in concentration, lost in his own stare. Mary Ann paused, watching him with keen interest.

"Mary Ann, is there any chance you and I could meet sometime, and get to know each other better? We could see if there's a possibility of developing a good and respectful relationship."

Mary Ann kicked at the snow piled near the curb, slanting him a glance. "Do you mean that you would like us to develop a possible romantic relationship, Oscar? Is that what you're trying to say?"

Oscar swallowed. She saw his Adam's apple move. When he spoke, his voice was soft and breathy. "Yes. Yes, that's what I mean, Mary Ann. I have always thought very highly of you, you know. Yes, a possible romantic relationship. Could we try that?"

He stared at her, and his eyes filled with feeling. She held his stare, smiling.

"Why not, Oscar? Why not?"

EIGHTEEN

Trudie managed to push Jon into the car, slam the car in gear and race out of the side entrance of Rusty's before the police car arrived. It came bouncing into the lot, braking, skidding to a stop. The crowd was already dispersing. Trudie wondered who had called the police. She recognized many familiar faces in the crowd, even if she wasn't friends with them. After all, she'd lived in Deer Lake her entire life and Rusty's was the most popular hangout. Would one of them tell the police she had taken Jon and driven away? Would Big Frank file an assault charge against Jon? Strangely enough, all that possibility excited her. At least she wasn't sitting at home reading a book by the fire. She was out having an adventure—a crazy one, yes—but an adventure nonetheless.

Trudie glanced over at Jon, who was slumped and brooding, the adrenalin draining from his body, the alcohol and the fight leaving him tired and blunted.

"Jon, are you okay? Are you hurt? Is your mouth okay?"

Jon felt his face and opened and closed his jaw. "Old Big Frank had a good right. He just didn't know what to do with it."

"Should I drive you to the emergency room?"

"No way."

"So you're okay?"

"Yeah, sure. Why shouldn't I be?"

"Because you were just in a fight with a big man who would have clobbered most men his own size."

Jon made an ugly face. "That guy? No way. He's out of shape, slow, stupid and drunk."

"You're drunk too."

"Yes, but I'm not fat, slow or stupid. Well, okay, I'm not fat or slow. Big Frank fought stupid and I knew he would. I've been in a lot of fights, both on screen and off. You get so you can read a guy. Big Frank was all mouth and puffed up confidence, with nothing to back it up. He thought he could take me with just his bulk. That was stupid."

"Where's your motel, Jon?"

"I don't want to go back there."

"Where then?"

Jon turned his face to her and, in the dim light, she again saw his raw yet sensitive good looks—the looks she'd found so attractive in high school. The good looks that hit the camera and the big screen with grace and force. His chosen roles were nearly always characters who were plucky, volatile and sassy. You couldn't pull your eyes from him when he was acting in a scene. You never knew how that character would respond—what he'd say or do. Just like the real Jon sitting beside her.

He was entrancing, frightening and wildly attractive, and Trudie was sick of her quiet, predictable life. She wanted a change. She needed and longed for a change, and she was determined to make a change. No more the careful girl, the cool withholding girl. The nice dental hygienist who lives in that old remodeled Victorian House like some Jane Austin character.

While watching the fight, she'd first been disturbed, then surprised, by her swift change of sensation. She wasn't upset or turned off by it in the least. On the contrary, she felt sexually aroused at the sight of Jon punching that big oaf in the side of the head and knocking him down. She had even cheered along with the others. Even Ray had given her a surprised glance, as if to say "Do I know you?"

She'd felt a thrill and an elation she hadn't felt in years. Jon had always done that to her, even in high school. Jon Ketch was a thrill ride in an amusement park. Jon Ketch was a drug that got you high. Jon Ketch was a charismatic wonder, like some spiraling planet far out in the universe about to collide with another planet. He was a black hole mystery. He was a super nova waiting to happen. And sometimes, you didn't have to wait too long.

"Where do you want to go, Jon?" Trudie repeated.

"I want us to go back to that ghost town and to the freaky house. The one we went to twenty years ago."

"Jon, that's over twenty miles away! It may not even be there anymore."

"So let's giddy-up, then, and find out. Twenty years and twenty miles. Sounds synchronistic or something."

Trudie obeyed. She found Highway 11, turned right, and drove off into the unpredictable darkness toward Shaffer, Ohio, an old boom-and-bust town once known for its mining and timber.

Jon's chin slowly fell into his chest and then his head rolled right, resting against the window, his hands folded in his lap. His snoring was soft and rhythmic. Trudie glanced over occasionally and smiled. During their senior year, Mary Ann had drawn up an astrological chart for

Jon, declaring that Jon had the potential to be known in the world, even famous. Trudie struggled to remember. Something about Jon's Jupiter being in the sign of Leo, which meant "the great actor", and his moon being "at the top of his chart," indicating possible fame.

Jon had laughed at her analysis, saying "When I *do* become a famous actor, I'll return to Deer Lake, Ohio and thumb my nose at every girl who refused to go out with me because I was too short or too damned nuts."

Trudie grinned, straining her eyes to see ahead. She wasn't entirely sure she knew where the old town was. There had only been a few shacks around twenty years ago. She remembered crossing an old bridge. As they'd rattled across it, Jon had said, "I can't swim, Trudie, so if this thing collapses, you'll have to save me. You *will* save me, won't you?"

"Sure, Jon. I'll always save you," she'd said.

Fortunately, Trudie saw a leaning green sign with fading letters that read HISTORIC BRIDGE AHEAD. That was it.

Minutes later they were bumping across the rickety wooden bridge that spanned a small scenic river, not that Trudie could see much of it. She pulled over to the side of the road and rolled down her window, hearing the rushing water. She recalled how she and Jon had looked over the bridge down into the water and had seen lots of shale lying along the bottom. Just upriver were some small rapids and now, with her window down, the memories all came back. Even in the faint light of a street light, she could see the hinge for a water wheel and the stone foundation where a mill used to operate.

Jon stirred, then awoke. "Where the hell are we?"

Trudie presented her face to the open window and filled her lungs with air. "Shaffer, Ohio, our little ghost town."

Jon wiped his face and sat up. "Good! Good! Let's see if our spooky, broken down house is still there."

Trudie rolled up her window, put the car in gear and drove up a steep hill. At the crest, she slowed down, and they both peered into the darkness, searching.

"It's up on the right, I think," Jon said. "Was it spring or winter that we came here?"

"Autumn," Trudie said.

The two-lane road was deserted. Theirs was the only car on the road.

"Really? I always thought it was spring. But how could that be? You had dumped me for Cole by then."

"I didn't dump you."

"Yes, you did."

"Okay, whatever. Keep looking. It might not even be there anymore."

"Wait a minute!" Jon said pointing right. "Look, over there!"

Trudie craned her neck right and saw the charcoal outline of an old structure, tucked behind some trees.

"That's it!" Jon said. "That is it."

"I'm not so sure, Jon."

"I'm telling you that's it, Trudie. Stop the car. Pull over!"

Trudie edged over to the shoulder of the road and stopped.

"Do you have a flashlight?" Jon asked, excited and fidgety.

"Yes, in the glove compartment."

Jon rummaged inside and grabbed it. He switched it on and off as the beam flashed, then pushed the door open and got out. Trudie emerged, slipping on her coat.

"It's cold out here, Jon."

Jon switched on the flashlight and swung the shaft of light toward the old house. "Yeah, that's it, Trudie. That's the freaky house. Come on."

Jon tramped forward, stepping in three inches of old snow, picking his way through reaching bushes. Trudie buttoned her coat and advanced behind him.

"Why exactly are we here, Jon?"

"You'll see," he said, glancing back.

Trudie's coat snagged on a tree branch.

"Are you okay?" Jon asked, starting back to her.

Trudie plucked the branch away and continued. "I'm fine. I've got to say…this place is scary looking."

"It's supposed to be scary, Trudie, it's a ghost town and these houses are probably haunted."

"Lovely. I didn't want to come here twenty years ago but you talked me into it. I can't believe I'm doing this again."

"Whine, whine, whine. They're friendly ghosts."

"How do you know?"

"Trust me."

"Right," Trudie said, doubtfully.

They scrabbled up a hill around gnarly tree roots, and then Jon took Trudie's hand and helped her up to the old stone path that led to the house.

"Almost there, Trudie."

Wind whistled through the bare trees, rattling the branches, adding to the eerie silence. Trudie heard the quiet music of the river below and a creaking shutter, swinging on its hinge. They traversed the winding stone path and emerged into an opening, finally standing before the old leaning shack, vapor puffing from their mouths. Jon looked at Trudie and grinned.

"Shall we go inside?"

"Is it safe? Look at that porch. It's mostly caved in."

"No worries. I'll find a good sturdy spot."

"Be careful."

"Me? Never. What fun would that be?"

Jon ventured forward, testing the first step of five. He put a little weight on it, bounced and tried the next. It snapped and he sank. "Forget that one."

"Careful, Jon!"

He tried the third and fourth steps and they held. He reached out his hand. "Come on, Trudie, let's enter our dream house."

"You are nuts, Jon."

"Yes, ma'am."

He urged her forward and helped her climb the unstable stairs, finally finding a four-foot square patch of safety on the porch. Jon swung the beam of the flashlight around, seeing the black trunks of trees, an old stone well and a leaning outhouse.

"Home sweet home," Jon said, pulling Trudie close. "Do you know how often I've daydreamed about you and me buying this house, remodeling it, putting in plumbing and a boiler and a fireplace...the works...and living here?"

Trudie looked at him, skeptically. "Why here, of all places? There are plenty of nice houses in town you could have dreamed about."

"I don't know. Call it my weird and whacky nature, but this is the house I've dreamed about. But you were always in that dream, sitting by the fire, reading or sewing or rocking the baby."

"Baby?" Trudie exclaimed. "You make me sound like some pioneer wife out on the western plains."

"Of course a baby. I always wanted to have a baby with you. I had the whole thing pictured in my mind. You and me in a big four-poster bed with a feather mattress going at it. You'd always ask for more and I'd always give you more. Every night, you and me making love in that back bedroom. Me on top, you on top. You and me wrestling and kissing and fighting."

Jon gave her a bold, but tender look. "Yep, you and me having babies together."

Trudie took a breath. "Jon, I'm not a prude, but you're embarrassing me."

"Why? What's wrong with that? What's wrong with making love to a woman you love and adore? What's wrong with loving a woman who turns you up and down and on? What, Trudie? What?"

Trudie looked away. "Nothing, I guess. I don't know. You just say things that are unexpected or something. I don't know what to say."

"That's me, Mr. Unexpected."

Jon tugged her toward the front entrance, shining the beam on the shaky floor boards. "I say, let's go inside and I'll make great big love to you."

"Here?"

"Yes! Right here. Right now. Let's make love and let's make a baby. Right here in our dream house."

Trudie pulled away. "Jon, you *are* out of your mind!"

Jon switched off the flashlight, lowering it. He looked out beyond her into the darkness, as he shoved a hand into his coat pocket.

They were completely isolated, and Trudie felt vulnerable and unsteady. Jon had always been good at making people feel unsteady and off balance. He had a talent for it. He'd done it again.

"Jon... do you love your daughters?"

"What kind of question is that? Of course I love them. Why wouldn't I?"

"Do they love you?"

He cleared his throat. He switched on the beam, held it below his chin, pointing the shaft of light up, so that his face looked strange and scary. "Yes, I think they love me. Can you believe that? God love them all, they love me and I miss them."

"Are they with their mothers?"

"Oh yeah. Beth wanted to come with me, but her mother wouldn't let her and it was Dena's turn to have them for Christmas."

"Did you love your wives?"

"Questions. Questions."

"Did you?"

"Yes, I did. The first one messed around on me and the second wanted to marry somebody famous. I mean, it's not like I'm George Clooney or Tom Hanks. I'm not a superstar, but she thought I'd be one. Then I found out I didn't like her all that much. And then she didn't like me much so... Pop goes the marriage."

Trudie studied him. "Jon, do you like your life?"

He breathed in. "Well now, let's see. Yeah, I guess so. I mean, the worst thing in my life is me."

Trudie laughed.

Jon seized her arm. "Okay, let's go inside."

They crept over the threshold, nudged the squeaking door aside and gingerly entered the house. His flashlight explored the rickety old furniture, the crumbling stone fireplace, a broken window, and a curtain billowing with a puff of wind. With the flashlight poised, they inched along, the darkness opening before them and then closing in its wake.

As the floor was revealed, they saw broken boards, shattered glass and old beer cans.

"Ahhh... Now that's sad," Jon said, focusing on the beer cans. "That's just sad to see the old dream so tattered and abused, like some old whore who used to be grand and fine."

"Not very romantic, Jon," Trudie said.

"Maybe not, but accurate."

Jon's shoulders sank. "Well, we certainly can't make love in here."

"I don't think so," Trudie said.

Jon turned off the flashlight. The darkness seemed alive in the cold air, the sounds creepy. Jon moved in close to Trudie. They were face to face, the same height, their breathing staggered. "You, my dear Trudie, I have always loved."

The words hung in the air, waiting.

Trudie trembled from rising emotion. They were close to a wall. Jon leaned in and kissed her. Trudie stepped back, her neck stiffened.

"Are you okay?" he asked, lifting his hands. "Nothing up my sleeve. Promise."

She nodded and then whispered, "Yeah, I'm okay."

He touched her shoulder and whispered. "Okay, then I'm going to kiss you again."

He pressed her against the wall and kissed her again. It was an open kiss, and she was excited by the wet, soft nibbling.

"I have always loved you, Trudie, my dream girl."

He moved in for another kiss and she felt him hard against her. She was flushed by sudden desire and she threw her arms around him, kissing him back, entranced by swift passion. But when she felt as though she were falling into a current of desire, she fought it. She backed away, gulping air.

Jon waited, watching her. "Come back to my motel room, Trudie. I want to make love to you. I have wanted to make love to you for so long."

Trudie's head was filled with flashing things: words, wants, needs, emotions, desires.

She leveled her eyes on him. "To hell with going back. Let's make your dream come true now, Jon. Let's make love here... in your dream house."

They played, teased and touched. The night seemed to close in around them, blessing them, allowing them isolation and a gentle intimacy. The wind, which had been moving and cold, calmed. Somewhere out in the trees a night bird called, as if awakened by strange music.

Trudie stopped and drew back.

"What?" Jon asked, surprised. "What happened?"

Trudie lowered her head. "Not here, Jon. Not now."

"But you said..."

She cut him off. I know... I know... But no."

The softness and warmth left his eyes. He stood perplexed. "Hey, whatever, Trudie."

"I'm sorry, Jon. It's just that I want more than... than this."

Jon buried his hands into his pockets, nodding. "Okay, I hear you. I've got that."

She wouldn't meet his gaze.

Jon reached, gently lifting her chin. "Hey, kid. It ain't no big thing."

Their eyes made contact.

"You and me, Trudie; well, we got lots of time to be lovers. I feel it. I sense it."

Trudie's eyes stung with tears and she swiped them away.

"Don't cry, Trudie."

"Oh, Jon, I wanted to be adventurous for you."

Jon laughed. "Trudie, for God's sake you saved my ass back there. If you hadn't been adventurous back there, I'd be in jail right now."

He leaned in and brushed her lips with his, her lips soft and shy.

Jon spoke at a near whisper. "Trudie... I love your lips, and I've always loved you."

They remained in that broken-down house for a time, whispering, kissing and touching until the wind kicked up and the cold returned, seeping into their bones, chattering their teeth. Trudie noticed that Jon's right hand was scraped from the fight, and had been bleeding. She kissed it.

Arm and arm, they started back down the hill to the car, silent and thoughtful. Tomorrow would come. Decisions would have to be made, and actions evaluated and analyzed, and their expanded souls and full hearts would have to be questioned. But on this unforgettable night, which stretched out unpredictably before them—a treasured secret—on this infinite and glorious night, the lovers drove back across the bridge, entranced, liberated and in love.

NINETEEN

On Monday morning, The Christmas Women sat around the dining room table, laptops open, cell phones close by, pouring over emails. There were hundreds of details to be covered and a constellation of issues to be resolved. The challenge was to weed out the less important, nail down the urgent, and assign someone the responsibility to follow through.

There were numerous requests for interviews from local papers, national news networks, blogs and TV stations as far away as Louisville and Cincinnati. They wanted to interview Mrs. Childs, The Christmas Girls and, of course, Jon Ketch. Everyone wanted an exclusive interview with him about his role in the show.

There were financial issues, logistical issues, personal issues, alumni issues. Were The Christmas Women giving more time to some performers and not enough to others? Could the crew get into the school auditorium early enough to build the sets, rehearse the music and map the lighting?

Money was coming in from all directions and it was growing increasingly difficult to manage. Connie needed help, and even though she was likeable and pleasant, she could be territorial and controlling. Still, she'd always been dependable and the girls knew they could trust her. So who should they send in to help?

Trudie had hired a small production company out of Columbus, Ohio to film the entire performance, so the DVD could be distributed to alumni and sold to the public. The production company had called to say they needed more money or they couldn't do the job. They were, essentially, backing out of a contract they had signed. Did Trudie really want to hire an attorney and spend the time and the money to sue them? Whose money? The scholarship money? Trudie's money? Meanwhile, she had to scramble to find another film company.

Besides all that, The Christmas Women had not been able to rehearse even one number. Ray kept emailing and texting, strongly encouraging them to meet with him so they could go over the old music and choose which pieces they wanted to perform.

Kristen took a sip of coffee and blew out a weary sigh. "If I'd known what we were getting into when we thought this whole thing up, I never would have said yes."

"Yes you would, Kristen," Trudie said, typing an email. "It will all be worth it when Mrs. Childs enters that auditorium, takes her seat and watches the curtain rise. Seeing her face will make it all worthwhile."

Kristen looked at her friend with renewed admiration. "You look different, Trudie. What is it? Your hair?"

Trudie dropped her eyes to her computer. "I slept well. I had a good sleep. Well, a pretty good sleep."

Kristen persisted. "Don't you think Trudie looks different, Mary Ann?"

"She does have good color. You seem more relaxed," Mary Ann said.

"Okay, I *am* relaxed. Like I said, I slept really well for what little sleep I got. Anyway, let's not forget that it's fine to see everybody and party and have fun, but we're doing this for Mrs. Childs."

Kristen nodded. "That's what I love about you, Trudie. You're so constant. So good."

"Stop saying I'm good, Kristen. I'm not that good, okay? I mean, I'm not always good. You're good too, Kristen, and Mary Ann is good. Everybody is good."

"Kristen isn't good," Mary Ann said, with a humorous wink. "She is all evil."

Kristen laughed. "You are so right, Mary Ann. But wouldn't Trudie be the greatest mother?"

Mary Ann glanced up at Trudie, knowing this was a hot button issue with her.

Trudie glared at Kristen over her laptop. "Let's drop this whole conversation and move on," she said, frostily.

Kristen shrugged. "Okay, Okay..."

Trudie looked at her phone and went rigid. "Oh God!"

Kristen and Mary Ann shot her a look of distress.

"What?" Kristen asked.

"Ray just texted. Mrs. Lyons, you know the high school principal, read about Jon's fight in the local paper and on the internet. She's furious."

"Furious?" Kristen asked. "Why? What's it to her?"

"Just a second. Ray's sending another text." Trudie scrolled. "He says she wants to see him and me ASAP. She said it reflects negatively on the high school and she's having second thoughts about allowing us to do the show."

"Bullshit!" Kristen shouted.

"She is a piece of work," Mary Ann said.

Trudie sat back and slumped. "This woman is such a pain in the neck. What am I going to say to her?"

"Don't say anything," Kristen said. "Let me talk to her."

"That's not the way," Mary Ann said.

"Don't worry," Kristen said. "I'll make it professional, just like in court. You're too nice about everything, Mary Ann. This woman wants to be in control and show everybody what a hard ass she is. Okay, fine. I'm going to ask her a few pertinent and uncomfortable questions."

Trudie stared into her phone. "Uh oh... Somebody at Rusty's took a video of the fight and put in on *YouTube*. Ray sent a link." Kristen and Mary Ann shot up and scrambled over. Trudie tapped the link and they waited nervously as the video loaded.

It started, and the three girls nosed forward. The quality was good. Jon was punching, weaving and dancing around Big Frank, who was stumbling backwards.

"Wow!" Kristen said. "Look at crazy Jon fight. Where did he learn to fight like that?"

"And that guy is big," Mary Ann said.

Trudie nibbled on her lower lip, feeling herself sink in despair. She turned to Kristen. "Do you still want to face Mrs. Lyons? You know she's seen this and is probably going to send it to the school board."

"You bet I want to see her. Let's go."

Kristen broke away, and then paused at the doorway, her mind suddenly awake with an idea. "I'm going to change into my black business suit. I brought it just in case. Meet me at the front door in about five minutes."

"I'm coming too," Mary Ann said.

"You don't have to," Trudie said. "She only asked to see me and Ray."

Mary Ann gave her a quick firm nod. "Hey, we're The Christmas Women, aren't we? Just like the Three Musketeers. All for one and one for all, or whatever they used to say."

Fifty-five minutes later, The Christmas Girls were perched on three wooden chairs in front of Mrs. Lyons' broad, gray, metal desk. Ray stood behind the girls, silent and contrite.

Mrs. Lyons placed steepled hands at her lips, her stern eyes taking in each girl, as if she were about to mete out guilty sentences. She ignored Ray. Trudie felt like she was sixteen again. Mary Ann was mildly amused. Kristen sat ramrod straight, ready for battle, running arguments through her head like she always did before a court appearance.

Mrs. Lyons had a commanding manner. Her grey hair was combed flat against her head, gathered into a bun. She wore a plain gray dress without jewelry, giving her a no-nonsense, prison warden look. The outfit had undoubtedly been calculated for effect and was successful. Mrs. Lyons appeared cool, austere and completely in command.

"I'm sure you ladies appreciate my position here at Deer Lake High School. As the head of the administration and the faculty, I must set and maintain high moral standards for our students. And thus far we have done so. We have no drug or alcohol problems at this school. We do not tolerate cheating or bullying or violence of any kind. If we are accused of being overly conservative and old fashioned, then so be it. We are proud of that. We admit that our goals for our students are high. Our standards are high and, as a result, our test scores are high: some of the best in the entire State of Ohio."

Mrs. Lyons lowered her hands, folded them, and placed them on her desk, as if some director had told her to do so for greater effect. Then, as an afterthought, she rearranged some papers on her desk and sat back, smugly, in her black leather desk chair. The overhead florescent light aged and hardened her pallid face—a snowy white face—the color of the snow flurries that drifted by outside her office window.

She lifted her chin, imperiously. "For all these reasons I feel you should find another venue for your Christmas show."

She paused, but raised a finger before anyone could speak, and continued. "Now I know Jon Ketch is a famous movie actor, but that is even more to my point. Just because he's a famous person, he does not have the right to fall into a drunken brawl at a local establishment and make our town appear, to the entire outside world, like an outpost for drunkenness and violence. If Mr. Ketch performs at this high school, it will appear as though we condone his behavior. And I can assure you, we do not. Therefore, I feel it is my duty to ask you and your alumni to find another location for your Christmas show. It cannot happen at Deer Lake High School."

Having concluded her discourse and delivered her verdict, Mrs. Lyons gave a little nod. She was about to rise, to conclude the matter, when Kristen's steady and firm voice stopped her.

"Thank you, Mrs. Lyons, for your opinion."

"I can assure you: it is not just my opinion. It is my decision."

Kristen wore a slim dark business suit, with a white blouse and black heels. Her dark glossy hair was perfectly styled, her makeup immaculate, her lips glistening.

"Mrs. Lyons, with all due respect, we do not agree with your opinion, nor will we abide by your decision."

Mrs. Lyons' eyes widened, first in surprise and then in narrowed irritation. "I beg your pardon."

"If you will recall, Mrs. Lyons, we gave you a proposal, which you and the board agreed upon. Then we presented you with an agreement, which you and the President of the Board both signed."

Mrs. Lyons protested. "Yes, but that was before this incident with Jon..."

"The incident doesn't matter, Mrs. Lyons. You signed the proposal and you signed the agreement, and the agreement is a legally binding document. You can consult with your attorneys on that point if you wish."

Trudie glanced over at Mary Ann, who was straining not to smile. Ray stood at perfect attention, his eyes sliding back and forth.

Kristen reached into her leather briefcase and extracted the agreement. "I have looked over that agreement and there is no provision for cancellation except in three instances: One, destruction of high school property by any member or members of said alumni group. Two, default on payment to Deer Lake High School for use of the auditorium, stage, makeup rooms, green room, lobby, basement, backstage area, etc., and, three, inadequate provision made for security personnel."

Kristen held up the agreement. "The fact that Jon Ketch had a fight off the high school premises has no bearing whatsoever on this agreement."

Mrs. Lyon seemed to screw herself more deeply into her chair. She lowered her smoldering eyes. "I will consult our attorneys and see what we can do about this agreement. Meanwhile, I will make every effort to stop your show while they deliberate. And our attorneys will deliberate until well after the New Year, I can assure you that."

"Yes, you can do that, Mrs. Lyons. But I ask you not to."

"And why not?" Mrs. Lyons asked, narrowing her eyes. "Your name is Kristen Anderson, I believe. I'm told you're an attorney."

"Yes, Mrs. Lyons, that is correct. Are you really personally prepared to cancel both Christmas shows? Are you prepared to take the anger and disappointment that will come from the town, from the mayor and from the school board? Are you prepared to face the national press? Because driving down here I saw three mobile trucks parked on Main Street. Do you really want to tell them, and many more journalists who will undoubtedly descend upon this town, that you are canceling this show, and all because Jon Ketch was defending his friend, Ray, and his high school sweetheart, Trudie, from drunken bullies?"

Mrs. Lyons sat up. When she spoke, her voice was tense. "I will tell them that..."

Kristen trampled on her words. "...Mrs. Lyons, Jon Ketch is a hero. A hero from this high school. A hero for defending his friends and for defending himself against an ignorant drunken oaf, who lives in an entirely different town. Are you prepared to become the antagonist in this national drama?"

Mrs. Lyons' jaw tightened and she closed her eyes, her mind spinning. The three girls waited, bodies stiff, hearts drumming. When Mrs. Lyons opened her eyes, she had regained her steely resolve.

"Yes, Ms. Anderson. Yes, ladies, I am willing to do whatever is necessary to protect this school and its reputation."

Trudie and Mary Ann exchanged nervous glances. Trudie's hands formed fists.

Kristen paused, surprised by Mrs. Lyons' answer, and by her persistent stubbornness.

She fumbled for words, but couldn't find the right ones. Mrs. Lyons waited, a look of controlled triumph on her face. Kristen looked at Mary Ann, who smiled. Then she looked at Trudie, who nodded, her steady eyes telling her she was doing fine.

Kristen turned back to Mrs. Lyons, displaying ice-cold class. "Mrs. Lyons, perhaps you have forgotten something."

"Oh, have I?" she asked, curtly. "And what would that be?"

"This Christmas show is *not* for us, *not* for the community and certainly *not* for Jon Ketch. This Christmas show is for Mrs. Childs, who is sick with cancer and who could die at any minute."

Kristen opened her hand to the window. "That's why all these people have come here. That's why the TV crews and reporters are here, because this is a beautiful and poignant Christmas story that is unfolding in our own lovely town, because I grew up here, Mrs. Lyons. The four of us all grew up in this town and still love this town. The four of us attended this high school and graduated from this high school."

Ray made a little nod. He swallowed.

Kristen had regained her strength. "How often does something like this come along, Mrs. Lyons? Never. This is a once-in-a-lifetime event that will be remembered, memorialized and talked about for years to come. We need to seize this moment. We need to celebrate it— this unique and poignant opportunity to bring Christmas happiness and joy not just to Mrs. Childs, but to the entire Deer Lake community. That's why Mary Ann and Trudie and Ray are here. That's why all the alumni are here."

Mrs. Lyons stared with chilly intensity. She didn't stir and she didn't look as though she was breathing.

Kristen took a few steps toward the principal's desk. "We are all here to give Mrs. Childs her well-deserved surprise Christmas present, because she has meant so much to all of us. She was a teacher here at Deer Lake High School, a teacher who made a difference in this high school, a difference with her students and a difference in this town. She is why we are doing this show, Mrs. Lyons. It's for Mrs. Childs. Do you really want to say no to this Christmas present for the entire community, and for Mrs. Childs?"

Mrs. Lyons blinked. She patted her hair and licked her lips, staring down at some papers on her desk, as if seeking some place to put her eyes, so she wouldn't have to look at Kristen.

Ray stood erect, heart thrumming in his ears.

The room gathered into an uncomfortable quiet. Mary Ann eased back in her chair, her eyes soft, her body relaxed. Trudie nodded, looking at her friend with pride.

"Mrs. Lyons," Kristen concluded, "we ask you, respectfully, and from our hearts, that you let these performances go ahead as planned. This is not for Jon Ketch or about Jon Ketch or about anyone else, except for our lovely and wonderful teacher, Mrs. Childs. And she is dying."

Trudie and Mary Ann gazed at Kristen with renewed affection and appreciation. Ray lowered his head, as if in prayer.

TWENTY

The Christmas Women descended the high school steps with Ray following, talking excitedly.

"Kristen, that was brilliant. I mean, what you said back there was incredible. I've never seen her back down on anything before. Once Mrs. Lyons makes her mind up, that's it. Holy Mackerel, I was so nervous."

Trudie laced her arm in Kristen's. "I was so proud of you, Kristen. You saved the show."

"Well done," Mary Ann said, taking her other arm.

Kristen pointed at a mobile TV truck passing by. "I haven't saved anything. Jon's fight video is all over the internet and I don't have a clue how we're going to manage this media circus. Those vans are coming from all directions. We're going to have to call for more security. And I don't know what Jon's going to say or do."

Trudie noticed traffic had thickened and the town was filled with people from out of town. "Let me handle him. Did the rehearsals start at 10 o'clock, Ray?"

They stopped at the curb, as they all checked their phones.

"Yes. School's open only a half day today, so at 2 o'clock we'll be able to move everyone over to the auditorium."

Trudie looked up, mostly talking to herself. "I wonder if Jon's at the church rehearsing."

He hadn't texted or emailed, and she hadn't spoken to him since she dropped him at his motel at two o'clock in the morning. Her stomach was in knots. Had he left town because of all the media trucks and vans? Had he regretted last night? Why hadn't he contacted her? She'd sent him three texts! It was so typical of Jon, always unpredictable and maddening. No wonder his two wives had divorced him. As she scrolled through her messages she saw one from Don Rawlings. She tensed up. Jon doesn't text, but Don does! What does that tell her?

Sorry U had 2 leave last nite. Thanks 4 the help. Missed U. C U at rehearsal.

Now *there* was a thoughtful, predictable guy! She wished she hadn't left the party. She wished she'd stayed with Don and, after everyone had left, they could have drunk wine and talked and kissed... and even made love. What was the matter with her?

She glanced up, startled by a police siren. "So is Jon at rehearsal?"

"He must be," Mary Ann said. "The girls texted that he picked them up."

Trudie shook her head, feeling acid stress pool in her stomach as they watched yet another TV mobile van driving by.

"Where are they all coming from?" Trudie asked in amazement. "And where are all those people going to stay? The motels are already full!"

"I don't know, but we have got to get a handle on this thing," Mary Ann said.

"Let's get over to the church and see what's going on," Trudie said, growing increasingly angry and hurt that Jon didn't have the courtesy or thoughtfulness to answer any of her texts. Didn't he realize she'd feel insecure the morning after?

Mary Ann slid into Trudie's car and Kristen hurried off to the parking lot to drive her rental car. Ray had to stay at school until 1 o'clock, when Christmas vacation officially began. He'd recorded his accompaniment and burned a CD, so the performers could rehearse without him.

Trudie started her car and started up Main Street. She found a hole in the traffic, gunned the engine and swerved off to a side road. She barreled the car up to 40, preoccupied and worried. Mary Ann was swaying and bouncing, watching the world speed by, her hands loosely clasped in her lap. Trudie pulled up short to a stop sign, and then slammed on the accelerator and shot ahead, bending around a curve, tires squealing. A dog galloped after them, barking his disapproval.

"Are you okay, Trudie?" Mary Ann asked.

"Yeah, fine."

"You're driving a little fast, don't you think?"

Trudie awoke from her hypnotic state, noticed the speedometer and quickly released her heavy foot from the gas pedal. "Oh... Yes, I guess I am driving too fast."

Trudie swallowed a breath, made a right turn and saw the white church steeple in the distance. "I need to call Julie to see how Mrs. Childs is doing. I meant to this morning, but it just slipped my mind."

"I called this morning," Mary Ann said. "Julie said her mother had improved over night."

"Did they get the results from the tests?"

"Yes. One rib is fractured, that's all. It could have been a hip or her pelvis."

Trudie glanced over, hopeful. "That's good news. What about the cancer?"

"They're still not sure if she should have more chemotherapy."

"Do you think she should?"

Mary Ann thought about it. "I don't know."

"What does the healer in you say?"

"Let me put it this way. I respect Mrs. Childs' wishes."

"Did Julie say her mother would be strong enough to make the show?"

"I asked her that. Julie said she didn't know. She was hoping to get her back home sometime today."

Trudie turned right into the church parking lot, found an open slot and parked. Just after she killed the engine, she looked at Mary Ann.

"I saw you with Oscar at the party last night."

Mary Ann nodded. "I feel like I'm in high school again. I feel like Oscar has asked me to go steady. He did admit that he'd like us to have a relationship—a romantic relationship."

"And what did you say?"

"I surprised myself. I said, 'Why not?' What the logistics of a long-distance courtship are, I have no idea. We didn't discuss it."

Their attention was suddenly pulled away by a TV van bouncing into the parking lot.

"Oh, God, Mary Ann. What are we going to do about all this?"

Mary Ann's face darkened. "Manage the problem, Trudie. Let's go."

They pushed out of the car, slammed the doors and walked purposefully over to the van that had parked near the church entrance.

An attractive, perky blonde emerged, blinking into the day. Snow flurries were still falling, settling on Trudie's and Mary Ann's heads and shoulders. They hurried over to the blonde, who dazzled them with a warm and welcoming smile.

"Hello," she said, showing perfect teeth, extending a hand. "I'm Sofia Taylor."

Trudie looked down at the hand but didn't shake it. "I'm sorry," Trudie said, directly, "this is private property and unless you have a permit to be here, I have to ask you to leave."

The blonde's smile remained. "Is this the church where the rehearsals are for the Christmas show in which Jon Ketch will be acting and directing?"

"You need to leave, Sofia."

Her lips puckered in disappointment. "Oh, I'm sorry." She brightened again. "Who are you?"

Trudie did not take the bait. "Sofia, please get back in the van and leave. You are not legally authorized to be here. This is private property."

Sofia had done her homework. She brightened. "You're one of The Christmas Women, aren't you?"

Mary Ann stepped forward and drew out her phone. "Ms. Taylor, I am going to call the Sheriff. End of talk."

The three women stood standing, staring, calculating. Finally, Sofia's smile vanished. She pivoted, yanked open the door and climbed in. Trudie and Mary Ann waited until the van had driven away before they swung around to the basement entrance, opened the door and entered.

Jon Ketch stood before them, legs apart, arms folded, ready to pounce. A Cincinnati Reds baseball cap was pushed back off his forehead and his florid face was pinched in anger. They stood in an open space, near some folding chairs and a lectern. In the background they heard the choir rehearsing *Hark the Herald Angels Sing.*

"I'm going to leave," Jon said, emphatically.

Trudie, already hurt and angry from his neglect after an unforgettable night, burned into him with her eyes. She folded her arms. "Really? Just like that?"

"Yep. Just like that."

Mary Ann spoke up. "We're managing all this media business, Jon."

Jon barked a laugh. "Managing it?! Don't make me laugh. Do you have any idea what the media are like? Professionals can't manage these vultures! They will chew you up and spit you out and then step on top of you to get to me and then chew me to pieces. Believe me, I know. I've punched a couple. I'm sure you've read about it. Anyway, they *will* get to me. You haven't got a chance."

Trudie gave Mary Ann a sideways glance. "Can you leave us alone, Mary Ann?"

Mary Ann ducked away and started for the back office.

Trudie motioned with her head for Jon to step into a quiet corner. He did so.

She lowered her voice, but there was strength and force in it. "Jon, you can't leave now."

"Do you want this show to be about Mrs. Childs or about me? Because I can tell you, before the show opens on Christmas Eve, it's all going to be about me. I didn't come here for that and I don't want that."

"I don't care. Mrs. Childs won't care. She'll just be thrilled to see us all up on that stage again. Then it will be about her, and only about her."

He started to protest, but Trudie threw up a hand to stop him. "I don't want to hear it. You made a commitment to us, to the community, to the alumni and, most importantly, to Mrs. Childs."

Jon canted his head to the right, his eyes large and cold. "That was before all this shit happened. Before the enemy charged."

"All this shit happened because you got into a stupid bar fight with some loser! Now it's all over the internet and *YouTube* and every crazy kid with a cell phone is coming to town. Stop thinking of yourself for once in your life and think of somebody else. Do something—one damned thing nice for somebody else for a change! Sacrifice a little of your precious fragile ego for Mrs. Childs. She might be dying, Jon! Dying! Okay? So you have to give a few stupid interviews. So what! Big Deal! Suck it up! Stop being a little whiny kid who wants to take his trucks and cars home because the world doesn't play the way he wants it to. Well, guess what? That's just the way it is. So deal with it!"

Jon stared at her, his eyes strangely beguiling. He searched her face, as if seeing it for the first time. Suddenly, a secret was revealed to him. His eyes opened wide in recognition. He grabbed Trudie's shoulders, pulled her forward and kissed her. Trudie wrenched away, furious.

"Stop that! Stop it!"

Jon stared, transfixed. "Trudie Parks, if you had shown that much passion, that much power, that much authenticity, twenty years ago when you were playing Maggie in *Cat on a Hot Tin Roof, you* would have wound up in Hollywood. That was outstanding! That was fantastic. You were... riveting!" He pulled her forward and kissed her again.

She twisted away, swung and slapped him across the face. The loud smack seemed to echo.

"Ouch," he said, his hand touching his cheek. "That hurt!"

"You are a selfish bastard, Jon Ketch!"

"And you, Trudie Parks, just gave a magnificent performance! The performance of a lifetime!"

"That was not a performance, Jon! I wasn't acting. Don't you know the difference?"

Jon shook his head, wiggling a finger at her. "All the world's a stage and all the men and women merely players, Trudie." He stepped back, placing his hands on his hips.

"Wow, you took my breath away. You really are something. I mean you've got fire and ice. You've got that WOW thing that I didn't even know was there!"

Trudie felt a rising rage. Her eyes locked on his. "Why didn't you answer my texts?"

Jon's eyebrows lifted. "Why?"

"Yes! Why!? You have to ask me why? Didn't you know I was freaking out after last night? Are you really that heartless, stupid and selfish that you didn't know I would need to hear from you after...?" her voice trailed off, and her eyes misted over.

She turned away, barely able to squeeze out the words. "You heartless little...shit!"

Jon shrank and sighed with regret, while pocketing his hands. He scratched his nose, lifting a helpless hand. "Trudie...I came by the house to pick up Carly and Lynn. I thought you'd be there and we could talk about last night. But you were gone. The girls said you went to the high school."

His voice turned quiet and intimate. "Trudie, look at me."

"No."

"Please. Look at me."

"I'm crying, okay. I'm not going to look at you. I didn't sleep much last night, my stomach's in knots and I already look like hell."

The choir finished singing, and the place grew religiously quiet.

"Okay, don't look at me. The truth is, Trudie." He paused, sighing heavily. He tried again. "The truth is, I wanted us to be alone together so we could talk about things. Hey, I was scared, okay? You scare me a little."

Trudie snapped a look at him. "What? I scare you?! That's a laugh. You scare the hell out of everybody, including me."

He pulled his hands from his pockets and spread them wide. "You do scare me. You always did. Hell, I love you and you scare the hell out of me."

Trudie stared, fuming. "Don't bullshit me, Jon. I'm in no mood for it."

"So help me God, I'm not. You do, in fact, scare the living daylights out of me because when I'm with you, I don't know who the hell I am. I feel all tangled up in love."

Trudie looked away, seeking answers in the air all around her. She adjusted the strap of her purse. "I don't even know what that means or what to say. I never do know what to say to you."

She fumbled into her coat for a tissue. She wiped her eyes.

Jon heaved out a sigh. "Okay, here goes. Last night was the most special and memorable and wonderful night of all my nights. Truth be told, it ain't gonna get any better than that unless you and I stay together. That was it! Boom, Bang, KaWhoosh! Love everywhere, and we didn't even really do anything. Bells, whistles, fireworks. Trudie Parks, Lady from Deer Lake, I love you like I've never loved nothing before and that scares the hell out of me, because I don't know what that is. I've played the part of being in love a few times on the big screen, and in a couple of plays, but I have to tell you, I don't think I was very good at it, because I never felt that real crazy, knock-you-on-your-ass love before last night."

Trudie stood, conflicted, suspicious and touched. Once again, she was speechless. She closed her eyes and massaged her forehead.

"Therefore," Jon said, finger raised toward the ceiling as if to make a proclamation, "I didn't know how to answer your texts. How could I tell you what I feel in a text? How trivial and pedestrian is it to write about love in a friggin' text. Maybe I send a text about love to Minnie Mouse or Miss Piggy, but not to you. To you it must be said face to face or up in a Ferris wheel or sailing under the Brooklyn Bridge at sunset. I was knocked silly by last night, Trudie. I felt foolish and hypnotized. And I wanted to run away. I still do want to run away. I'm scared. What the hell do I do with that kind of love?"

Trudie opened her eyes and shook her head. "Jon... you are just plain nuts. Do you know that? How the hell do I know what you should do with it?"

He nodded. "I have really blown a fuse."

Trudie stood erect and resolute. "Well, I don't care what you feel or how crazy you are. You can't leave town. Not now. You can run for the hills after the last show on Christmas Eve if you have to, but not until then."

Jon pursed his lips, slid his hand inside his shirt, shifted his hat sideways and thrust his chin out, giving an excellent impression of Napoleon. He spoke in a French accent.

"I have conquered many lands and many women and yet, Mademoiselle Parks, you, yes *you* and only *you*, have conquered my martial heart. Will you, as they say in French, come with me to the boudoir, where we will drink Burgundy wine, eat greasy Bistro food and make love?"

Trudie blotted her eyes, shaking her head in exasperation. "Will you please stop performing for one damned minute and just tell me you'll stay and do the show, Jon? You're driving *me* nuts!"

He gave her a grand, sweeping bow. "After your superlative performance, at my expense, mind you, what else can I do? Because you have once again captured and, indeed, conquered, my hopelessly-in-love panting heart. Yes, I will stay and do the show and agree to do those friggin' interviews just for you, because, Trudie Parks, I love you."

TWENTY-ONE

Tuesday morning, the Deer Lake Auditorium was a buzzing hive of activity: singing, hammering, piano playing, sawing, shouting, line readings, crying and answering ringing phones. There was the smell of paint, coffee, bacon, turpentine, makeup and Cole Blackwell's musty cologne.

Six beefy security guards stood by all six entrances to the high school. Four more patrolled the parking lot. Two additional guards, with heroic faces and bodies, stood on either end of the high school front steps, next to blue saw horses and yellow CAUTION tape blocking the entrance. One very imposing security guard was assigned to stay with Jon Ketch at all times. Two cars from the county deputy's office were parked in front of the high school with their blue dome lights quietly sweeping the area. All the cops and security were needed.

Jon Ketch's fans had descended on the town en masse, coming from all over the state and beyond, and they were trying to swarm the high school to catch a glimpse of him. The high school phone lines rang constantly, many from callers who'd just heard about the Christmas shows and wanted tickets. When they were told the performances were sold out, they demanded an additional show be added. When they were told there wouldn't be additional shows, some callers hung up before learning about the DVD of the performance which would be available for sale by the start of the new year. Proceeds would help boost the scholarship fund.

Mrs. Lyons paced the school and the auditorium like a general looking for any slight infraction. Whenever she peered out of a window and saw the surging masses of people surrounding the high school, she bitterly castigated herself for ever allowing this kind of thing to happen. How could she have been so negligent? She'd already received calls from every single member of the school board. All said they were "concerned."

It was inevitable that the Deer Lake Sheriff would pay the high school, and Jon Ketch himself, a visit. Sheriff Jake T. Mason arrived in a dark blue sedan with blue roof lights. He inched his car through the crowds, being waved through by security guards. He pulled up to the rear exit door, next to a little mountain of plowed snow, and switched off the engine. He emerged from his car, grabbed his belt and tugged up his pants, taking in a scene he'd never before witnessed—and never wanted to witness again. Swarms of people were being held back by yellow crime scene tape, saw horses and security cops. He'd seen it in the movies, but never in his town. He didn't like it. It felt chaotic and unstable. Anything could happen when you have this many people together. And most of the crowd looked young and antsy.

And all of this was playing out because a few alumni from the high school and a famous Hollywood actor, who'd grown up in Deer Lake, had some stupid idea about putting on a Christmas show for a retired teacher.

How could something so simple turn into something so complicated?

And then there was the issue of the fight at Rusty's. Jake didn't care that Big Frank had gotten his ass kicked, he was even happy about it, but he didn't want a repeat performance from the actor. Another fight like that could set the whole town into riotous chaos. Copycats could make his Christmas Eve very ugly indeed.

This was not a movie. It was not *It's a Wonderful Life*. This was real, and Jake had to deal with it. He'd be up for re-election next year, and he liked his job. He'd been doing it for a long time, and nothing like this had ever happened before, something that could jeopardize his job. So, if he wasn't prepared and very careful, this whole business could blow up in his face.

He'd already called in deputy support from some of the surrounding counties, and more counties had offered their help. He might call them in too. He was taking no chances.

Jake T. Mason had graduated from Deer Lake High School, 25 years before. He did not know any of the players in this Christmas show farce and he hadn't taken drama from Mrs. Childs. He barely remembered her. He'd played football and baseball. He'd gone to Ohio State on an athletic scholarship. He lost it when a knee injury finished his football aspirations.

Jake was broad and thick in the neck. He had a comfortable paunch, a lumpy face, no-nonsense dark eyes and a sallow complexion. Though he stooped a little, he maintained he was still over 6 feet. Dressed in a brown uniform, chocolate brown leather coat, black cowboy hat and black cowboy boots, he nodded at the security guard at the door and entered the school, wishing there was something he could do to stop the show and get Jon

Ketch out of town. Before the actor left town, though, Jake wanted to meet him. He liked some of his movies, especially *Killers Crossing,* a gritty drama about a small town sheriff, Jon Ketch, who was caught in a web of murder, lies and corruption. Yeah, he liked Jon in that movie. He'd even bought the Blu-ray edition.

Sheriff Mason hoped he'd get someone to snap some pictures of him and the actor together, so Jake could display them proudly on his office walls. If all went well on Christmas Eve, he'd be able to use those pictures during the next election, and that couldn't hurt. It would also give him something to brag about at Joey's Truck Stop out on Highway 11. Yeah, that would be nice: Sheriff Jake with the famous home town boy, Jon Ketch. Nothing wrong with that.

Sheriff Mason strode down the hallowed halls he remembered so well, passing the glass trophy case where he paused to glimpse his old football team photo and championship trophy. He squared his shoulders, smiled, and lifted his proud chin.

He moved on, hearing the echo of his heavy footsteps. Being in the school always brought back good memories: the games, the girls, the old glories. He hoped nothing would happen in the next two days to change all those good memories. He even whispered a Christmas prayer, asking for a little Christmas help.

As he approached the auditorium, he heard voices— lovely voices—singing *White Christmas.* Now wasn't that nice? As he reached for the center door handle to the auditorium, he began whistling the tune, just the slightest bit off key. It sounded fine to him, and it cheered him.

Inside the auditorium, The Christmas Women were being yanked in all directions, answering questions, phone calls, texts and emails, racing about the auditorium to critique performers, staging, lights and sets. They were trying to cram weeks of work into one and a half days. Wednesday afternoon was Christmas Eve and the two performances would go ahead as planned, ready or not.

Trudie had scheduled three interviews for Jon, letting him choose who would conduct those interviews. He and all three girls had sat down to come up with a list of pertinent content they wanted him to include in his answers.

1. Yes, the performance was dedicated to their former drama teacher. It was the main reason they had all come together. Mrs. Childs was the focus.

2. Yes, her health was improving.

3. Yes, she'd had a strong influence in his life. She was his first acting teacher.

4. Yes, he'd gotten in the fight at Rusty's to protect his friends.

5. No, no charges were filed by him or against him.

6. No, he had no plans to write a movie script about the incident.

7. Yes, he'd loved growing up in Deer Lake.

8. Yes, Mrs. Lyons had been invaluable and helpful during the entire undertaking.

9. No, he was not in love with his old high school sweetheart. (Trudie insisted on this.)

10. Yes, he was playing Ebenezer Scrooge in the play and he was going to be performing in the Rockettes' style kicking routine along with The Christmas Women.

Whether Jon actually kept to the scripted answers was anyone's guess. Trudie was sure he wouldn't. He never had, so why would he change now?

Oscar worked feverishly on the Santa Claus-at-home set, complete with a giant Christmas wreath stage center, a fireplace and mantel, stockings and a rocking chair. Mary Ann would play Mrs. Claus, reading the classic poem, *'Twas the Night before Christmas*, while rocking and knitting a sweater.

Oscar was also overseeing construction of the set for *A Christmas Carol*, which was being built by three high school seniors and two alumni. They were all enthusiastic about the project, despite the constraints on time, materials and money. The set would consist of various pieces of old office furniture, the fireplace from the Santa Claus-at-home set, a large multi-framed window with frosted panes, and a blue backdrop that would serve as a screen where images could be projected: old Victorian England and its darkly lit streets, and a night sky with gleaming stars and ghosts swirling and diving, their ugly faces contorted with grief. It would also project a foggy graveyard when *The Ghost of Christmas Future* points Scrooge to his gravestone.

Cole Blackwell was to play the *Ghost of Christmas Future*, since everyone knew he was a bad actor and his character spoke no lines. At 6 feet 6 inches tall, wearing 2-inch boots and a long black hood and robe, he would tower over the diminutive, withered and stooped Jon Ketch, playing Scrooge. Jon was delighted by the dramatic and visual possibilities of their scenes together.

By late morning, Trudie, Kristen and Mary Ann finally got to rehearse with Ray and the 16-piece alumni and high school orchestra. While they were on stage singing and practicing their dance steps, they were all aware of Jon, speaking with Sheriff Mason in the back of the auditorium. They were distracted, making mistakes. Ray finally lost his patience, threw up his hands and shouted.

"What is the matter with you three! For crying out loud, you're missing notes and steps all over the place.

Can you please concentrate! You look awful. You're going to embarrass me, the rest of the cast and Mrs. Childs. Don't forget, this will be filmed and burned on DVD, and we will probably be on the nightly news, all over the state of Ohio."

Kristen threw her hands to her hips. "Okay, okay. Bitch, bitch, bitch. Give us a break. We're 20 years older and we're wondering if the Sheriff is going to haul Jon off to jail."

Ray shaded his eyes, gazing out to the rear of the auditorium. "How many interviews has he given?"

"Two," Trudie said. "God only knows what he said about us all."

"Don't worry about Jon. He always comes through. He's a pro."

Trudie rolled her eyes. "Ray, sometimes I don't even know who you are."

Mary Ann sank down. Seconds later, Trudie looked over to see Mary Ann's head bowed and her forearms braced on her knees. She was struggling to catch her breath. "How did we sing and dance and smile all at the same time without passing out? I am exhausted."

Trudie sat down on the stage cross-legged, stretching out her right leg. "And how did we do it in heels? Are we nuts?"

Kristen rolled the stiffness out of her shoulders and played the role of the dance coach. "Come on, you two, we have to get this. Tomorrow is it. We can't look like complete klutzes in front of Mrs. Childs and the whole world. Get up!"

Grudgingly, they did. They practiced on, with straining effort and explosive snorts, sometimes cursing, sometimes screaming out in triumph when they got it right. The stage lights were hot, but they grunted and sniffed on, moving in a sluggish, heavy-footed prance, arms swinging, smiles vanishing, sweat popping out and rolling down.

Their feet were swollen, their chests were heaving, their faces were flushed and their bodies were slick and smelly. At last, they'd had enough. All they could do was collapse on stage in various undignified positions, fighting for breath and self-esteem, painfully aware that they'd had a small, silent and disenchanted audience.

As they were leaving the stage, using the towels they'd flung around their necks to blot their faces, they saw a large figure rise from the center of the auditorium. They descended the side steps to the auditorium, and watched as Sheriff Jake T. Mason strolled down the aisle to meet them.

"Uh-oh," Trudie said. "And I smell real bad."

"I smell like a horse," Kristen said.

"And I feel, and must look like, a fat cow," Mary Ann said, under her breath. "Jon is in the back giving another interview. It can't be all bad if the Sheriff hasn't taken him away in cuffs."

"Do you know the Sheriff?" Kristen whispered.

"No. It's not like I spend a lot of time in the county jail."

"Just asking."

"Good afternoon, ladies," the Sheriff said, hat in hand. "I'm Sheriff Jake T. Mason."

They greeted him with tentative smiles and hellos.

"You look real nice up there. I like all that kicking. I was in New York five years back and saw the Rockettes' Christmas show. You could sure give them a run for their money."

Kristen spoke up. "You are very nice, Sheriff, but I think we've overestimated our abilities. We're not the 18-

year old girls we used to be, and our feet and cardio- vascular systems are a testament to that."

The Sheriff gave them a tight smile. "Well, you look good to me." Then the Sheriff's face fell into seriousness. "Ladies, I'm told by Mrs. Lyons that you three are in charge here. Is that right?"

They nodded in agreement, speculating where the Sheriff was going with this.

"Well, I just need you to assure me that you will keep everything snapped down here, so to speak. I appreciate the extra security you're paying for, and we've added extra deputies out there in the streets, but I do hope I can count on you to keep Mr. Ketch from repeating what he did the other night at Rusty's."

Trudie nodded, aggressively, aware that her hands were clammy. "It won't happen again, Sheriff. We promise."

The Sheriff glanced back over his shoulder to see cameras rolling and spot lights bathing Jon, as he gave his last interview. "Well, he has assured me he will behave himself and I'll take his word for that. I just want you ladies to be in the loop and know that I am standing by to make sure your little Christmas show goes on without incident."

"We want the same thing," Mary Ann said. "We just want this to be a very special night for our former teacher and for the people of Deer Lake."

"Well, that's fine. That's real fine. Don't let me stop you from your work now. You go on and have a good show. I hope you don't mind if I wander around the place during the performances."

The girls shook their heads in perfect unison, as if they had choreographed it. Sheriff Mason studied them curiously, nodded, then turned and exited up the aisle.

Trudie watched his retreating figure. "If anything goes wrong, do you think he'd throw us in jail?"

"Oh, yeah," Kristen said. "I've seen that look down at the courthouse. Yep. He will definitely throw our tired, sweaty asses in jail."

TWENTY-TWO

The entire cast and crew would have to pull a near all-nighter at the theatre. The sets weren't completed, the dancers were struggling, actors were dropping lines and Jon was fuming.

"These lines should have been memorized long before I came to town. Now get with it, people! Don't embarrass me and get me excommunicated from Hollywood!"

Liz Tyree, the thin, spike-haired stage manager, yelled from off-stage right. "That would be the best thing that ever happened to you, Jon. Your last movie sucked."

Jon turned to her, smiling graciously. "Critics are to artists as pigeons are to statues, Madam Stage Manager."

The cast and crew laughed. Liz flipped him the finger.

The Christmas Women had rehearsed until 8 o'clock and were exhausted. They sat back in the auditorium rubbing their sore feet, watching the cast of *A Christmas Carol* stumble through their blocking and fumble their lines.

Kristen looked discouraged. "From what I've seen here today, we're not going to cheer Mrs. Childs up, we're going to depress her."

"We need more time," Mary Ann said. "Jon is the only professional up there. We're all amateurs. And, in my case, out-of-shape amateurs."

"We don't have more time," Trudie said. "I don't mind if we make a few mistakes. It will make it seem quaint and simple. But we can't look like fools."

Kristen winced at a painful blister on her big toe. "Did Julie say we could go over to the house and see Mrs. Childs?"

"Yes. She took her home from the hospital at 4 o'clock. I told her to make sure the TV wasn't on. She said her mother never watches TV. She watches old movies and reads, so we're okay there."

"Are we sure no one in the hospital told her about the performances?"

"No, we're not sure," Trudie said. "Julie said Mrs. Childs was shocked by the crowds in town as they drove home."

Kristen leaned over. "What did Julie tell her?"

"That there was a concert being held at the high school," Trudie said.

"Did she believe her?" Mary Ann asked.

Trudie shrugged. "I don't know. I hope so. We'll find out when we go over to see her."

"After we eat, we have to come back and join the group to rehearse *The Hallelujah Chorus*," Kristen said.

"I never could sing that thing," Trudie said.

"I always want to sing the base part," Mary Ann said.

They sat back, enjoying their break. Trudie closed her eyes, hearing Carly, as *The Ghost of Christmas Present*, speak her lines perfectly, with character and emotion.

Jon was ecstatic. "That was absolutely perfect, Carly. Excellent! You are a good actress. A wonderful actress!"

Mary Ann smiled proudly, watching Lynn follow Jon around with a clip board, taking notes and reading Jon's blocking back to him, reminding him where he wanted the actors to stand and to move.

"Jon's okay, isn't he?" Mary Ann said.

Kristen chuckled. "Jon's a nut case."

Trudie didn't open her eyes. "Jon is definitely *not* okay."

"You were with him last night, weren't you?" Kristen said.

Trudie kept her eyes closed. "Let's not go there."

Cole started down the center aisle, wearing *The Ghost of Christmas Future*'s black robe, minus the hood. He slid into the aisle just behind the girls and sat behind Kristen.

Kristen turned to look at him.

"It's going well," he said, indicating toward the stage. "Jon is a slave driver, but he's good."

"Have you memorized all your lines?" Kristen asked, jokingly.

"Very funny," Cole said. "You know my character doesn't speak. He just points and looks frightening."

Mary Ann twisted around. "You look very imposing up there, Cole. You're going to scare a lot of kids."

"How's Mrs. Childs?" Cole asked.

Trudie opened her eyes and turned to him. "We don't know if she's going to be well enough to come."

"What will we do? All this is for her," Cole said.

Trudie slid down in her seat. "We were talking about it. We decided we'll take the show to her."

"At her house?" Cole asked, leaning forward.

"Yes, or the hospital. Wherever. It won't be the same, and we'll have to do an abbreviated version, but we'll do what we have to do."

"I see," Cole said, focusing on Kristen. "Kristen, can I see you for a moment?"

Kristen stared down at the floor, avoiding Mary Ann's and Trudie's eyes. Without speaking, she got up, side-stepped her way out to the aisle, and then headed to the back of the auditorium, with Cole, a dark apparition, towering above her.

Trudie and Mary Ann didn't turn around.

"Is she really that thoughtless?" Trudie asked.

Mary Ann shifted around to look at Trudie. "She's having a pre-40 crisis. I know how she feels."

"But you're not married."

"No, but I understand how she feels."

They turned their attention toward the stage and watched Jon transform himself into an old man. In an instant, he was bent and shuffling, his face crumpled in solemn resentment, his voice edgy, husky and irritable. It was an amazing metamorphosis: Jon became Ebenezer Scrooge incarnate.

"If I could work my will," said Scrooge indignantly, "Every idiot who goes about with 'Merry Christmas' on his lips, should be boiled with his own pudding, and buried with a stake of holly through his heart."

Trudie watched him with warm eyes, feeling stiffly nostalgic as she recalled the boy of 18. Had he truly always loved her? *"What a talent,"* she thought. *"What a wacky, exciting man, with a remarkable talent."*

"He'll bring the house down," Mary Ann said.

"I hope you don't mean that literally. He's quite capable of doing it."

Mary Ann laughed.

Oscar left the stage and ambled over, slapping the sawdust off his jeans. "It's coming along," he said. "It's going to take the rest of the night to finish, but we'll be ready by tomorrow afternoon."

"That's cutting it close," Trudie said.

Oscar turned back to look at the stage. The large Christmas wreath was still hanging above center stage. "Yes, but it will be done right. We want to do most of the painting tonight, so there'll be time for the smell to dissipate."

"You've done wonders," Mary Ann said. "Are you going to be able to make it snow during the finale?"

"Yes, I think so. Worst comes to worst, we'll put a couple of high school boys up on the catwalks slinging the stuff. We've done that before."

Trudie sat up. "It was nice of you to come, Oscar, and to do all this. You're a life saver. You would have been a great set designer."

"I love doing it," he said, looking at Mary Ann with happiness. "I love being here with you all again. I haven't felt this good in a long time. I just hope Mrs. Childs can make it. She once told me that a set designer can make or break a show. I want to *make* this one and I want her to be able to see it."

Mary Ann looked at herself self-consciously. Her chubby belly showed under her tight black leotard. She sucked it in as she sat up.

"Mary Ann, how about we go somewhere for a sandwich or something?" Oscar asked, adjusting his glasses. Trudie thought he looked like the quintessential professor of physics or mathematics.

"I should take a shower, Oscar. We've been dancing for hours. I'll use the one in the women's dressing room. I'll just be fifteen minutes."

"I'll wait. I've got things to do."

After Mary Ann left, Trudie and Oscar made small talk. Finally, Oscar grew quiet and thoughtful.

Trudie waited, checking her phone, seeing texts from Don Rawlings and Julie Childs.

"Trudie..." Oscar said.

Trudie struggled to concentrate, waiting to open the texts. She saw he needed to talk.

"I'm very... well... I have always admired Mary Ann." There were little hesitations and pauses, as he carefully composed his words. "I often regretted not staying in touch with her. Of course, I was happily married but... Well, I could never really shake Mary Ann from my mind. She's a good person. A kind and thoughtful person. And then when my wife passed away, so many memories came back into my mind. I remembered so many things that Mary Ann and I had done in high school. Little conversations... private moments."

He was silent for a time.

Trudie kept listening, torn between Oscar's conversation and the texts. "Mary Ann cared a lot for you, Oscar."

Oscar looked up, hopeful. "Did she?"

"Yes, she did."

He nodded, and then stared beyond her into the darkness of the theatre. "Well, I hope she and I can pick up where we left off. I hope so."

After he had wandered away, Trudie read the texts. Julie's first.

"Mom wants to see Mary Ann. Alone. Didn't say why. Is she free?"

Trudie texted back. *"Yes, I'll let her know and she'll get back with you."*

Trudie wondered what that was about. She forwarded Julie's text and added. *"You can take my car."*

Next Trudie read Don's text. *"Will b at rehearsal soon! Will you b there?"*

Trudie glanced up, watching the play continue on.

She texted back. *"Yes. I'll be here."*

Trudie stood up barefooted, stretching her tight and aching muscles, her feet feeling raw and sore. *How would she be able to dance two shows tomorrow?*

When Mrs. Lyons marched down the aisle, Trudie wanted to run in the opposite direction. *What now?*

"Hello, Mrs. Lyons," Trudie said, forcing a smile and wishing she'd slipped her heels back on.

"Good evening, Trudie. Have you seen the crowds outside?"

"Not recently."

Mrs. Lyons was standing at attention. "They're growing. The restaurants and bars are packed with people, and traffic is becoming impossible. People are calling, upset that they can't see the show. I suppose you can't add another show at this late hour?"

"No, Mrs. Lyons. We're pushing it as it is. Everybody's already tired and we'll have to work all night just to be ready for tomorrow. We couldn't anticipate all this. It all happened so fast."

"Yes, well, there's no use complaining now. Listen, I have an idea and I want to know what you think about it."

Trudie took an uneasy breath, bracing herself. "Yes, Mrs. Lyons?"

"What if we could broadcast the show outside? Maybe your people could rig up some stage microphones, and, I don't know, hang some speakers outside and just broadcast the entire show so that the people outside can at least hear it."

Trudie couldn't believe her ears. Was Mrs. Lyons actually offering something constructive? She stared, blankly.

"Trudie? What do you think? Can it be done?"

"Well, I don't know. I guess so. We may have to call some sound people, audio people. It's short notice, but we can try."

She looked at Mrs. Lyons again, suddenly realizing what a fantastic idea it was. She smiled with gratitude. "Thank you, Mrs. Lyons. I like the idea. I like it very much. At least they'll be able to sing along and hear Jon perform as Scrooge. Yes, I'll get right on it."

Mrs. Lyons almost smiled. The right corner of her mouth lifted about an eighth of an inch. "I think it will help to calm the crowd and make them feel more a part of the show," she said.

"Yes, Mrs. Lyons," Trudie said, enthusiastically. "Yes, I agree."

After Mrs. Lyons had withdrawn, Trudie climbed the stage to ask Oscar what he thought, if it could be done on short notice. He was thoughtful. "We'll have to call professionals in for that, Trudie, and tomorrow is Christmas Eve. It's going to be tough."

Trudie stared down at her bare feet, lost in thought. Just then, a name bubbled to the surface of her mind. Her face lit up. She snapped her fingers. "Wait a minute!"

Oscar looked on, hopeful.

"I may know someone. It's a long shot, but maybe."

She quickly thumbed her contact list until she came to Larry Watson, one of the high school students she tutored at the library. A few days back he'd mentioned that his brother set up audio for rock bands. Well, maybe?

She pressed the call button and waited, nibbling her nails.

"Hullo..." Larry's bored voice answered.

"Larry! This is Trudie Parks."

Silence. "Am I in trouble?"

"No, Larry, you're not in trouble. I need to ask you something."

After she had explained what she needed, Larry said his brother was in town for the holidays, staying there with his parents, but he wasn't home at the moment. He was out with friends. Trudie asked for his cell phone number.

An hour and a half later, Hugh Watson, Larry's brother, was on his way to the high school to evaluate the space. Hugh had graduated from Deer Lake eight years before, and he remembered the space well. By the time he arrived, he'd already sketched an audio plan based on Trudie's explanation. Hugh was tall and rangy, wearing a faded orange T-shirt, jeans and heavy black boots. At first, Trudie found him intimidating, with his shoulder-length brown hair and Aztec black tribal sleeve tattoos on both arms. He was brisk, humorless and strictly business. But he exuded confidence.

"I can do it," Hugh said, with a firm nod, as he paced the stage, taking in the auditorium. "But it won't be cheap."

Liz Tyree was standing nearby, touchy and tense, watching Hugh with wary suspicion. She'd been calling out light cues, cursing her partner, Kelly Stokes, for missing two in a row. By profession, Kelly was a very successful marketing manager for an ad agency in Chicago.

"Come on, Kelly, it's not that late," Liz called. "Maybe you need a double espresso or a swift kick."

Kelly hollered back. "Liz, you should have had a personality lobotomy back in high school."

Hugh saw them, but ignored them. "We'll have to hang lots of ceiling mics. Sensitive ones. We may have to use racks of power amplifiers and four to six monitors. Watts... 500 to 1000. I'll be at the mixing board. We can set that up in the back of the house, out of the way. No problem. And my guys will be walking around making sure everything works. The outside speakers are no problem. We'll hang six. We'll have to work most of the night and into tomorrow morning. I'll need 3 guys and my brother, Larry."

Trudie braced for the estimate. "How much?"

Hugh touched some figures into his tablet and quoted his fee. Then, as an afterthought, he said, "Hey, I'll tell you what. The show is for your old teacher, right?"

"Yes."

"Okay. That's cool. I'll take 10% off."

Trudie had to make the decision on the spot, with no time to consult the others. Kristen had disappeared with Cole, and Mary Ann had gone to see Mrs. Childs. It was still pricy, but Trudie was certain that Hugh would do the job right.

After Hugh left, Trudie wandered the stage. She was achingly curious as to why Mrs. Childs had wanted to see Mary Ann alone. Was Mary Ann truly her favorite?

TWENTY-THREE

Julie was wordless as she accompanied Mary Ann to her mother's bedroom. She lingered for a moment, patting her mother's pillows, rearranging the flowers and then finally, at her mother's urging, she left them alone. It was obvious that Julie still wasn't comfortable with Mary Ann's "New Age" healing approach.

When Mary Ann first entered, Mrs. Childs was lying in bed, reading Charles Dickens' *David Copperfield.* After Julie exited, she laid the book aside and her soft, drowsy face became alert. She smiled warmly.

"Hello, Mary Ann. You look a little flushed."

"Yes, well... I've been exercising today. I'm a little out of shape."

"Sit down, please. I want to talk to you."

Mary Ann did so, folding her hands in her lap. "You look healthier," Mary Ann said. "You have some color. That's good."

"I do feel better today. Christmas has cheered me up. It always did. I suppose it cheers most people up, unless they're alone or they've lost a loved one."

"It *is* a happy time," Mary Ann said. "I've had to squeeze in some Christmas shopping in the last few days.

I was way behind. My daughters want clothes and new phones. When I was their age, it was clothes and a Mariah Carey album."

"I'd love to meet your daughters. You should bring them to see me. I'd love to meet them."

"And you will, I promise."

Mrs. Childs settled back into the pillows and closed her eyes.

"It's getting late, Mrs. Childs. You must be tired."

"No... I was just thinking."

Mrs. Childs opened her eyes and tilted her head. "Mary Ann... the last time you were with me, something rather strange happened to me."

"What happened?"

"It was extraordinary. I was aware of you standing above me, with your eyes closed, and you were whispering something."

"Yes. I was saying a prayer for you."

Mrs. Childs smiled. "How nice. How nice to know that one is remembered in someone else's prayers."

Mrs. Childs shut her eyes again, as if to summon the memory. "Do you know that as you were praying, in an instant, I saw my whole life play out before me, just as if I were watching it unfold on a stage? Just like it was all a great drama, a play. I saw my childhood, roaming around my father's old drugstore, and I heard him say things I'd long forgotten. I saw my mother shouting at me because I had never become the actress she wanted me to be. I saw my husband's kind face, my kids playing in sparkling green grass on a warm summer day, and I saw so clearly my teaching career. I saw every student's face. Every one of them—even the jocks who hated coming to my class, and who didn't particularly like me."

She opened her eyes. She looked enquiringly at Mary Ann. "I saw you, Mary Ann, when you were 18 years old. You were standing downstage center and I was seated in the Deer Lake auditorium, front row center. And then you spoke to me as if you were repeating a monologue you'd memorized. But it was authentic. It wasn't stiff or contrived."

Mary Ann leaned forward. "What did I say?"

Mrs. Childs became emotional. "Oh, my, tears again. I'm afraid I have grown old and silly. I never used to cry."

Mary Ann reached for a tissue and handed it to her. She waited for the emotion to run its course.

Mrs. Childs tried again. "Mary Ann... you said, 'Mrs. Childs, you have truly made a difference in all our lives, and we love you.'"

Mrs. Childs' voice thickened. "I heard you say, 'Mrs. Childs, the love you feel while watching your life unfold will nourish you, bless you, and heal you. Just relax into that love and be healed by it. That is the power of true love.'"

Mary Ann was still, listening, smiling.

Mrs. Childs took a little breath. "Well... Do you know that the doctors have changed their minds about giving me more chemo? Did Julie tell you that?"

"No, she didn't."

"Well, she was surprised. She kept asking them questions. Anyway, I have felt so much better since your prayer, Mary Ann. Truly better. Oh, I'm not ready to get up and dance a jig or anything, but I do feel stronger and I don't have the heavy fatigue and pain I used to have. I even got out of bed and walked around my room for a few minutes this morning. It felt so good to be up and moving again."

"I'm so glad, Mrs. Childs."

Mrs. Childs met Mary Ann's calm, unblinking eyes and she searched them, trying to read them. "Do you have a gift for this, Mary Ann? A gift for healing?"

"I don't know, Mrs. Childs. If it *is* a gift, it is a gift I try to pass along and give to others. I keep practicing."

Mrs. Childs nodded, not really understanding. "I'm going to die soon, aren't I, Mary Ann?

"We're all going to die, Mrs. Childs."

"Yes, of course, but I saw my death. While you were praying for me, just before I fell into a deep sleep, I saw a very bright light coming toward me. It was a calm and comforting light. I wasn't the least bit afraid. I saw my father, and he called to me. I saw my mother, too, and you should have seen her. She was wearing the prettiest red dress and dark patent leather shoes, and she had her hair all done up in curls on top of her head, in that 1940's style she loved so much. Then she did something I don't remember her ever doing: she reached out to me. She reached out with both hands, smiled warmly and said, 'Myrna...you were the bright star of my life. I love you so much.'"

Mrs. Childs sighed and lay back, soothed by the memory. "Such a nice experience, Mary Ann. It didn't seem like a dream. It felt real. Well, anyway, I felt so much better."

Mary Ann touched her arm. They sat in silence for a few minutes, and then Mary Ann stood. "I should go now. You probably need to rest."

Mrs. Childs' tranquil eyes were filled with gratitude. "Thank you, Mary Ann. Thank you for easing my pain."

Mary Ann reached for her teacher's hand. "Before I go, I'm going to whisper another prayer, Mrs. Childs. A simple one. Is that okay?"

"You know, I've never believed in this kind of thing—the occult and New Age this and that. But I'm pleased I can let myself go along with it. Maybe I've grown a little in my old age. Maybe I'm not as stubborn as I used to be. There was a time, you know, when I would have not so politely asked you to leave."

Mary Ann laughed. "Yes, I know."

They grew quiet and then they closed their eyes. The air became charged with tenderness, as currents of serenity washed over them. And by the time Mary Ann left the room, closing the door softly behind her, Mrs. Childs had drifted off to sleep.

At the front door, Mary Ann was working into her coat as Julie stood tentative and awkward.

"She says you've helped her," Julie said.

"If whatever I did helped ease her pain, I'm glad," Mary Ann said, buttoning her coat. "Will you bring her for the 8 o'clock show?"

Julie glanced back at the bedroom. "She says she's going to die soon, but she seems stronger. I guess we'll just have to see what happens."

Mary Ann stared down.

Julie licked her lips, trying to find the right words. "Mary Ann, can you tell if she's going to die soon?"

"No. My feeling is... and you'll excuse me for saying this, but I feel, intuitively, that she's ready to go, or at least preparing to go. But... I don't know."

Julie's lower lip quivered. "Well, thank you for all you've done. If she feels as well as she does tonight, I'll try to take her to the show. I wouldn't want her to miss it, and she'd never forgive me if she learned about it afterward." Julie wiped her wet eyes and made a brave little smile. "I don't want to miss it either."

Mary Ann lingered for a moment. She touched Julie's arm, affectionately, and left.

The traffic was heavy as Mary Ann drove back to the high school. She'd never seen so many cars or so many people packed into all the fast food restaurants; never heard the impatient blaring horns at red lights, or the blue sweeping dome lights from police cars, as deputies directed traffic at Rusty's and the mall entrance.

Many, no doubt, had come to see Jon Ketch, or at least to try to get a look at him, because he was "their" home town boy, but many others came because they remembered the Christmas shows, and those shows had somehow enhanced their Christmas season experience.

Many others came to honor Mrs. Childs, and they had contributed to her scholarship fund. The word had spread quickly, thanks to Ray, Connie and Don Rawlings. She smiled to herself as she thought about her good and loving friend, Trudie. Would her frightened and reclusive friend reach out to Don Rawlings? Or would she and Jon try to make a go of it? There was no question that Jon loved her, in his own nutty way. Trudie was not an easy person to read, but Mary Ann sensed that Trudie was ready to take a leap—maybe even a radical leap—and run off with Jon. But, would she?

Mary Ann crept toward the high school, feeling uneasy about her visit with Mrs. Childs. Mary Ann was not the master healer her healing/meditation teacher had been. Not by a long shot. But Mary Ann had felt an energy— Mrs. Childs' energy—seeping away. There was simply more mass than life force. Would she last the night?

Mary Ann was recognized by security and waved into the parking lot.

She parked, unfastened her seatbelt and saw a text from Trudie.

"Had to make a big decision. Jon sent the girls home with Ray. How's Mrs. Childs?"

TWENTY-FOUR

The next morning, Kristen noticed a bottle of *Advil* on the dining room table, undoubtedly placed there by Trudie late last night before she'd staggered off to bed, racked by pain and fatigue.

It was December 24th, and the first Christmas show was scheduled for 5 o'clock that afternoon. Kristen was up first, as usual. Grateful for Trudie's thoughtfulness, she picked up the bottle, popped the cap, shook out two and swallowed them down with orange juice. Texts and emails were still flowing in. She ignored them, placing an elbow on the table, dropping her aching head to rest in her hand. She felt worst than if she'd had a hangover.

Trudie emerged from the kitchen to the dining room a half hour later, limping, coffee cup in hand. She saw Kristen. Kristen lifted a weak hand of hello. Trudie grunted. It didn't sound like hello. Her gaze took in the *Advil* and her eyes widened with sudden interest. She reached, shook one out and swallowed it down. She sat, grimacing, her back in knots.

"What time is it?" Trudie asked.

"Six forty-five," Kristen mumbled.

Trudie reached for her phone and checked messages. She scrolled, ignoring most, searching for Julie or Hugh Watson. None from Julie: Good? One from Hugh. He'd sent it at 5:54 a.m.

"On schedule. Some problems hanging two speakers outside. We'll solve it. Can u tell your stage manager to get off my ass?!"

Trudie sighed.

"Problems," Kristen asked, half-heartedly.

"Always. Liz, of course."

"Why did we let her stage manage? She's such a bitch."

"Yeah, and she's the best. She knows it, and we know it. There will be no mistakes. She and Jon make a great team. They're both wacky perfectionists."

"What time did you get in?" Kristen asked.

"A little after three. You?"

Kristen stared into her empty juice glass. "I couldn't sleep last night. I was in bed by two, but I don't think I slept more than an hour."

Trudie wrapped both hands around the large white mug, enjoying the warmth. She sipped her coffee. "Do tell why... if you want."

"I don't want, but I made a big decision at 4:42 this morning."

Trudie pinched her cotton robe at the neck. "It's cold in here. I should turn the thermostat up, but I just can't move right now."

"It's cold outside, 28 degrees. And guess what? It's supposed to snow tonight."

Trudie grunted. "How much?"

"Two-to-three inches."

"Oh, that's nothing. A white Christmas Eve. Perfect."

"Just for Jon. Just like in a movie. Snow for the Christmas show," Kristen said, grinning at her clever little rhyme. "Did he go back to his hotel last night?"

"I doubt it. He was still rehearsing when I left. I couldn't believe it. He'd sent everybody else home and he stayed on that stage by himself, with Liz at the light board. He was trying out voices, movement and dialogue and she was right there with him, creating lighting effects. He was still going at three, and when I asked him if he was leaving, he said he was going to sleep in the theatre."

A little bell "dinged" and Kristen got up and went into the kitchen. "My bagel's ready." She returned with a cup of coffee and a toasted cinnamon raisin bagel. She sat down with a wince. "Damn, every part of my body hurts and my feet are killing me, and I'm in good shape! How are we going to dance two shows?"

Trudie's forehead lifted. She closed her eyes in resignation and shook her head. "God help us all, everyone," she said parodying Tiny Tim from *A Christmas Carol.*

Kristen spread butter on one half of the bagel and grape jelly on the other. She didn't look up. "When this is all over, what are you going to do about Jon?"

"I can't even think about Jon right now. Thank God he hasn't mentioned it. He is completely absorbed in the show."

Kristen persisted. "When Don showed up to rehearse, I was sitting in the back of the auditorium. I saw he brought you flowers."

"Yes, they were lovely. A dozen red roses. I found a vase and left them in the dressing room."

Kristen licked the jelly from the bagel. "Interesting. Two men. Two possibilities."

Trudie looked away. "Two more problems I don't want to deal with right now."

Mary Ann descended the stairs, bypassed the kitchen and padded into the dining room. Her face was puffy and her eyes were red. She walked unsteadily to a chair and dropped down with a heavy sigh. "I'm 38 years old and I feel 78. Pass the Advil, please."

Trudie did. Mary Ann held it tightly in her hand, but she didn't open it.

"Are the girls still sleeping?" Trudie asked.

"Yes, Carly will sleep till noon if I let her."

"So let her," Kristen said.

"Jon wants the entire cast at the theatre by 10 a.m. He wants to do a full run through, twice."

"He's going to wear everybody out before the shows begin," Trudie said.

"He said he does not want to incur the wrath of Mrs. Childs. He pointed out, rightly, that she'll be studying every detail, and she'll let him have it if she sees anything that's not perfect."

"You didn't talk much about her last night," Kristen said, taking a nibble at the buttered half of her bagel. "Does that mean you're not sure she's going to make it to the show?"

Mary Ann got up and disappeared into the kitchen. She returned with a glass of water. After she swallowed an Advil, she looked pointedly at her two friends. "Julie is going to bring her unless, of course, Mrs. Childs takes a turn for the worst."

Trudie massaged her stiff neck. "Do you foresee a turn for the worst?"

Mary Ann stared down at the table. "Last night I thought I did. This morning... I don't know. Has Julie texted any of you?"

They shook their heads.

"Then I guess she's doing fine," Mary Ann said, with a feeble smile.

Trudie looked at her two friends. "Before we go to the theatre today, I have a request."

Mary Ann and Kristen looked up.

"You remember the old ice skating rink out on Highway 11?"

"Out near Grove Point?" Kristen asked.

"Yes."

"I can't do it," Mary Ann said, anticipating what Trudie was about to say. "There's no way these feet and this body are going to be able to get up on the ice and skate. It just ain't gonna happen."

"I'm with you," Kristen said. "No way, Trudie."

"Then let's not skate. But let's go, just for the memories. We can sit and talk and spend time together. We'll just get away from it all for awhile—before everything ends and you both go away again. Remember how much fun we used to have ice skating together?"

Mary Ann nodded. "It was fun, even if I was the klutz and you two just went gliding along like something from a dream."

Kristen took a bite of her bagel, her eyes suddenly far away. "I remember the last time we went skating. It was just before we did our last Christmas show."

"Yes," Trudie said. "So let's just go. Let's just sit and talk and relax for awhile."

By 8:30, the women were at the Grove Point ice skating rink, dressed in coats, caps and gloves. Mary Ann had awakened her daughters at eight to tell them that Ray would pick them up at 9:30, and she reminded them to eat some breakfast. It would be a long and exciting day.

Outside, the wind was calm. The sky was a quilted silver gray. Flurries were drifting down, glazing the tops of parked cars and the gray roof of the ice skate rental house.

Grove Point was an oval rink that sat off the highway down in a little valley, surrounded by birch and elm trees, with an old red barn visible on the crest of a distant hill. The rink didn't open until nine, but the girls didn't care. They roamed the area, circling the place, pausing to settle on a long wooden bench at the far end, where they had a good view of the area.

They didn't speak for minutes at a time, content to feel the cool flecks of snow on their faces and tongues, happy to snuggle close, arms locked together, feeling sane and sweet, away from the frantic world.

When they got cold, they walked and chatted about their lives. When they sat again, falling into a new silence, they were caught by the serenity and snowy beauty of the area, by the festive decorations of holly, wreaths and Christmas lights.

Skaters appeared at 9 o'clock, some sailing gracefully past, turning and pivoting, some stumbling, reaching and falling to the music of *Sleigh Ride!*

To Trudie, it was an irresistible impulse. She shot up, exclaiming that she had to skate, sore and tired as she was. Kristen and Mary Ann enthusiastically followed.

Soon all three were gliding across the ice, feeling wildly young again, as the wind swept across their faces and chilled their bones. When one fell, the other two helped her up, and they cruised on, laughing, chatting and free. Their muscles ached and their feet complained, but they drifted on, unwilling to give up the high adventure, all too aware that they'd soon be back in the hectic world of the show… and then their inevitable separation would come.

They'd part once again and carry on with their distinctive, challenging lives. So for those few enchanting moments, they skated on, arms raised, faces turned to the sky, feeling joyful, free and easy.

Finally, the flying minutes told them they had to leave. Before they returned to their car, they asked a young woman to take their picture. The fussy woman threw herself into the production, snapping photos at different angles and poses.

Their favorite was the one of them leaning slightly into a snow bank. Each was snuggly tucked close to the other, at a three-quarter angle, ski caps pulled low over their foreheads. They were laughing, eyes squinting, but gleaming with delight and affection.

When they arrived at the theater, they were swarmed by questions, problems and quarrels. No one had gotten much sleep, and tempers flared over the slightest issues. Jon was onstage with the full cast in costume, arguing with Liz about the way she was lighting the end of the show.

Hugh Watson was testing the hanging stage microphones, traipsing across The Ghost of Christmas Past's difficult and technical scene, oblivious to everyone, ignoring complaints and anxieties. Hugh had simply shut them out, concentrating on his job with all the focus and one pointed meditation of a Zen master.

Ray was down the hall, rehearsing the musicians in the band room. He discovered he was missing parts for the trumpets and first violins. He would have to run home to search his old music trunk to see if they were there. And, of the 16 musicians present, seven were students who attended surrounding high schools that had music programs, but these students were far from professional.

The band's rendition of *The Hallelujah Chorus* was off-key and clumsy.

Molly Cahill had her chorus and dancers in the woodshop room, drilling dance steps, but dumbing them down when she saw the group couldn't keep up.

Oscar and the set designers had run out of paint, wood and nails and Connie was nowhere to be found to issue the necessary petty cash so they could make a run to the hardware store, only open until 1 p.m. And on and on...

The Christmas Women dived in, solving each problem, while fighting off a colossal anxiety that the entire show was about to fall flat on its face, be a stinking disappointment to Mrs. Childs and the community, and be a dismal failure for the return of The Christmas Girls.

By two o'clock, all three women were seated in the auditorium. They were fighting exhaustion, and they still had to rehearse their numbers with the orchestra in full costume and makeup.

At 4:15, the girls were again sitting in the auditorium, struggling to recover what little optimism and energy they had left. Jon had vanished. Oscar and his crew were still hammering and painting. Ray was in the orchestra pit rehearsing the musicians, pleading with the violins to play in tune. Hugh Watson was in the back of the house at the mixing board, working assiduously to solve the problem of why two outside speakers were still not broadcasting.

A rambling crowd had formed around the school, especially when the word got out that the show would be broadcast live from the stage.

The Christmas Women wore their short, tight, red dresses, white faux fur hats and 3-inch red heels, just as they had 20 years before. Their cheeks were rosy, fake eyelashes long and sexy, their makeup heavy.

"I'd love a very wet gin martini," Kristen said. "There's a bartender named Doug, who works at a hotel on the West Side of Manhattan. He makes the best martinis."

"One hour of sleep," Trudie said. "Just one single hour. I'd pay big bucks for one hour of uninterrupted sleep."

Mary Ann batted her lashes slowly. "I wish my Christmas shopping was done. No way anybody on my list is going to get anything until January, except the girls. I've never seen them happier. They are having the time of their lives."

Kristen and Trudie looked at her, affectionately. "They're wonderful girls, Mary Ann," Trudie said. "You are very lucky."

Mary Ann nodded. "Yes, I am."

Trudie glanced down at her phone and saw the text from Julie. She sat bolt upright. "It's a text from Julie!"

They all sat up, waiting.

Trudie tapped and read.

"I told Mom I was taking her out. She said no, she's not going anywhere. I texted Jon. He's here. He's taking her. Told her, Santa Claus is coming to town! We'll be there!"

Trudie showed the other two the text. They applauded, hugged and kissed.

Kristen shot up, and unkinked her neck. "Okay, kids. Let's go do a show. Ouch! Everything hurts!"

TWENTY-FIVE

At 4:45, the dressing rooms were crackling with nervous laughter and excitement. Liz was still in the theater running light cues. Hugh had solved the speaker problems, and the sound coming through the outside speakers was pure and clean.

Ray paced backstage, agonizing over the orchestra, unable and unwilling to accept comfort and encouragement from anyone.

Oscar and his team were sliding the sets into position, making final alterations, using large fans to help disperse the fresh paint smell. Fake snow had been delivered and Oscar pointed up to the catwalk, instructing two high school athletes what to do and when to do it. There was no time to rehearse.

Jon had returned, telling the three girls that Mrs. Childs was weak, but he'd said just enough to make her interested and intrigued. She was coming to the 8 o'clock show. He'd leave right after the 5 o'clock show, under police escort arranged by Sheriff Jake T. Mason, and accompany her and Julie back to the theatre. He and the Sheriff would escort her down the aisle to her center aisle seat.

At 4:55, Trudie carefully drew back the stage curtain and stared out. The auditorium and balcony were filled to capacity, including standing room. Her knees got rubbery, as she heard the low buzz of the anxious crowd and saw ushers seating the last of the audience. She was amazed and grateful that it had all come together so fast. She felt a catch in her chest, and she swallowed hard.

The lights slowly dimmed, and the restless audience fell into whispers. Ray entered the pit, and a spotlight bathed him. There was thunderous applause. Trudie saw the terror in his eyes as he lifted his piton, pulled out a handkerchief and wiped his face. They were not professionals. They were not used to being in the spotlight. It was all supposed to be a simple little Christmas show. None of them saw this behemoth coming, sweeping them up in emotion, fear and challenge.

The cymbal crash startled Trudie—she jumped. The orchestra erupted into a lively version of *We Wish You a Merry Christmas*. And then it all came rushing back to her. Twenty years were erased in an instant and she was 18 years old again, excited, thrilled, ready to perform in the Deer Lake High School Christmas show, featuring The Christmas Girls!

She merged with the chorus as they prepared to spill out onto the stage for the opening number. Trudie saw Kristen and Mary Ann across the stage, stiffly waiting for their cue from Liz. It seemed to happen in slow motion. Liz called the cue and gave the signal: a pointed gun of her finger. The show was off and running!

There was a hypnotic quality to the performance, as singers and musicians merged, dancers twirled and leaped, and then exited the stage for *A Christmas Carol*.

Jon and his cast moved through the play with ease and fluidity, capturing mood, atmosphere and most of Jon's direction. There were glitches of course: some sets took too long to appear. Bob Cratchit and Jacob Marley dropped lines. Don Rawlings started playing his sax before the girls were on stage. The musical accompaniment to Mary Ann's recitation of 'Twas the Night before Christmas was too loud and the audience had trouble hearing her. The chorus forgot some of the words to The Twelve Days of Christmas, and, during the finale, snow fell abundantly on stage right, but not on stage left. One boy up on the catwalk had gone off to the bathroom, misjudging the time. That caused the chorus on stage left to instinctively look up, until Ray motioned for them to focus on the audience.

The musicians struggled with Frosty the Snowman and The Hallelujah Chorus, and The Christmas Women's finale kicking chorus routine was a bit off and awkward. But they spiritedly swung through the steps, with broad toothy smiles and lively singing that struggled to stay on pitch.

When the burgundy velvet curtain finally came down, the uproarious applause was deafening. The entire cast received a standing ovation, returning for four curtain calls.

After the show the entire cast met behind the stage, in the Green Room. There was little time for back patting and celebration. After a few quick bites of pizza, the tension swiftly returned, as the cast listened closely to the aggressive stage notes from Jon (delivered by Jon's assistant, Lynn, because Jon had fled to retrieve Mrs. Childs). There were voluminous music notes from Ray and many dancing notes from Molly Cahill.

Jon had slipped out via the back door of the school, waving at the cheering crowds that were held back by yellow CAUTION tape and security guards. He piled into the Sheriff's car and, with its roof lights flashing, they traveled off to Julie's house.

The Christmas Women stood in bare feet before the cast, Mary Ann and Trudie with shawls wrapped around their shoulders, and Kristen sipping coffee. Trudie spoke for the trio.

"We thought you were all wonderful out there! The three of us and Ray want to thank you for coming and for being a part of this reunion and celebration of Mrs. Childs' life. Whatever happens out there during the second show, I hope we can all just enjoy ourselves, have fun and pretend there aren't three cameras capturing every move, every word and every step our poor aching feet take."

The group laughed. Trudie saw Oscar and Mary Ann exchange affectionate glances. She also noted that Kristen and Cole were not. They were avoiding each other's eyes.

Trudie folded her hands. "Seeing you all here again has been one of the best Christmas presents of my life. Thank you all again, and Merry Christmas and Happy New Year!"

After the applause faded, the cast emptied the room and prepared for the final show. The strain of so many concentrated hours was showing on many faces, including those of The Christmas Women. Now that it was certain that Mrs. Childs would be in the audience, the cast had to tramp down nerves and trepidation. Like The Christmas Women, the performers wanted this night to shine, to inspire and to leave Mrs. Childs, and indeed them all, with nothing but pride and good memories.

Liz gruffly called everyone into position. "Curtain in 10 minutes."

Trudie went to her. "Is Mrs. Childs here yet?"

"Nope."

"We may have to delay the curtain."

"Curtain is at 8:00 sharp," Liz said, crisply.

Trudie gained instant aggressive height. "We do not raise that curtain until Mrs. Childs is firmly in her seat, Liz! That is final. No argument. No debate. The show is not about us. It's about her!"

Liz's eyes burned. "Whatever you say, Ms. Boss."

Trudie stormed away across the stage, struggling to regain her composure. She inched forward to peek through the side curtain. Just as she did, she heard screams of joy and wild applause. Trudie peeled back the curtain to see the entire audience rise to its feet.

There she was! Mrs. Childs in a wheelchair, being ushered down the center aisle by Julie and her brother, Nick, with Jon and the Sheriff behind, chests puffed out, faces filled with masculine pride. The applause was deafening.

Mrs. Childs glanced about, struggling to take it all in, struggling to understand, her lips compressed in tight concern. Her eyes widened in speculation as she advanced.

Near her designated seat of honor, Jon and Sheriff Mason helped her up, walked her a couple of steps, and eased her down in her chair.

"Okay, Teach," Jon said. "Sit back and enjoy the show."

Mrs. Childs was speechless, searching her daughter's and her son's eyes as they sat down beside her. The applause continued, as the lights slowly dimmed.

Just before the lights came down, Trudie saw something that startled her. She saw a handsome man in his early forties and a teenage boy start down the right aisle, with an usher leading them to their seats. The boy was

Kristen's son, Alexander! No doubt. Trudie recognized him from *Facebook* and Christmas card photos. The man with him must be Kristen's husband, Alan! Trudie had seen only the occasional photo of him on *Facebook*. Now it made sense: Kristen's decision at 4:42 in the morning. She and Cole avoiding each others' eyes. Kristen had called her husband and son and asked them to come.

Trudie glanced right to see Kristen peering out from stage right. She'd seen them too. Trudie noticed Kristen's private smile of satisfaction as she released the curtains and stepped back.

At 8:13 p.m., the curtain was drawn back and a large white screen descended. A recent photograph of Mrs. Childs was projected onto it. It revealed a mature face, with carefully styled gray hair, a friendly smile and lively eyes. The audience erupted into loud applause, as a dedication was superimposed over the photo.

This Christmas Show is Dedicated
to Mrs. Myrna Childs.
Offered with Love and Devotion
by Her Former Students at Deer Lake High!
Thank You for Making a Difference in Our Lives!
And
Merry Christmas!

Mrs. Childs absorbed a wave of affection and was nearly overcome with emotion. So many fond memories rushed back, of all the wonderful music and dancing and acting, those Christmas shows that had made her so proud. Her breathing choked and tears came into her eyes.

The screen was raised as a spotlight struck the orchestral pit. Ray emerged, and he was showered with applause. He stepped up on the conductor's podium and pivoted to face his former teacher. He placed a hand over his heart and bowed.

Mrs. Childs began to tremble. She swallowed back emotion, even as the first cymbal crash announced the start of the Christmas show.

The overture bounced through the melody with energy and verve, setting a tone of high celebration. When it concluded, the stage lights flashed on and the entire cast swept in from the wings, dressed in bright winter sweaters, scarves and hats, singing *It's the Most Wonderful Time of the Year*. Their voices were sure and strong, and the orchestra struck every note right. Ray was sweating and beaming.

The Christmas Girls materialized, joining the chorus, each seizing the arm of a man, strolling across the stage dancing and singing.

As the opening chorus drew to a close, Liz, with headset on and hard eyes focused on Oscar, called the next scene.

The lights went to black, and Oscar and his crew flew into action. They placed the fireplace, Scrooge's office furniture, Bob Cratchit's desk and Scrooge's safe on the set. The crew fled the stage as Liz called the next scene.

In the balcony, the projector shot images of old Victorian England onto a backdrop, revealing church spires, gothic towers, hansom cabs, turrets, gables and foggy streets.

A dim spot caught Jon Ketch enter stage left, dressed all in black as old Ebenezer Scrooge, white hair sticking out from a stove pipe hat. The audience applauded their home town boy who had made good, and they watched the wizened, irascible figure groan and complain through his scenes. He stooped about, miserable and grumpy, barking out his hatred of life and everyone in it. His eyes moved in fury and contempt, his body passing through raw emotion, fear and regret.

Mrs. Childs watched raptly as the play progressed, gaining power and poignancy until, near the end, all of Scrooge's bitterness was shattered into humility and pathos, when the towering and frightening Cole Blackwell, as The Ghost of Christmas Future, pointed his crooked, wiggling finger at Scrooge's own tombstone, demanding that he see it and learn from it.

Stunned and terrified, Scrooge staggered about, face in his hands, sobbing and pleading, " No, Spirit! Oh no, no! Spirit! Hear me! I am not the man I was. I will not be the man I must have been but for this intercourse. Why show me this, if I am past all hope? Good Spirit, your nature intercedes for me, and pities me. Assure me that I yet may change these shadows you have shown me, by an altered life! I will honor Christmas in my heart, and try to keep it all the year. I will live in the Past, the Present, and the Future. The Spirits of all Three shall strive within me. I will not shut out the lessons that they teach. Oh, tell me I may sponge away the writing on this stone!"

The play ended in happy celebration, as Scrooge regained his love for life, people and Christmas, and when Tiny Tim exclaimed, "God bless us everyone!" the curtain came down.

Mrs. Childs erupted into heavy applause for her old student, clapping until her hands hurt. She continued applauding anyway, feeling her body awaken with pride and gratitude.

"Wasn't he magnificent?!" Mrs. Childs exclaimed to Nick and Julie. "Isn't he just the greatest actor?!"

During the second half of the show, Don Rawlings, along with Carly and Lynn, brought the house down with his squawky, yakety-yak sax rendition of *Rudolph the Red*

Nose Reindeer. The girls' wild and careless dance behind him brought squeals of laughter, as they swung their arms about, kicking left and right, their red noses blinking on and off. Mrs. Childs laughed so hard that tears ran down her cheeks.

The lights dimmed as the applause roared on, allowing the stage hands to roll the fireplace, now with mantel stockings, onto center stage. Mary Ann sat in a rocking chair dressed as Mrs. Claus, half-reciting, half-singing *'Twas the Night before Christmas*, encouraging the audience to join in. They all shouted the final lines with her: "Merry Christmas to all and to all good-night!"

Like clockwork, the stage hands pushed the set back, and the chorus entered from stage left and right, singing a medley of songs, starting with *I'm Dreaming of a White Christmas.* The finale came when The Christmas Women exploded onto the stage singing *Jingle Bells*, using The Andrew Sisters' arrangement. The auditorium joined in singing and clapping as the girls fell into their Rockettes' style kicking chorus. Jon shot out from stage left, dressed as Santa, shouldered in next to Trudie, and began kicking and laughing right along with them. Up on the catwalk, the two high school boys slung out handfuls of fake snow. It drifted down lazily.

To Julie's and Nick's shock, Mrs. Childs struggled to her feet, yelling out her approval. The girls and Jon waved back to her as they kicked on, hearts racing, faces flushed, sweat pouring down, feet stabbing them with pain.

Two cameras rushed in, capturing the exceptional moment, and the girls kicked even higher, with Jon barely able to hold on, his face fixed in a strained comical grin.

The roaring applause lifted them, the crash of the cymbals excited them and still The Christmas Women thrilled the audience with their relentless precision dance. Ray was all swinging arms and grins as he lifted the orchestra to new heights, yelling at them to give him more sound—and they did—cheeks puffed, faces red, violin bows skipping across the strings, timpani booming like thunder.

When the last note fell into a cymbal crash, the audience shot to its feet in rowdy applause. High on adrenalin and joy, The Christmas Women hugged, Jon threw kisses to the audience and Ray charged into the introduction of *The Hallelujah Chorus.*

The entire cast and crew packed the stage, and indicated to the audience that they should join in. The singing was loud, soaring and triumphant. Even Charlie Wills, the B-flat trumpet player who'd never managed to hit the right notes before, nailed all the high notes and sent them ringing off the ceiling and walls. For long seconds the remnants of Handel's masterpiece reverberated around the auditorium.

When it was finally over, the audience settled back into their seats, hearts racing. Ushers appeared at the aisle, handing out LED votive candle lights. The house lights came down and the room fell into a silence. The soft glow from hundreds of starry candle lights brought a sacred peace, and when Ray cued the orchestra, they began to play the introduction to SILENT NIGHT.

Outside, the masses joined in, singing and swaying gently to each verse. They had gathered in the parking lot, on the front lawn, in the streets and on the sidewalks. They'd come from the mall and from the restaurants and from the churches that had already concluded their services. They'd come from the surrounding towns and villages and from as far away as Columbus and Cincinnati.

Taxi cabs parked and drivers emerged and listened. Some joined in with the singing. TV crews hovered and listened, and some of them sang. Security guards and deputies quickly noticed a sudden change in the playfully raucous crowds. When the carol began, the crowd suddenly fell into a hypnotic dream of tranquility. They sang, smiling and swaying, kissing and holding hands.

Sheriff Mason witnessed the astonishing scene from atop the high school steps, hands on his hips. He suddenly knew that he was experiencing a once-in-a-lifetime event, one he'd probably never experience again.

The entire town had come together to sing a Christmas carol of comfort and peace, and the Sheriff felt it. Sheriff Mason, who wasn't particularly religious, suddenly had an inexplicable religious experience. As he gazed out into the world of gently falling snow, Christmas lights, crowds singing *Silent Night*, and a cool night wind caressing his face, he experienced a ONEness, and a perfection in all things. Everything he heard, saw and felt was somehow connected to ONE extraordinary being, and he was a part of that miracle of being. For that brief moment in time, there truly was peace on Earth and goodwill toward all people. Sheriff Mason joined the chorus of singers, raising his deep bass, off-key voice to the heavens, feeling joyful and blessed.

Inside, Mrs. Lyons stood in the back of the auditorium singing, misty-eyed. There was something in the air that night and she had effortlessly plugged into it. She didn't try to define it or understand it and, for once in her life, she didn't want to. She just sang, feeling a warming affection for all humanity.

After the carol came a deep and rich silence. Mrs. Childs sat still, her eyes closed. It had been an emotional night and she needed time to rest. When she heard her name called, her eyes opened on The Christmas Women and Jon standing next to her, waiting.

"We're taking you up on the stage," Trudie said.

"I can't walk all the way up there," Mrs. Childs said.

"No worries, Teach," Jon said. "These are modern times. They have an access ramp."

They helped her into the wheelchair and Jon pushed her up the access ramp, through the wings and out onto the stage, positioning her downstage center, while the audience thundered with applause. Mrs. Childs was swarmed by her former students, who hugged her, kissed her cheeks, and presented her with presents, cards, and dazzling bouquets of flowers.

The audience was on its feet, in a standing ovation. Mrs. Childs struggled to adjust to the reality, one moment smiling, the next moment wiping tears. Jon leaned over and whispered in her ear.

"How was the play, Teach?"

She gave him a stern look. "I saw five glaring errors."

"Only five, Teach?"

"I'll give you my notes before you leave town," she concluded, with a little amused wink. "Next year, when you do it again, it will be perfect. And I'll be here to make sure of it!"

Jon laughed, and then did a little tap dance.

Mrs. Childs reached for The Christmas Girls—her Christmas Girls—and she took their hands and, because the applause and the whistling and the celebration were so loud, she mouthed the words, "Thank you. I love you all with all my heart."

The alert male photographer appeared. He gathered the entire cast and crew together and began snapping multiple shots, capturing smiles, funny faces, kisses and hugs.

Finally, he placed Mrs. Childs, The Christmas Women and Jon together. He was about to snap the first shot when Trudie turned to see Ray, standing off in the wings, looking on. She motioned for him to join them. He held back. Mrs. Childs followed Trudie's eyes. She commanded Ray to come, with a firm wave of her hand and her persuasive piercing eyes. Ray obeyed, and the group cheered him.

Mrs. Childs stood in the center, flanked by Jon and Trudie on her right side and Mary Ann, Kristen and Ray on the other.

"All my favorites," Mrs. Childs said, as the photographer snapped the last photo. "You are all my favorites."

TWENTY-SIX

The cast party at Rusty's was loud, jumping and joyful. There was dancing; there were platters of food; there were champagne corks popping; there was impromptu singing and there were dramatically told recaps. Highlights from the show were already playing on several laptops. Liz Tyree was praised for her flawless stage managing, and she reveled in it, gulping down a glass of champagne someone had shoved into her hand.

Ray toasted his orchestra, praising their musicianship. The bass player jumped from behind the bar and sprayed him with a popped bottle of champagne. Ray's hand flew up to his face as a stream of foam splashed into the side of his head.

Don Rawlings' act had been a big hit. Many of his co-workers and clients had been at the show and they were busy buying him beer and praising his talent. "Ah! If it hadn't have been for Carly and Lynn," he yelled, "you would have all booed me off the stage."

Trudie was working her way through the crowd to congratulate him, when she noticed an attractive brunette hanging off his arm. Trudie saw them kiss a couple of times. They weren't sisterly kisses. Don pulled her in close and kissed her again. Perplexed and off-balance, Trudie asked one of Don's friends who the woman was.

"Oh, that's Stacy. They broke up a little over a month ago. But she was at the show tonight and she loved it. I guess she and Don just got back together."

Trudie retreated to another part of the room, deflated and confused. She was quickly pulled away by Kristen to meet her husband, Alan, and their son, Alexander.

"These are my men," Kristen said, proudly. "I called them in the middle of the night and told them they had to come. And the sweethearts did."

Alan was classy, refined and complimentary. "I'm so happy to finally meet you, Trudie. Kristen thinks the world of you."

Trudie smiled at her friend. "As I do her."

Alexander was formal and a little shy. Trudie thought him a very handsome boy and she told him so. He thanked her and then reached for his cell phone.

"We're leaving for Breckinridge at six in the morning," Kristen said. "Oh, and Alan found us a room at a hotel close to the airport, so we'll all be staying there tonight."

Trudie hid her disappointment with a forced smile. "Oh, that's convenient. Good. Good."

The party thundered on. Mary Ann was sitting in a red booth in the café with Oscar and the girls, eating pizza. Carly wore the lacy chiffon dress she'd found in Trudie's attic, and Lynn proudly wore a vintage 1960s red and white polka dot dress she'd unearthed from the same trunk.

Carly had braided her hair into one elegant pigtail, and the long matte green dangling earrings she wore added class and elegance.

Lynn's hair was wild and careless. Her earrings were 1960s yellow plastic with white daisies. Trudie wondered what they would be like in five or six years.

The girls glowed with satisfaction, their faces still fresh and alive from the exhilaration of performance and applause. Trudie watched them, longingly. They were beautiful young women and Mary Ann was so lucky. It had been such a treat to have them as guests. It had given Trudie a much-needed lift to have them all living in the house. She would miss them all.

Trudie browsed by a second booth that held Hugh and Larry Watson. Both were biting into hamburgers, French fries spilling out over their plates.

"Hugh," Trudie said, pausing. "I just wanted to thank you for all you did. You really helped make the show a success. The check will be in the mail first thing next week."

"That's cool," Hugh said, with a mouth full of fries. "Cool."

Larry glanced up with red-rimmed eyes and a sagging face.

"You must be tired, Larry. Did you pull an all-nighter?"

"Yeah. I'm really tired."

"He's okay," Hugh said. "It will make a man out of him."

Larry made a miserable face.

Trudie smiled. "Thanks, Larry. See you at the library right after Christmas vacation?"

He nodded and Trudie moved on, suddenly feeling lost and weary.

Cole Blackwell had already left town, as had many others. They wanted to spend Christmas with their families and share the experiences of the Christmas show with them. Mary Ann would fly out tomorrow as well; she was heading to Florida, to spend Christmas with her parents. And Jon? Where was Jon? Trudie didn't know, and she was a nervous wreck about it. Everyone was asking her where he was, and when he would show up. But that was like Jon. He always made a surprise appearance. That was his style and everyone knew it.

Trudie took a glass of champagne and wandered back into the bar, over to a wooden booth where Ray was still talking excitedly about how well the orchestra had played. He stood, and kissed her, congratulating her again on the success of the show. She listened and smiled, feeling herself start to sink. Where was Jon?

Now that everything was over and everyone was leaving, what would she do next? Just continue on with her life as it was? How could she? Everything had changed. But had it really? If things hadn't changed outside, they had definitely changed inside. She was different. She was very different.

She felt her phone vibrate. She snatched it up. It was Jon! She slid out of the booth and moved to the side exit door. She pushed out into the chilly night. Snow was falling and there were two inches on the ground, glistening under the tall, parking lot lights.

"Jon? Where are you?"

"At the Columbus Airport."

Trudie shrank, as if the air had been kicked out of her. "Oh... We thought you were coming to the party. Everybody's waiting."

"I'd be mobbed, Trudie. Have you seen the crowds and the reporters? Anyway, I've got three little girls who want me home for Christmas Day. I'm their Daddy and I've got to play Santa Claus. I love them and I've got to be there. My flight leaves in an hour."

Trudie didn't speak.

"Hey, Lady Parks. You all made it happen. And what a happen it was! It was a great night, Trudie. A spectacular night. Thanks for letting me be a part of it."

Trudie struggled to find her voice. "Jon..."

"Yes, Trudie."

"Jon..." she decided against saying what was in her heart. "It was a good night, wasn't it? Mrs. Childs was so happy."

"She was, Trudie, thanks to you all. I went home with her after the show and gave her a good night kiss. I love the woman, Trudie. I love her like a second mother. I just love Teach. I'm so glad we all got back together again, and you helped make it all happen."

Trudie felt sick. She had to get off the phone before she got emotional. "Well, you have a good flight back to L.A, Jon, and remember me sometimes, okay?"

"Hey, Trudie, wait a minute. I want to tell you..."

But Trudie had hung up. She felt the flow of tears.

Her phone rang. It was Jon again. She didn't want to talk to him. She couldn't.

She leaned back against the door and before she could stop them, the tears pumped out of her and she sobbed, her shoulders rolling, her body in a spasm of disappointment and pain.

EPILOGUE

Trudie Parks sat in the living room on the cushioned window seat, staring out the bay window at the falling snow. She was dressed in her blue cotton flannel pajamas and heavy cotton housecoat. It was a gentle snowfall, the eleventh snowfall of the season, and it was only December 31st. But it was beautiful, as it sugar-coated the limbs of the trees, glazed the bushes, and dusted the tops of parked cars. She heard the scraping sound of a snow shovel up the street and it somehow comforted her.

It was New Year's Eve day and she didn't have to go to work. She could lie around next to the fireplace and read, bake some cookies and call Mary Ann and Kristen. Mary Ann was back in California and, since Oscar had Christmas week off, Mary Ann had invited him to stay with her and the girls. She said she was moving slowly ahead with Oscar, ensuring that Carly and Lynn were comfortable with the new relationship. So far, they were. The Christmas show had helped to bond them all together. Mary Ann confided that Oscar was a kind and good man and they were becoming quite close.

Kristen was still in Colorado skiing. She'd emailed just last night.

Alan and I have recommitted ourselves to the marriage. I'm so glad I turned Cole down and that I didn't do anything I'd regret right now. Being with you and Mary Ann again gave me a new perspective on life. It helped clear my head. Trudie, let's all get together again soon, little sister. It will do us all good. I love you, Trudie, with all my heart and always will. Happy New Year!

Trudie watched the steam rise as she sipped her hot coffee. How wonderful it had all been. How miraculous it was that Mrs. Childs was feeling so much better! After the show, she seemed to gain strength and vitality. It seemed that her long battle with cancer was over, and she had won, at least for the time being. Her recovery was all the more remarkable because it had happened around Christmas. Even Julie had called it a Christmas miracle.

Trudie had asked Ray to email the entire cast the great news after Julie called to tell her. Julie's voice was excited and cracking with emotion.

"The doctors are amazed, Trudie. Just amazed. I told them it was that Christmas show. The Christmas show totally resurrected her. She's already planning next year's show, so look out!"

Trudie would be sure to stop at Julie's before she joined Ray and others to celebrate New Year's Eve at a new chic restaurant in Columbus. She'd bring in the New Year with good friends and the best of good memories. She had a lot to be grateful for.

Trudie turned to look at the house. It had been so quiet since everyone left. What a delight it had been to have the old rooms filled with life for those few marvelous days. How natural it had seemed to have Carly and Lynn romp about its rooms, and Kristen's forceful but good-hearted personality awaken the sleeping ghosts, and Mary Ann's gentleness soothe and heal them all. How lucky she was to have such good friends.

Trudie faced the window again, uttering a little sigh of satisfaction. She missed all of them. She missed them living in the house.

Suddenly, her eye was drawn to something. A man appeared from nowhere, bundled up in a heavy coat and scarf, a red ski cap pulled low over his head, obscuring his face. He was hunched and braced against the whistling winds. Was he hurt? Did he need help? Trudie stiffened. He dashed under the shade of the porch for cover, and then she heard him ascend the stairs to the front door. Trudie pictured him sick and cold. Where had he come from? Was he dangerous? Should she call the police?

She raced to her hall closet, grabbed her winter coat and slipped it on. She released the door lock, making sure the lock chain was secure, and then opened the door, cautiously, only a couple of inches. She peeked out. There, looking back at her, was the grinning face of Jon Ketch!

"Hey there, Lady Trudie. It's your old lover boy, Jon."

Trudie's face was blank with shock. "Jon! What in the...?"

He shrugged, loosely.

"How...? Why are you here?"

"I'm here because I love you and I want to marry you."

Trudie made a little sound of surprise. "What?!"

"It's true. You wouldn't take my calls and you ignored my texts. So here I am and I want to marry you." He pointed at his chest. "I, Jon Ketch, want to marry," he pointed at her, "you, Trudie Parks. You and me! Jon and Trudie. Wife number three, yes, but my one and only, always."

Trudie stood in bewildered silence.

"You can close your mouth, Trudie. It's okay."

She did close her mouth.

"We can go steady for awhile if you want. I'm sure your folks would approve of me. I'm so lovable and normal. Hey, and I have a good, steady job. So should we? Go steady?"

He took out his old high school ring. "I have my high school ring and I'm happy to put it on your finger. Shall I?"

Trudie didn't move. She couldn't move. She couldn't think.

Jon studied her, his eyes narrowed on her. "You okay, Trudie?"

She still didn't speak.

"Can I come in?"

Trudie didn't move.

"Will you please speak to me?"

She finally found her voice. Her expression darkened. "Jon... why did you leave without kissing me goodbye? Without coming to see me?"

He frowned down at the cement porch. "I should have. I'm sorry. I was all messed up and confused. I was going to tell you all that but you hung up on me. Now that was rude, Trudie. Anyway, there you were and there was Mrs. Childs, who I thought was dying and I'd never see her again. Meanwhile, my girls were waiting for me, texting me every 5 minutes to see if I was coming for Christmas. Pleading with me to come home. I was a mess, okay? And then you hung up on me and wouldn't take my calls. Okay, so I thought you needed some time, and I needed some time to think things through. I'm not the greatest judge of my own character you know."

"Yes, I know, Jon. You are very... very..." Trudie was at a loss for words. "I don't know what you are."

"I prefer to think of myself as a textured kind of guy."

"You are that, alright," Trudie said.

"Okay. So I went home and thought about things."

"And?"

Jon seemed to melt a little. His eyes captured and then held hers. "I'm crazy for you, Trudie Parks. Always have been. Always will be. You just do it for me."

Trudie breathed in uncertainty. "Can I trust you, Jon? Can I?"

Jon reached into his coat pocket. He presented her with another ring. He held it up to the light. It was a stupendous diamond ring that glittered and sparkled. Trudie stared, breathless and mesmerized.

"Yes, you can, Trudie. You can trust me, and here is the ring of my commitment. I love you and I want to spend the rest of my mad and silly life with you. Please? Please, Trudie, my love? Say yes?"

Trudie didn't budge. She stared at the ring, her eyes expanding on it. "Is that a real diamond? It's huge."

"Yes. It is as real as I am. It's prettier, yes. But not as original. I can afford it, Trudie. I just signed a contract to be in a movie with George Clooney. He's the good guy and I'm the bad guy. He shoots me at the end, but I get paid a lot of money. We'll be filming in the Caribbean, London and Paris. I'd love to have you with me. I think we'd have lots of fun together. Now, let me have your hand."

Trudie snaked her arm out of the still-chained door, extending her hand. Cold wind whistled in as Jon slipped the ring over her delicate finger. It dazzled, and she watched the dancing play of light.

"I love the look of that," Jon said, smiling, warmly.

Trudie suddenly felt drugged and dizzy. A diamond ring? The Caribbean? London? Paris? Marriage?

"Well, do you like it?" Jon asked.

Trudie cleared her throat. "...Yes... Yes. It's beautiful, Jon. Just beautiful."

"Now, can I please come in?"

Trudie tried to blink away anxiety. The past 20 years had been safe and predictable, and all her actions and choices had helped to define her. She knew who she was. She had a meaningful and uncomplicated routine. Was she ready to be yanked away into a chaotic life with Jon Ketch? Was she ready to jump out of an airplane without a parachute?

Jon stood in humble anticipation. "Trudie? Will you be my wife?"

Trudie began to tremble. "But how can we, Jon? I live here. You live there. You're a famous movie star and I'm a nobody dental hygienist."

Jon turned serious, pointing a stern finger at her. "First of all, you have never been, nor will you ever be, a nobody. You are Trudie the Sweet. Trudie the Beautiful. Trudie, my Great Love, among many other wonderful things."

Now Trudie melted. "Jon, that was so sweet."

Jon spoke earnestly. "Trudie, we can live here sometimes. We can live there sometimes. We can live wherever sometimes. The important thing is we live somewhere, anywhere, together. We have fun together, we love together. We have a kid or two together, preferably at least one son."

Trudie considered his words, while staring down at the ring. She lifted her eyes to see Jon's hopeful face.

"Well, Trudie?"

Trudie looked beyond him, her face revealing nothing.

Jon shivered. "Trudie! Can I please come in? I'm freezing my ass off out here."

A puff of wind blew snow across the porch. Jon ducked away, protecting his face from another gust of buffeting wind.

A slow, lusty expression changed Trudie's face. She stepped back, released the chain and swung the door wide open. Her voice took on strength and conviction.

"Yes, Jon Ketch, you can come in now. But I warn you. It will be a long, long time before you get out."

He hesitated, thinking about it. He nodded and entered.

Trudie slammed the door behind him.

Thank You

Thank you for taking the time to read *The Christmas Women*. If you enjoyed it, please consider telling your friends or posting a short review. Word of mouth is an author's best friend and it is much appreciated.

Thank you,
Elyse Douglas

Other novels by Elyse Douglas that you might enjoy:

The Christmas Diary
The Summer Diary
The Other Side of Summer
Daring Summer
The Christmas Eve Letter (A Time Travel Novel) Book 1
The Christmas Eve Daughter (A Time Travel Novel) Book 2
The Lost Mata Hari Ring (A Time Travel Novel)
The Christmas Town (A Time Travel Novel)
Time Sensitive (A Time Travel Novel)
The Summer Letters
The Date Before Christmas
Christmas Ever After
Christmas for Juliet
The Christmas Bridge
Wanting Rita

www.elysedouglas.com